PIXIE DUSTED

PIXIE DUSTED

FRACTURED FAE
BOOK THREE

SARAH J. SOVER

This book is dedicated to the memory of Dr. George Hewett Joiner, Jr., without whom I might never have traveled this path. True magic is in the way we touch lives, and Dr. Joiner was a magician of the highest order, leaving an immeasurable impact on the world.

It started off like any other case—a dead pixie in a dumpster. Chessa Moon sat across from the victim's brother, a tight-lipped teen who reeked of vodka and kept scowling in the direction of Quincy, the half-ogre who'd pushed him through the door of C&F Investigations.

"I told you. I don't know anything." The teen was about half a foot taller than Chessa, but he looked like a bug with Quincy lurking over his shoulder. The way the pixie shrunk into himself on the worn plaid couch didn't help matters. His stringy brown hair fell into his face, and he didn't move to push it back.

"Look kid, you're the one who was running your mouth to anyone with ears at Pub Nine. We ain't cops or we'd book you for underage drinking." In his youth, Cross-Eyed Quincy had earned his stripes getting into all kinds of trouble on the streets of Boston. Chessa knew he wasn't going for intimidation, but his green mohawk, the jagged scar over his right eye, and his sheer size were enough to spook the most experienced street toughs around. Truth be told, it was part of why Chessa worked with Q—he provided the muscle she needed on occasion. That, and he owned a quarter of the firm, whether she liked it or not.

"Hey, Q, can you go for a walk?" she asked, pointedly glancing at the cracked apartment door that served as the entrance to the PI firm she'd started just over two years ago with her best friend Gwen. Not that *Her Grace* stopped by much these days. Chessa couldn't blame Gwen—she had her hands full as the Queen who vowed to overhaul the Seelie Court way of life—but that didn't mean she didn't miss the hell out of her. Quincy grunted as he turned and stomped out of the apartment. Once he was gone, Chessa could see the tension melt from the boy's shoulders.

"I'm sorry about him. He can be a little intense," she said. She handed the teenage pixie a can of Coke she retrieved from the mini-fridge under the desk. She didn't offer up Gwen's bottle of Jack, though she was sure he would much prefer it. "What's your name?"

"Xander." He popped the can open and took a big swig before setting it down on the rickety side table. His hair needed a trim, and his translucent wings twitched behind him as if he were contemplating using them to bolt out the window. It would be an unfortunate move if he tried it—that window had been painted over long before C&F Investigations took up residence.

"Okay, Xander. Quincy didn't tell me much about you before he hauled you all the way across town. Do you have anyone who will be looking for you?"

Xander's eyes widened as if processing a threat, but he shook his head. His body language was concerning. Chessa wondered just how rough Quincy had been bringing him into the office.

"Tell me Q didn't kidnap you off the street."

"From the bar," replied the kid, his eyes cutting back toward the doorway. "He grabbed me by the shirt and took me right out the door. Stuffed me in his motorcycle bag. Nobody even tried to stop him."

Chessa suppressed a sigh and made a mental note to discuss proper client recruitment with Quincy later. "I apologize for his rudeness. He means no harm."

Xander looked dubious, and Chessa didn't blame him. Rude was a hell of an understatement when it came to kidnapping. Well-acquainted with the Pub Nine clientele, she knew there wasn't a single patron or staff member who would stand up to Quincy if the half-ogre set his mind to something. The best she could hope for was to downplay the whole thing and hope the kid got over it quickly.

"Believe it or not," she continued, "Q has his reasons for everything he does, even if his execution is somewhat sloppy. Do you know why he brought you to me?"

Tears filled Xander's light blue eyes, a stark contrast to the firm set of his jaw. "My brother was stabbed to death, and the Korranthia Police won't do a damn thing about it."

The pieces clicked into place. Chessa had seen the headlines on all the news webpages and had even started writing up a piece for *Crime Wave*, the blog she kept as a side hustle. A pixie had been found dead in Dorchester last week, not far from the house he shared with friends. According to the authorities, it was a crime of passion, a domestic situation involving a scorned ex-girlfriend. Looking at Xander, Chessa got the distinct feeling there was more going on here.

"Your brother was Mandrake Aster?"

Xander nodded, biting his bottom lip. "He wasn't killed by a jealous lover. He never dated anybody. He was ace."

Chessa was skeptical. Most young men she knew didn't share every detail of their love lives with their teenage siblings. "Asexual doesn't mean aromantic. You're sure he wasn't involved with someone he'd kept secret from you?"

"You think I don't know that? You think I don't know my own brother? Drake lived in an artist community. He had family, born *and* chosen, and he didn't need anything else. He had enough love for everyone, and everyone loved him. He was happy with things that way."

Chessa took a deep breath. She didn't mean to offend a grieving brother, but she needed details. If the authorities were pegging the crime on a romantic partner, then she needed to find out why. "I believe you, Xander. If I'm going to take your case, I'll need all the information you can give me. I'm going to bring in my associates and have you start from the beginning. I want you to tell us everything you can about Mandrake and everyone in his life. Can you do that?"

Xander nodded and his bottom lip quivered. "Yeah. But I don't have any money."

Of course not, Chessa thought, stifling a sigh. Very few of the clients C&F represented did, and that's why she needed to keep her side gig as a crime blogger. If Quincy was going to literally abduct business off the street, he needed to set his sights on more profitable marks.

"We'll worry about that part later. Is it ok with you if Quincy comes back?"

The teenager nodded, but Chessa could see fear flicker in his icy eyes. Still, she needed everyone on the same page. She hit a button on her desk, and Norman, her assistant, popped in from the back room where he'd been hiding since the half-ogre partner busted in with a client-slash-victim. He wore his wizard robes, an oddity he'd developed since arriving from Glastonbury last summer. The look was quite striking with his scraggly white beard and pointed hat.

"Norman, this is Xander. He's our newest client."

The kid gaped at the wizard, who flashed a friendly smile and stuck out his hand. "Magical to meet you, mate!" The Cockney accent was at odds with the formal robes, and Chessa knew the impact his appearance had on folks. Boston wasn't exactly teeming with Gandalf cosplayers. She'd been meaning to bring it up but hadn't yet figured out how. Now free of his Unseelie crime family's influence, Norman was desperate to find himself. If that meant dressing like Merlin for a few months, who was she to make him feel bad about it?

Xander took his hand and his stress seemed to ease up for a moment. Interesting.

"Norman, could you stick your head out in the hall and call Q back?"

The moment of peace was over for the young pixie. By the time Quincy returned and Norman shut the door, Xander was wound up tight again. Even so, he started talking.

"Drake always looked out for me. He was more than my big brother; he was like a second Pa. When he went to live with his friends after college, I was torn up. I always thought he'd come home, you know?"

Norman tapped away at his laptop, even through the pauses while Xander talked.

"Do you still live with your parents?" asked Chessa.

"They died. Last year." The way he tacked on the qualifier was pointed, and a lump formed in Chessa's throat. The battle between the Seelie and Unseelie Courts had inflicted a hefty toll on communities across the globe, but Korranthia had taken the biggest hit, partly thanks to the number of fae loyal to both Gwen and her.

Chessa still suffered nightmares about everything she'd experienced. That week of hell was more traumatizing than being in the crosshairs of a serial killer, a comparison few others could make with any confidence. The Seelie won, but some scars would never fully disappear. Quincy cleared his throat, bringing her attention back to the subject at hand.

"I'm sorry for your loss. We all lost so much in the battle. So, you're alone?"

"Yeah."

Quincy grunted. "How old are you, kid?"

"I'll be sixteen next month." Xander's eyes went wide as if he'd just thought of something. "But don't say anything to the authorities. Please.

I'm fine on my own, I swear. Drake sent me enough money to live on while I finish school, and there's a trust for later."

"We ain't in the business of turning anyone in," replied Quincy before Chessa could say anything. "Are we, boss?"

She hesitated. On one hand, gaining a reputation for snitching would be murder for business, but on the other, Xander was just a kid. He shouldn't be made to tackle the world alone. Could she guarantee that foster care would do any better by him? In the end, she caved to the glare Quincy was shooting at her. He knew the dangers of being a teenager alone in the world better than anyone, so who was she to go against him? "No, we're not."

For the first time, Xander smiled at Quincy.

Norman held up his hand as if he were a school kid waiting to be called on, a motion that looked ridiculous considering his visage.

"Yes, Norman?" said Chessa, adopting the upbeat tone of Ms. Krupps, her third-grade teacher.

The wizard looked up from his screen and twitched his nose in a rabbit-like motion that had become his habit of late. "Should I strike that last bit from the record?"

"For the love of Danu, man, of course, you don't put that in your notes!" Quincy ran a hand over his green mohawk, which rebounded perfectly. "Fucking flatlander."

"Oy, what does that even mean?" Norman's face was beginning to flush, and Chessa knew better than to let this escalate.

"It's okay, Norman. I'd rather you asked if you didn't know," she said before returning her attention to Xander. "What else can you tell us about your brother?"

An hour later, Chessa felt like she had just as much information as when the boy first came through the door. A sorceress confessed to killing Mandrake after he broke off a romantic relationship with her, and the KPD made the arrest and then closed the case without further investigation. Open and shut. But the picture Xander painted of Mandrake Aster didn't line up with what the authorities were claiming. If it were her brother, she'd be upset too.

"Say I agree that the sorceress didn't kill your brother and is taking the fall for someone," Chessa said once Xander wrapped up his story. "Is there any reason someone else would want to harm him? Someone she'd want to protect, perhaps?"

"No. Everyone loved him. Please, talk to his housemates. They'll tell you the same thing."

Chessa nodded, having expected the answer. She wrote down the address to the house Mandrake rented with friends out in Dorchester as well as the address of the home he'd inherited from his parents, where Xander lived in Brighton. She had a lot to follow up on. While Xander made it seem like Mandrake was a Sprite Scout, working hard and sending money home to support his little brother, Chessa felt in her bones that he was holding back.

Xander's grief was sincere, of that much she was sure. She was never good at turning her back on someone's pain, but the nail in the coffin was the nagging feeling that, despite the kid being torn up, there was something decidedly off about the whole situation. For starters, nobody was as clean as Xander made Mandrake sound. No matter how good of a person you were, there were always those who hoped for your downfall. Another thing that struck her was the question of why Mandrake didn't move home to take care of his teen brother after their parents died. Chessa's own sister had made bigger sacrifices to care for her when their mother was overwhelmed by life, and it seemed like the right thing to do if she bought the image Xander painted of his 'second pa' of a brother.

She studied Xander's face. He twitched, his puffy eyes darting toward the door. The niggling feeling intensified. Something else was going on here, and everything inside of her screamed to leave it be. So, naturally, she planned to do the opposite. If there was dirt to find, Chessa would sniff it out.

"We will do everything we can," she said. Only then did Xander seem to relax. He met her eyes for a fleeting moment before looking down at his feet.

"Brighton is a long way to go alone," she continued. "Do you want Quincy to take you home?"

"On the bike?"

The big half-ogre grinned. "Nah, with my wings."

Xander laughed, and Chessa caught a glimpse of the child in him still. She watched Q walk him out. The kid was alone in this world, and there was nothing she could do about it. The only solace she could offer was to hunt down whoever was responsible for killing his brother.

2

Quincy didn't like leaving the kid alone at a time like this, so he didn't. Chessa had told him to take the boy home, so she must have sensed it too—there was something off about Xander Aster. Quincy had been around enough angry young'uns to feel this kid spiraling like he was going down the drain, and in his experience, the only kind of flush that was ever any good was the kind you held in your hand after going all-in. Xander was all-in all right, but not in the way that would ever hit the jackpot.

Nah, leaving him alone wasn't an option.

Instead of staying on Hwy 90 to drive out to Brighton, Quincy took the exit onto 93 North, the little pixie clinging to the small fae belt on the back of the motorcycle, wings strapped to his back to keep them from being damaged by the wind. Hoping he was smart enough to hold tight, Quincy bet Xander wished for the comfort of the motorcycle bag now. If the client fell off the back of the bike, it would make the job a lot simpler.

When they pulled up to Pub Nine, Q's spot on the pavement was vacant, as it ought to be. He parked and gave Xander a moment to get clear before dismounting himself, pulling off his studded helmet, and locking the kickstand in place with his thick, black, steel-toed boot. Quincy spit in his hand and ran it over his mohawk to pop it back in place.

Xander stood on the curb, looking at him sideways.

"You coming in, or what?" said Quincy, walking toward the establishment that served as his home away from home.

Xander hesitated, the little helmet Quincy let him borrow still strapped to his head. "This doesn't look like home."

"Sure it does! It's my home. Are you going to stand there all day or are you going to come in for a pint? It ain't like anyone's waiting on you."

Quincy knew he shouldn't be contributing to the delinquency of a minor, but he also knew there was nothing like the temptation of a misdemeanor to keep a wrong-headed kid around. Besides, it's where he'd encountered Xander in the first place.

"Uh, sure. I guess I can come in for a drink." Xander struggled to get the helmet off before tucking it in the bag on the side of Q's Harley and scurrying in on the half-ogre's heels.

"Fallan, get my friend here a Bud Light on my tab," Quincy called to the elf behind the bar.

Fallan opened his mouth as if to object before snapping it shut and grabbing a pixie-sized glass to hold beneath the tap, the skin on his face darkening to a deeper shade of purple. Quincy tried not to let his relief show. He learned a long time ago that most people would do as he said if he issued orders rather than asking favors, but he still sometimes got blowback. Though not from part-time bartenders working to make it through grad school. It was the combination of Q's ogre size and intimidating sneer, he'd wager. That sneer had gotten him out of, and into, a lot of situations over the years. Speaking of wagers, his regular poker buddies were sitting at the end of the bar eyeing him expectantly. Damn it. Was it Tuesday again?

"Sorry, boys, I'm on a case," Quincy said, earning him some disgruntled looks. Krik leaned into Sherrie and said something, and they both shook their heads. Quincy almost felt bad for the amount of time he'd been putting in over at C&F Investigations. Almost. These guys should be able to get by without him.

Jarvis made a disapproving tut sound followed by some off-handed barb Quincy couldn't make out, and Dudlin clapped him on the back. The young necromancer's head came loose and fell on the floor. Xander gasped in horror, unaccustomed as he must be to the work of sloppy necromancers, and Quincy couldn't help but laugh. Strictly speaking, the dead-raisers weren't legally permitted to practice outside of an academic setting for reasons like the one rolling through beer puddles and dirt on the floor of the pub. Q didn't see the harm in it, even if Jarvis did keep coming back a bit worse for the wear.

"Don't worry about him, he's fine." How many times had that kid's frat brothers brought him back by now? Three? Four? By all rights, he shouldn't be around to disapprove of Quincy's activities. Dudlin picked up the head and set it back on Jarvis' shoulders.

"Don't let me keep you from your, um, friends," squeaked Xander, his eyes wide.

Quincy smirked. "They'll be alright without me. Here." He slid the miniature glass over to Xander, who looked ridiculous sitting on the barstool. Most small fae opted for the tables set up on the bar's surface, but this kid didn't seem terribly experienced with bar etiquette. Quincy would make sure nobody sat on him.

"I can pay for my own drinks," replied Xander, his eyes going hard.

"So you said. You're loaded, right? Trust fund and everything. Where'd Mandrake get the cash?"

It was easy to act self-sufficient when someone else was footing your bills. Quincy never got a dime from his family. He was out on the street as soon as he could wipe his ass. But what he did know about the financial workings of Korranthia was that an art school dropout living in an artist commune didn't have the dough to buy a latte, let alone set up a trust fund.

"I'm n-not sure. He probably had a job or something."

Well, now that was interesting. Xander had claimed to know all about Mandrake's personal life, but he didn't know how big brother paid the bills? Seemed fishy. But Quincy didn't want to spook Xander. That kid was one wrong word from turning into the Road Runner. Putting people at ease wasn't Quincy's forte, so he decided to keep him off-balance in a less precarious way.

"Come to think of it, you said you ain't got cash to pay for our services. My boss, she takes folks at their word. You ain't pulling her wings, now are you?"

"You're the one who took me to her! I didn't want to hire a detective."

"We ain't detectives."

Xander dropped his voice to a near-whisper. "Personal investigator, then. And no, I don't have *that* kind of cash, not until I'm twenty-five."

A trust fund he couldn't touch until he was a responsible adult took away any motive he would have to off his own brother. At least, on the surface, it did. But if he'd done Mandrake in himself, why would he be crying about it at the local watering hole? Xander might be squirrelly about money, but Quincy didn't like him for murder.

"Yeah, I suppose you've got the right of it. See, when things don't add up around here, I like to know why. It's why I went into this line of work in the first place. That, and trying to go straight."

"Straight?"

"Let's just say, my employment endeavors haven't always been on the up-and-up, if you know what I mean. So, if your brother was getting paid for some unsavory work, I wouldn't hold it against him. I just need to know the facts if we want to solve the case."

Xander took a long swig of his beer as Quincy stared at him. When he set it on the bar, he didn't make eye contact.

"I told you. I don't know what he did for money. Can I go home now?"

Damn. He'd pressed too hard.

"Yeah, kid. You can go home. I'll drive ya."

"No. That's ok. I'll fly." When Quincy shot him a questioning look, he tacked on, "I could use some time to clear my head."

Quincy shrugged. He wasn't the kid's old man. Chessa had Xander's contact info, and he said as much when he walked him out. "Look, I can't make you do anything, but I want you to be careful. Keep an eye out for anything that seems off. We don't know why Mandrake was killed, but if they snagged a patsy and the real killer catches wind of you sniffing around, it could go sideways for you on a dime."

Xander nodded and swallowed hard. "Thanks for the beer. You're the first person who's been nice to me in a long time."

If Quincy had a heart, that would have hurt. "Do me a favor? Meet me back here tomorrow night."

Xander agreed, but Quincy wasn't sure he meant it.

3

Chessa started her morning with a chai latte and a bag of delicious baked gold from Dela's Donuts to prepare herself for the long flight down to Dorchester. Gwen preferred to drive everywhere, and Chessa had considered taking her friend's old blue Subaru out to the artist commune, but flying over Boston during morning rush hour made her glad of her decision to wing it. Besides, the temperate September morning air was good for the soul.

Dela's wasn't far from the police station, but she wanted to meet Mandrake's roomies before hitting up her KPD contacts. She loved Sammy, the griffin who was more of a big brother in her eyes than a sergeant detective, but she didn't want him to influence her thoughts regarding the people in Mandrake's life. Chessa preferred to go in blind, free to connect directly without any preconceptions clouding her judgment. As far as she knew, this was a loving group of friends, a chosen family for all.

Pixies were better sprinters than marathoners, so she had to take frequent breaks on traffic lights or tree branches to catch her breath. By the time she reached Dorchester, Dela's was a fond memory. She thought about grabbing a bite to refuel but was eager to get to work.

By all technicalities, the house on Montello Street would be considered a single-family dwelling. The walkways on either side of the building were only wide enough for air conditioning units and service utility repair people. Pale blue paint was chipped off the stone façade in many places, the wood around the windows looked rotten, and the plants in the window boxes were all dead. The state of the house matched its neighbors'.

Chessa was surprised to hear yelling filtering through the cracked windows.

Families can be contentious, she reminded herself as she gave a strong knock on the door, not trusting the doorbell to be in working order.

"Fuck you, Lance! You never cared about anyone but yourself!" It was a woman's voice, and by the sound of it, she was letting Lance have it. The yelling ceased just before the door creaked open.

A goblin's face appeared in the doorway, his pale yellow eyes narrow with suspicion, the chain keeping the door from opening wide enough for even a pixie to slip through. "Can I help you?"

Chessa could tell this guy would be spooked by a private investigator, so she thought fast and offered up her street name, bestowed upon her by Quincy back when he used to say she grew stories for *Crime Wave* like one of those Chia Pets. "Hey, there," she said with a big smile. "I'm Chia, and I heard you might have a room available for a struggling writer."

"This isn't a good time," replied the goblin, shifting to close the door.

Chessa put her Chuck Taylor in the gap, a move more aggressive than she preferred to take with someone so skittish, especially someone large enough to crush her, but she saw her opportunity for intel gathering closing with the door. If worst came to worst, she could survive in a cast for six weeks. Thankfully, it didn't come to that. The goblin hesitated, and Chessa let the words flow. "I'm sorry, man, but I really don't have anywhere else to go. I've got the first and last month's rent in cash." She proffered up her most apologetic smile in an attempt to disarm him.

Emotions flashed on the goblin's face—first surprise, fear, anger, then something else. "Hang on," he said as he turned away from the door. Chessa waited a beat longer than she expected to, trying to decipher the muffled voices emanating from the other side. Then the goblin undid the chain, opened the door, and invited her in.

"I'm Lance Gruber," he said. "I'm sorry about that. We've had a hell of a week. Our roommate just, ah, passed away. Who did you say sent you?"

"I didn't. I'm actually a friend of Mandrake's brother Xander. He's the one who told me you might have a room." It was a gamble, Chessa knew, but she had to come up with something plausible.

"I don't know if this will be a good fit," said Lance, his face guarded. His eyes darted toward the door.

"Don't be foolish, Lance," said a woman as she glided into the parlor. Chessa wasn't usually one for embellishment, but there was no other way to describe the way the other pixie moved—her wings barely disturbing the air as her sheer chiffon robe trailed behind her, her long, wavy blonde hair somehow floating around her head. "We have plenty of room for a fellow creative. Hello, love, I'm Abigail Marquis. You don't recognize my name yet, but you will."

For the first time in her life, Chessa didn't know what to make of someone. Abigail was at once friendly, approachable, and the absolute picture of feminine beauty embodied by a pixie. Whatever reservations Chessa'd had from Lance's turbulent demeanor melted away.

"Oh, cut it with the theatrics, Abi," said Lance, rolling his eyes.

A slight pout made Abigail somehow more attractive, her eyes a deeper shade of blue and her strawberry lips more plump.

"I have no doubt I will," replied Chessa, ignoring the goblin. Abi was her way in and a delightful one at that. "I take it you're an actress?"

Abi gasped and floated down to the floor. "How could you tell?"

In a house full of art school grads, it wasn't hard to pin this one down as a drama kid. "I'm a writer. I have an eye for detail. Besides, you've definitely got that 'it' factor going on for you. Do you sing too?"

"Why, yes, I do." Abi turned to Lance. "She's good!"

The goblin looked like he might burst with laughter. "Since when do you sing?"

Anger flashed over the pixie's face. "I've been a singer since I was ten, thank-you-very-much."

"Is that what you call the caterwauling I hear every time you get in the shower?"

"Fuck you, Lance."

Lance grinned. "There's our Abi."

Despite being entertained by their banter, Chessa decided to break it up before she wound up in the middle of whatever argument they were having when she'd arrived. She needed to seal the deal.

"Who else lives here? Xander told me you were like a big, loving family of artists."

At that, both Abi and Lance burst out laughing, their disagreement forgotten.

Chessa glanced quizzically from one to the other until Abi took pity on her. "I'm sorry," she said between breaths. "It's just, if this is a family, it's the most monumentally fucked up one I've ever seen."

"For once, we agree," said Lance. "But welcome aboard the crazy train. Speaking of which, here's your engineer now."

A tall humanoid man who appeared to be about twenty - though fae blood made guessing ages a dangerous exercise - appeared at the bottom of the stairs leading from the entry up to where Chessa presumed the bedrooms were located. Pointed ears hinting at elf blood peeked through his strands of long, dark hair, which framed even darker, charcoal-lined eyes set in a pale face. A long leopard-print faux fur jacket draped over narrow shoulders, with torn, stone-washed skinny jeans disappearing into patent leather, knee-high heeled boots. Beads adorned braids lurking in his otherwise unkempt tresses, and the stench of bourbon hung in the air around him. Between him and Abi, Chessa felt like she was backstage at Coachella.

"Who have we here?" said the elvish humanoid, his voice thick like melted Velveeta.

Chessa perched on a worn, puke-green armchair by the window, a move that served to cover her unease as much as to get her farther into the house. Her survey of the room, furnished with a hodge-podge of thrift store quality offerings, provided very little intel. "I'm Chia, and your housemates were just describing the spare room you've got on offer."

"Were they now? And you'd like to join our little…family?"

Chessa wasn't clear on whether the newcomer had been listening in on the conversation or if he just happened to pick up the lost thread, but his eyes sparkled as he took her in, almost like he was a predator eyeing his next meal. She could use that. Summoning her most innocent voice, she answered.

"I would like that very much." The smile she flashed was genuine. She wasn't about to make any judgments just yet, and in truth, she was intrigued by this little group of misfits.

"We could use the extra cash, Dom," said Abi, her demeanor much more subdued. It appeared this guy, Dom, was the head honcho. Chessa wondered what his real name was and just how much submitting she would be expected to do before she got any answers.

"We run a democracy around here," he replied, flicking a wrist. The parlor's curtain swished closed in response, casting the room into darkness. "That's better." Maybe he wasn't entirely elf.

"Yes, we'll have to put it to vote. Has Honey emerged from her cave today?" asked Lance, glancing around. Abi chuckled and Dom rolled his eyes. It would take Chessa some time to get a bead on the group dynamics. Her gut told her something was off, but every time she thought she figured out what, the mood shifted.

"I'll give you some time to talk it over," Chessa said as she rose from the chair. "Take my cell number so you can let me know what you decide. I'm just a struggling writer looking for an affordable place to crash."

"What do you write?" asked Dom with a flourish of the hand.

"Mostly true crime, though I dabble in fiction from time to time." It was the understatement of the century. Chessa ran the hottest fae crime blog on the internet in addition to her relatively recent foray into private investigations. What she did was more than true crime, it was an art form in and of itself. If she told them she was the infamous Chessa Moon, they'd lock up tighter than the Kingdom Archives, so she'd pass as Chia, the writer, for as long as she could.

"Ooh, edgy," cooed Abi.

"Hey, Abs, maybe she'll get famous and you can star in one of her snuff films. You'd be good at that." Dom laughed, but he was the only one.

"Thanks for talking to me, and I'm sorry about Mandrake," Chessa said, making her pointed comment sound offhanded. Perhaps everyone wasn't ok with joking about murder considering the circumstances. The air seemed to get sucked from the room.

"Yeah, thanks. We'll be in touch," said Lance, standing to walk her to the door.

Once she was outside, Chessa didn't break stride. She could feel someone watching her from the upstairs window, and she didn't want to blow her cover or risk spooking her secret admirer. She decided to run by a QuickFlip for a hotdog before heading back downtown to pay Sergeant Detective Samson Wayne a visit.

4

The Korranthia Police Department precinct was buzzing with activity when Chessa arrived. She checked the time on her cell. It was just past five. Things were usually calm around now as the beat cops were out on patrol and the detectives were off to dinner in pairs or small groups. Chessa's sleuth sense tingled. Something must be up.

"Hey Pox," she said to the young humanoid at the reception desk. He looked agitated like he'd rather be doing something other than greeting citizens off the street.

"Oh, hiya Chessa. If you're here for your checkers game with Sergeant Wayne, it'll have to wait. He's in the middle of something."

Chessa flitted up to stand on the desk. "What's going on?"

"Off the record?"

"Of course. You're the one who filed my NDA."

She thought Captain O'Toole was ridiculous for requiring her to keep a blanket NDA on file for each year, but it was the only way he'd let his detectives work with the PI firm so long as its proprietor still maintained *Crime Wave*. Pox nodded, his sandy blond hair flopping just a bit. Chessa was surprised the captain didn't haul him off to the barber for a buzz cut directly after offering him the job. "There's a body. It was found just a few hours ago, and everyone's waiting for Dr. Plum to finish the autopsy."

"Another one? Is it related to the Aster case?" Chessa knew she shouldn't play coy, but she needed all the intel she could get. Besides, she wasn't looking to write a piece—she was on a case.

"We don't know yet. This one's female. She was found in a hotel room by housekeeping this morning after she failed to check out. It's nothing like the Aster except that the vic is another pixie."

"There are thousands of pixies in Korranthia," mused Chessa.

"Right. That's why they're thinking it's unrelated, especially since we got Aster's killer. But what are the odds that we'd go so long without any stiffs coming through the door, then get two over the course of two weeks? And both pixies?"

Chessa nodded. It was quite the coincidence. There hadn't been any violent crime since before the Battle of Avalon. Korranthia had lost more citizens than any other kingdom, and, once the mourning was over, everyone just wanted to get back to some semblance of normal. Gwendolyn Evenshine, Chessa's best friend and silent partner in C&F was now the Seelie Queen, largely thanks to the sacrifices of the Korranthian fae. There had been a series of political changes felt around the world, even here, but the ripples were more political than violent, at least at this stage. The community had lost too much, both on the Seelie and Unseelie sides, and fae were still licking their wounds and burying their dead.

"Have they established any kind of other connection between the two victims?"

Pox shook his head. "Aster was a beatnik. This new one, she was something else. You'll have to get details from Sergeant Wayne if you want more. O'Toole wants us tight-lipped on her identity."

That was an interesting little tidbit. Thankfully, Samson wouldn't hold back, even if O'Toole wanted him to. Not from Chessa. That griffin acted with his heart. It was one of the things Chessa loved about him. Confident she'd get the full scoop later, she switched tactics.

"You seem awfully invested. What are you doing on admin duty?"

Pox sighed and pushed his hair back. "Someone's got to hold down the fort, and I'm still the most junior detective in the precinct. Samson's been pushing for some new hires, but you know O'Toole."

"He can be a tad stubborn."

"That's putting it nicely. Anyways, Sergeant Wayne is in his office, but the captain's in there with him. You might want to give him time to clear out."

Pox had a point. Chessa was generally loved in the precinct, but not by O'Toole. Her connection to Gwen and notoriety with *Crime Wave* made her a major thorn in his side, no matter how many times she'd tried to win him over. She decided to make the rounds to see what other information she could log while she waited for the coast to clear.

She spent the early evening buzzing around the bullpen, shooting the shit with the cops on duty. Pox was right, they were mostly hanging around waiting on the autopsy report. This new victim must be somebody important. Shortly after Chessa's arrival, Officer Danvers sent Pox out to pick up a sack of Bogey Burgers, sliders that morphed into whatever sandwich was desired by the person who unwrapped them. You sure could tell a lot about someone with a Bogey Burger in his hand. The chain operated out of the back of established human mom-and-pop sandwich shops, and there just happened to be one a block away from the precinct. Chessa felt bad for Pox, who would rather be in the thick of things than relegated to errand boy, but there wasn't really much to be a part of at the moment. Samson was holed up with the captain and everyone else was sitting around, waiting.

By the time she saw O'Toole stomp down the stairs and off in the direction of his office, she'd learned that Mandrake Aster had trace amounts of pixie dust in his system, a factoid that would likely shock his brother and that the new vic had also been stabbed.

She also learned that Darla's son was living his best life in college, that Holcomb was recently promoted to senior detective, and that Tinslow was expecting her third litter, something that her mate struggled with since he already had his paws full as a stay-at-home sire. Chessa loved stopping by the station and catching up on everyone's lives, but she was growing impatient. Once the captain was out of sight, she zipped up the handrail and into Samson's office.

"Heya sweet cheeks. What's the word on the street?" asked Samson, not bothering to look up from his desktop monitor. Images flashed by on the screen, the light glinting off the round, red-rimmed spectacles perched above Sammy's beak, but she couldn't make out details from this angle.

"You tell me," she replied, keeping her distance. Samson would see right through her if she attempted to hide the fact that she was there for information, but he also wouldn't appreciate her staring at his screen. Their friendship had started off rocky, him resenting her exploiting her KPD connections to mine stories for her blog, so she'd had to win him over with absolute honesty. That and a jailbreak from an Unseelie holding cell.

"Which Chessa am I speaking to today?" he said, finally glancing up and narrowing his big, yellow eyes at her.

"The PI. I'm on a case."

Samson made a clicking noise, a sound that Chessa assumed was standard griffin communication, not that she had the privilege of knowing any other griffins in her twenty-eight years around the sun. "Off the record, then?"

"What's *Crime Wave*?" she replied. "Never heard of it."

"Come on around. I just got the autopsy from our new case. Portia Kolsch. You heard of her?"

Heard of her? Portia Kolsch was Korranthia's "It girl," the socialite heiress to the Wallow World empire. No wonder Pox had been guarded. The murder would send the stock market into a nosedive. With the little rush of adrenaline Chessa got when presented with a new mystery, she zipped over to stand on Samson's desk for a better view.

"Who hasn't?" she asked with a touch of sadness. It felt like a lifetime ago she and Gwen were watching Portia on that trash reality show about disinherited, bratty rich girls trying to make it in the big city.

Samson pointed to the photograph on his screen, his talon showing Chessa where to look. "Looks like a pro job. Whoever popped the pixie was trained to kill. It was a clean stab to the base of the skull, straight into the brain stem. She was dead before she dropped. I don't know who this pixie pissed off, but they made short work of her."

Chessa sucked air in through her teeth. As much death as she'd been around over the past few years, she was never prepared to face its imagery. Pox had warned Chessa that it was a stabbing, so she wasn't surprised by the blood that soaked Portia's salon-dyed blond hair, but she didn't expect the young socialite to look like an uncanny doll left outside to rot in the elements. Her jaw hung open, her eyes stared off into nothing, and her skin was tinged gray. Chessa never understood how Gwen could handle running her hands over corpses, using her empathic touch to pick up clues about how they died. The mere idea made her stomach lurch. It wasn't that Chessa was squeamish, it was more the disconnect between who the victim used to be and the pile of tissue and bone they'd become that she found so deeply upsetting.

She looked away. "Who do you think would pay to have her killed?"

"That's the strange thing. This doll doesn't have an enemy in the world. At least, that's what everyone says. She was a party girl, but harmless."

"It has to be something related to her family," Chessa replied.

"Bingo. O'Toole doesn't want this getting out until we understand how. The Kolches aren't a family we want to put behind the eight ball."

Chessa gave a low whistle as possible headlines ran through her mind. "The press is going to have a field day with this one."

"This stays off *Crime Wave*." Samson's voice was stern as if he were reading her mind. She could feel the advertiser cash slipping through her fingers. If there was ever a story she could monetize, this was it. Everything the Kolsches touched turned to gold, even in death. Especially in death.

Chessa grumbled some kind of non-response, but Sammy didn't press her for more. They both knew her non-disclosure agreement would keep her in line. It wasn't the threat of legal action that scared her, it was losing everything she was building with C&F Investigations. Chia the writer might not need the KPD, but Chessa the private investigator sure as hell did.

"Are you working the Mandrake Aster case?" she asked.

"Nobody is. That case was shut the minute it landed on my desk. There's a confession from a jilted lover and an arrest. Don't play dumb. It doesn't suit you."

Chessa smiled but gave herself an internal kick. She knew better than to play an angle with Samson. "Are you sure it's not a false confession? His brother claims Mandrake was ace and never had an interest in any kind of relationship."

Samson clucked. "Xander's been to see you, huh? That kid worries me. Reminds me a bit of someone we both know."

Chessa immediately knew Samson was referring to Gwen. She might be Seelie Queen now, but there was a time when she was just a Seelie royal reject, an ex-fairy godmother, broken by the murder of her princess, and out for blood. If Xander was anything like Gwen, they were all in for a world of hurt.

"So, you understand how much he needs our help," she replied.

"My wings are tied, kid. Bambi Boros confessed to killing Mandrake right there in the alley. They had a one-night stand, and he ghosted her. It was the latest in a series of rejections, and the sorceress just snapped."

Chessa pulled her electronic notebook out of her messenger bag and jotted down the name Bambi Boros. The papers hadn't given that information and neither had Xander. "Is there any chance I can talk to Bambi?"

"I'll shoot you over a copy of her confession. It's cut-and-dried, textbook. There's not much more to ask, but I'll let Pox know you've got the green light for an interrogation. Just file the paperwork with him."

"Will do. Oh, and Sammy, do you think you could get me into the morgue?"

Samson picked at his wrist feathers with his talons, a nervous tick that told Chessa he was uncomfortable. "You sure you want to do that? You're not thinking about trying out that new mojo of yours again, are you?"

Chessa shook her head. She wanted to crack a joke, but she still couldn't bring herself to make light of the raven brand seared into her palm, the mark of Morgan le Fay. It was Morgan's magic that saved Gwen during the Battle of Avalon, and it was Morgan's magic that brought Chessa's cousin Laural back from the dead, casting out a demon in the process. But when she'd tried to use it to resurrect others, the magic failed and hurt like hell in the process.

"No," was all she could muster.

"Good, because we still don't know what it does to you. Could be scrambling your cells, for all we know. Or worse."

Samson's yellow eyes bore into her.

"You don't need to tell me. It hurts like a bitch and doesn't do a damn bit of good. Norman's been combing through the Academy library for information. He told me to keep it under wraps until we understand what we're dealing with."

"Smart man, that Norman. He's got a good melon on his shoulders."

Chessa nodded in agreement and pulled on a pair of gloves. Every time she was around the dead, the brand on her palm glowed white hot and burned. She didn't need to draw attention, at least not until she understood what it all meant. "I still want to see Mandrake up close."

"If you're sure, let's shake a tail feather," replied Samson. He walked her down to the morgue. The low crime rate in fae communities combined with the high level of specialization required by fae medical examiners made it common practice for police departments to keep morgues on-site, where they fell under the direct jurisdiction of the Chief of Police, or, as in the case of the KPD, the captain. This time when Chessa passed the bullpen, nobody called out. It was probably the grim look on Samson's face. Chessa was used to it. When she was alone, everyone was her best friend, but when Samson or Gwen walked with her, it was like she was heralding the apocalypse.

As they approached the door leading to the morgue, her hand began to tingle. By the time they entered the morgue, it felt like she was holding it over a hot stove. She cussed under her breath, drawing a dubious look from Samson, but the griffin kept his beak shut.

The medical examiner, a goblin Chessa had only met in passing a few times, was young for the position, but had graduated at the top of his class. Zelnag Plum was the one creature at the KPD Chessa hadn't gone out of her way to befriend. She still couldn't bear that he had replaced Corrin, the C in C&F Investigations, her sweet, brilliant, and very dead cousin.

Zelnag must have felt the tension because he usually went out of his way to avoid her too. Upon her unannounced appearance in his lab, he stuttered and stumbled. "Sergeant. Ms. Moon. How c-can I b-be of service?"

"We're here about Mandrake Aster," said Samson. "Chessa would like to give him a once-over."

The combination of being in Corrin's old workspace and the searing pain in her hand made breathing difficult, so Chessa remained quiet.

"Right away," replied Zelnag, practically leaping up from his desk.

The office area was no longer set up for a pixie the way it had been when Corrin was around. In place of the small desk was a larger one, topped with a desktop computer and legal pad. Notes were scrawled across the paper in Zelnag's tilted writing, and Chessa could just make out the name "Kolsch" at the top of the page.

"And Portia Kolsch too, while we're here," she choked out.

Zelnag stopped in his tracks and turned to look back. "I'm afraid I can't discuss Ms. Kolsch without Captain O'Toole's approval."

Samson's feathers puffed up around his neck. "Are you pulling my pin feathers? I'm lead detective on that case," objected Samson.

"And I sent you over my findings per protocol," said the goblin. "That's all I can do. If you have questions about the autopsy, you will need to email them and CC the captain. Once he gives me the approval to answer, I will. I'm afraid I'm under strict orders on that."

Samson cocked his head but didn't respond. Chessa could tell he was fuming. Corrin never would have pulled this shit. "Can we hurry up and look at Mandrake then?" she asked. The sooner she was out of there, the sooner the searing pain in her palm would recede. She wouldn't be able to shake the other ache so easily, but one problem at a time.

"Of course. You're lucky you made it today. He's scheduled to be sent for cremation this evening," said the goblin, scurrying over to the clinical side of the room partition. "The funeral was yesterday."

That would explain why Xander had hit up Pub Nine. Aster's remains were contained in a drawer sized to accommodate larger fae, which made the pixie's two-foot tall body appear even smaller. There were multiple stab wounds to the torso. It was certainly messier than the photos that Chessa had seen of Portia Kolsch.

"Did someone hold him down?" asked Chessa, taking note of bruising on the bicep area of both arms.

"That's certainly possible. Or they grasped him tightly. It's not my job to make conclusions, only to document facts. The bruising on his arms is consistent with fingertips, however, if the assailant were a sorceress," said the goblin. "There are many other fae species in that size range as the suspect as well as mortals."

It sounded just like the kind of answer Corrin would have given, open to any possibility that fit within observable parameters. Chessa scowled and glanced at Samson, who remained quiet. It was hard to focus when she felt like her hand had been thrust into molten steel.

"Ok. Thank you. I'm done here," she said, eager to get out of the building.

Once they were far away enough from the morgue for her hand to feel normal once more, Chessa asked Samson about the bruised arms.

"Boros claimed they had an argument that turned physical. You know how angry dames can get."

Chessa shook her head. Other than Samson's misogynistic point and refusal to strike the word 'dame' from his hardboiled vocabulary, something else about the bruising was bothering her. "But they were facing the wrong way. It looked like he was grabbed from behind."

Samson padded and clacked along next to Chessa down the pathway leading around the precinct building, the city-wide glamour keeping their true natures disguised from prying mortal eyes. "I know you want to find something here, kid, but as far as the KPD is concerned, we've nailed the killer. Keep digging all you want, Danu knows I can't stop you, but do me a favor? Take it easy on Plum. He's a good kid, even if he is laced a bit tight."

That was rich, coming from Samson. Before Gwen came along, Chessa was confident the detective hadn't stepped a talon out of line.

"Sorry, Sammy. I get within ten feet of a stiff, and it hurts more than you can imagine," she said, rubbing the brand on her palm with her other hand.

"You haven't figured tops or tails of it?"

"No." Chessa looked down. She didn't like to admit that she was terrified by the power branded into her flesh. She'd raised the dead with better success than any necromancer alive, yet she had no idea how or why this power had been granted to her other than it was connected to Morgan le Fay, the first Unseelie queen. It was like the pain was begging her to use the power to bring back those they'd lost, but Danu knew, she'd tried. Gwen had to have her physically removed from the grove after the Battle of Avalon because once Laural and Gwen were safe, she'd spent hours trying to revive others, all to no avail. Still, her inability to help wasn't the only reason she was hard on Plum. "Besides, that place…"

She trailed off, but Samson must have understood. "I know. It's not his fault he's in that office. You acted like Gwen back there. And Korranthia isn't big enough to handle double that kind of abuse."

Chessa laughed. She loved Gwen, but man, did Samson have the right of it. "I miss the way she used to stalk through the KPD like she was about to light it on fire," said Chessa.

Samson shook his head. "The fires of vengeance burn the hottest."

"Well, she got much more than that. If she were here, we'd have more leads to run down."

Samson nodded. "That gift of hers is a double-edged knife, though. The sensory data she brought in was murder to decipher, and it got us all in some pickles."

The good detective was on a role with those understatements. It was Gwen's magic that helped them get the jump on the brain scraper, and the senses she'd picked up at various crime scenes saved their asses more than once. But it was that same magic that put a target on her back. If she were here now, Chessa had no doubt they'd have more information, but they'd also be in a world of trouble. It was for the best that Gwen's talents were being used for something more removed these days. Chessa hoped she was better protected, even if the stakes of her work couldn't be higher. "I'm not envious of what fate had in store for her."

"Me neither. But I sure am proud."

They rounded the corner and entered the building through the main entrance. Chessa thanked Samson, gave him a quick peck on the cheek, and said her goodbyes as he walked back toward his office. She stopped by the reception desk where Pox was sitting to fill out the form requesting an interview with Bambi Boros, then left the precinct.

5

On the way back to C&F, Chessa ran over both cases in her mind. Other than timing, choice of murder weapon, and fae species, there was nothing to connect the Kolsch murder with Mandrake Aster. Still, something in her gut told her there was more to it. This was the part she loved, the puzzle of it all. Since she was at a standstill with Mandrake until she heard back from the occupants of the Montello house, she decided to do a little digging on Portia. If there was one thing she could count on when dealing with a rich socialite, it was social media, so she headed to the office that doubled as home to snuggle in for an evening with her laptop.

When she arrived, Norman was sitting in his usual spot, a desk he'd had brought back from Avalon and which was now placed front-and-center in the living room of the apartment-turned-PI firm. Her own desk had been moved to the bedroom that used to belong to Gwen but now served as Chessa's sleeping quarters so she could more effectively run the company. There were times when she'd give anything to return to her old apartment over the industrial club and drift off to the bass beat reverberating through the walls.

"Hey Norm, any word from Q?" she asked, breaking the silence. She removed her jacket, carefully extracting her wings from the slits in the back that made flight possible without freezing half to death in the Boston winds, and gave them a quick flit to shake off the cold.

"He was in earlier. He said something about meeting the client 'round the rub a dub tonight but didn't fill out any paperwork."

Chessa grinned, partly at Norman's phrasing and partly at the idea of Quincy ever sitting down to fill out a form in preparation for hitting up Pub Nine. "Does he ever?"

"Fair point. I will get a full report from 'im tomorrow. Oh, and you had a call from Officer Pox at the KPD. Says he got you on the books to talk to Bambi Boros tomorrow at ten a.m. He also told me you went to the morgue today."

That last bit held a note of accusation.

"I didn't touch the body if that's what you're thinking."

Norman looked away from the computer to give Chessa his full attention. "Did it burn?"

She nodded.

He held out his hand, and she set hers in it, palm up. He inspected the brand as if he expected it to start glowing again. "Death calls to you," he said.

"I wish it would get another number," replied Chessa.

"That call means something. Morgan's power was unlike anything we know. All creatures of magic are born of Faerie, but most can't wield it. Fairies can."

Chessa wasn't sure where this was going, but she'd learned that sometimes, she just needed to let Norman get to the point in his own time. "So can you," she pointed out.

"That's different. Mortal practitioners like me get their powers from earth magics filtering in from the fae realm, but fae practitioners are powered by different things: the cosmos, the elements, the energy that moves the particles around us. But Morgan was more than a mere fairy like Gwen or Curtis. She was the mistress of death itself."

"You've really been hitting those history books, haven't you Norm?" Chessa said with a smile. She liked seeing him in his element. Whenever he was on the trail of a discovery, it was like he wore blinders. He wasn't much different from Chessa in that way, only his discoveries involved old books rather than alleyways and sketchy informants.

"If I could get my mitts on the books in the restricted section at the Academy, maybe I could learn more about whatever 'er magic has done to you," he said. "Here." He held out an old book with a faded cover. It was titled *The Necromancer's Guide to Lifegiving.*

"Where did you get this?"

"On my way back from the Academy, I stopped by Rise. They're a lot less precious with their books."

"You think a textbook from the school for necromancy is going to help me? You said that what I did with Laural and Gwen was something else. For one, I haven't heard that either of them has dropped an appendage."

Most fae considered necromancy a dead art, and what she had done on the battlefield surpassed anything necromancers had accomplished since Faerie was sealed off from the mortal realm many generations back.

"Turn to page 48," said Norman flatly. "Just because necromancy doesn't work right doesn't mean they haven't spent centuries learning. I think maybe they hit on something."

On page 48, Norman had marked a paragraph with a sticky note. It read:

Rule 23: Like energy, magic cannot be created nor destroyed, only harnessed. The magic used to raise the dead remains with the resurrected so long as they draw breath. No student shall use internal magics in the art of necromancy or they risk losing their own power for an indeterminant period of time. Only magics of the earth can be harnessed in such a way, and once the risen returns to the earth, so too does the magic.

"That makes sense, I guess," said Chessa, "but I still don't see how it helps."

"It would explain why you can't do it again. If you left bits of Morgan's magic in Gwen and Laural, then maybe you don't have enough to bring anyone else back."

Chessa nodded. It did feel like she'd used up a part of herself when she raised the ones she loved, but she didn't mind. It was more than worth the sacrifice.

"And it also answers a question I had about Morgan meself. She used the power to bring Arthur back from the dead. By all accounts, she loved 'er nephew Mordred more than anyone alive. If she could just go around resurrectin' folk, why didn't she bring 'im back after he and Arthur killed each other at the battle of Camlann? Maybe she couldn't."

He might be onto something. "You enjoy this stuff, don't you? I mean, the learning part."

Norman blushed. "I get lost in the research, that's all."

Speaking of research, Chessa had a socialite to cyberstalk. Thankful she had Norman working on whatever was going on with her, she went back to focusing on others. Not before asking him to order a pepperoni and pineapple pizza, though. She was famished.

Chessa had just collapsed into her oversized, overused recliner with her laptop when her cell dinged. The text was from Lance, and it only said two words: You're in. She decided to give it a few hours before replying. If she'd aroused suspicion in any of the housemates, she didn't want to push them over the edge by looking too eager. As far as they were concerned, she was just a writer looking for a crash pad. They could wait until she'd done some recon.

Sorcha, the pet shunni Chessa inherited from Gwen, formed from the shadows in the corner of the room.

"Hey there, girl," Chessa cooed absentmindedly as the shadow feline made figure eights around her ankles. It was a rare visit. Sorcha came and went as she pleased, and with Norman and Quincy always around, she preferred the Korranthia alleyways more often than not.

Chessa gave her a scratch behind the ears, eliciting a purr as the shadows bent around her fingertips, then got back to work while the shunni curled up on her lap.

By all appearances, Portia Kolsch was a typical rich pixie. Her feeds were filled with video clips and photos of her in various lavish and stylish places with B-list celebrities, influencers, and the occasional business mogul. The girl was good with her filters and angles, never appearing too processed but always managing to look like she was glowing and beautiful. Yeah, the tabloids would have a blast with this.

Chessa scrolled through her various pages and apps. She wasn't sure what she was looking for—mainly, she was trying to get a sense of who Portia was. She wasn't getting that. The girl was so careful not to let her mask slip, even Chessa's trained eye couldn't find many points of authenticity.

There.

One post from three months ago looked a little more real than the others. Chessa clicked on it and watched a clip of Portia sitting alone on her bed, surrounded by stuffed animals and pillows.

"Today is the day," she said, her voice flat. "Milo and Roberta gave me an ultimatum. They said I need to be more responsible, and they're cutting me off. Can you believe that? Like they've had to work a day in their lives!" Portia got a little gleam in her eye as she spoke.

"But they don't understand that I've already got a job. My job is to entertain you all! Last I checked, my follower count was in the hundreds of thousands. So, let's show them, let's show their entire dinosaur generation, that being an influencer *is* a real job! Thanks for your support, my lovelies!"

She gave a little wave and the clip ended. Portia Kolsch had been cut off from the golden faucet before, at least according to the PR statement that preceded the show of the same name a few years back, but maybe it was going to stick this time. Portia seemed to think so, but Chessa doubted it.

The next video was more of a cosmetics ad than a real post. Interesting. Portia was taking some advertising cash then. Chessa scrolled through all her more recent videos, all monetized product placements. The girl might know how to make herself look good, but she was terrible at making her videos appear organic. The gaps between posts grew wider as well.

Chessa took a note: *Interview Kolsches about Portia's financials.*

She spent the next hour combing through videos and photos to make sure she didn't miss anything. Sorcha abandoned her lap at some point, retreating to the shadows. Once Chessa finished internet stalking the young socialite, she did a quick search for her future housemates, but without last names for anyone but Lance, she didn't find anything beyond a mundane and abandoned social media profile for the goblin. Apparently, he was really into Family Guy ten years ago, long after its popularity had waned. Under normal circumstances, she would ask for identification for anyone she was planning to move in with, but her gut told her that too many questions would spook this lot. There was something going on with them, and she was pretty sure it was related to Mandrake's death.

She checked her phone to ensure enough time had passed then shot back a message. *Sounds great. I'll be by tomorrow afternoon.*

A thumbs-up appeared on her message. She saved Lance's number and then dug into the pizza Norm had left on the table by the door.

The pixie was late. If he was coming at all.

"Yo, we going to play or what?" Dudlin was sitting at the bar nursing a beer and waiting for Quincy to lead their little poker group into the back room. For his part, Quincy didn't want to be out of sight should Xander make an appearance. It wasn't that he cared about the little pixie; it was just that he was a half-ogre of his word. He'd told the kid he'd be here, so here he would remain.

"Not tonight."

"You've got to be shitting me! You blew us off last night, and we gave you a pass. You've changed, Q, and not for the better," said Dudlin, shaking his head.

Before he could say another word, Quincy lifted him by the flabby flesh of his into the air, Dudlin's stubby legs kicking. "You wanna test how much I've changed?"

Dudlin made a garbled sound, and Quincy dropped him on the ground and let him scramble away. He turned to Elda, the bartender. "This fuckin' guy," he said, motioning to the empty space where Dudlin stood moments before.

She shook her head and went back to drying glasses with a bar towel. She would never cross Quincy, even if he'd strangled Dudlin on the spot, but he made it a general practice to stay on the good side of his bartenders, especially those as wicked hot as Elda.

"Sorry about that," he said. I'm a bit on edge lately. You seen a pixie come in here today? The one I had with me last night?" Quincy put on his most polite voice, but he couldn't help but stare at the witch's cleavage. He'd have to leave a good tip tonight to make up for it.

Elda gave a little chuckle. "You mean the boy who just turned wing when he saw you assault another customer?"

"Shit." Quincy pushed through the pack of sorority girls clogging the dance floor and jogged out the front door just in time to see Xander flying off over the bushes.

"Xander! Come back! I ain't going to hurt ya!" Quincy called. "Dudlin's perfectly fine. He's a buddy of mine."

"Next you're going to tell me that there's a team of necromancers standing by to bring him back after you kill him!" Saying it out loud must have taken some of the steam out of the teen because he slowed to a hover.

Of all the rotten timing. "It was nothing but a little squabble between friends." Quincy hoped he could win Xander back over.

"If that's how you treat your friends, I'm not so sure I want to be one." Xander's mouth twitched as if he were fighting back a smile, and he lowered himself to the ground.

Quincy chuckled. "You'd get it if you knew Dudlin."

It took more coaxing than Quincy was used to delivering to get Xander to go back into Pub Nine, but eventually, he was able to lure the teen with the promise of another beer. Chessa would accuse him of contributing to the delinquency of a minor, he had no doubt, but then, the boss wasn't around, was she? Once they were settled into a booth, Quincy yelled across the bar to where his poker buddies were huddled.

"Dudlin, you're aight, ain't ya?"

The goblin rolled his eyes and made a show of turning his back. Quincy might have to smooth things over later.

"See, he's fine."

"Why did you want me to come here?" asked Xander. "I'm sure it wasn't for the company."

"Why are you so sure about that?" asked Quincy. It was always a shame when a young person didn't know their own value, but Quincy realized his misstep as soon as he saw the look on Xander's face.

"Oh, uh… You're not going to… I mean, you're not looking for…"

Quincy burst out laughing. "Calm your nads, you ain't my type. Now that, over there, she's more my speed." He motioned in the direction of

Elda, bent over the bar in her micro-mini skirt and a sequined low-cut top. Yeah, she would look boss on the back of his bike. But Quincy wasn't here for a hook-up. He was on a case. Sort of. Besides, he had a firm rule of never fraternizing with the staff of Pub Nine. It was bad for business.

Xander seemed to visibly relax, melting back into the side of the booth designed for small fae and taking a swig from his glass. "Ok, then, what do you want with me?"

"Two things. One, I want to get as much information about your brother as I can. Fae don't just drop dead in the alleys of Korranthia."

The tension returned to the young pixie's features. "And the other thing?"

"I want to make sure you're okay. I know you got money to care for yourself and all, but a kid your age shouldn't be alone in the world. Believe me. I know."

Xander's eyes cut to the door, and Quincy realized he needed to get him talking before the kid made some excuse to bolt. "Can you tell me anything else about the weeks leading up to Mandrake's murder?"

The answer to that wasn't much. Xander had been alone a lot longer than Mandrake had been dead. Big bro sent cash, and there was a weekly phone call, some texts exchanged back and forth, but other than that, Xander had very limited contact with his guardian. The more he heard, the more pissed Quincy got. By the time they'd finished their drinks, he was thinking that good old Mandrake might not be the saint Xander portrayed him to be. He certainly didn't step up for his little brother.

"So, you've been living in your family home alone since the Battle of Avalon."

Xander nodded, his brown hair falling over his gray-blue eyes.

"That ain't right. How are your grades?"

"My what?" asked Xander.

"Your grades. In school," replied Quincy. "Did I stutter?"

"Oh, no. I mean, I didn't think you'd care about that."

"Why? Because I'm a low-life half-ogre barfly? Answer the question." In truth, Quincy wasn't sure why he cared. This kid was nothing to him. But he knew how hard life could be for a teenager on his own in this town.

"I've got straight As."

That got Q's attention. "You're some wicked smart pixie, huh?"

Xander shrugged. "It was one of the things Mandrake insisted on. He said school was important."

Quincy nodded. "What else did he insist on?"

"You know, the usual. No drugs, safe sex." The teen took another swig of his beer.

"Your brother was right," said Quincy. "That's all important shit."

"Well, he's gone."

"But he would have wanted you to stay in school. Keep those grades up. Want another round?"

Xander laughed.

"What?" said Quincy. He didn't think he'd said anything particularly funny.

"It's Tuesday night," Xander replied.

"So?"

"So, you're here telling me how important school is while you order me drinks in a bar on a school night."

Quincy cursed. The kid had a point. Come to think of it, how many beers had the pixie downed? "How old are you anyhow?"

"Fifteen."

Quincy took the glass out of Xander's hand with his thumb and forefinger. It was tiny to him, but it was the size of Xander's head.

"Hey!"

"You're right. You need to go to school in the morning," said Quincy, thinking it might have been a good thing for the kid to see him about to whoop Dudlin's ass.

"Damn it, man, make up your mind!"

That was just it. Quincy couldn't make up his mind. He wasn't sure what he was doing here. Was he shooting the shit? Checking up on the kid? Working a case? Perhaps he was doing a bit of it all.

"Tomorrow, we meet at the library," he said. "Now go home and get some sleep."

Xander shot him an unreadable look but didn't object. "Which library?"

Quincy thought for a minute then remembered the old building his grandmother used to take him to before his life went to shit. It was the one place his father would never think to go, so it always felt safe.

"The one on Tremont. Right after school."

"Fine."

What the fuck am I doing? thought Quincy as he watched Xander leave.

"What the fuck are you doing?" asked Dudlin, sliding into the booth and sloshing his beer in the process.

"You should be asking what I'm gonna do. I'm about to cream the lot of you in poker," growled Quincy. He motioned for Elda to put a round of drinks on his tab, his peace offering, then led his posse into the back room.

7

The next morning, Chessa pulled a suitcase together in record time. She needed to pack enough for her ruse to be believable, but not so much that it looked like she was planning to stay long-term. She didn't want to bring her favorite things because there was no telling how this was going to go, and she'd be pissed if she had to abandon her shimmery blue club dress or the Ramones shirt she'd stolen from Gwen.

She was decked out in her second-tier duds, carrying a suitcase filled with more of the same when she got out of the taxi she'd taken to Dorchester. It was a much more relaxed way to travel than flying or tempting the fates by going Leaf Pass, even if it did get costly. While she wanted to support fae businesses, she just didn't have the luxury of hoping the flunky wizards and witches using elemental magic to move small fae from stop to stop would get it right this time. Last time, she'd been trying for Starbucks but ended up on top of a sand dune near Lake Michigan.

The key was under the planter just like Lance had told her it would be, and the house was eerily quiet. She let herself in and headed to the top of the stairs to scope out the room they'd set aside for her, the last room on the right just past the bathroom. It was still filled with Mandrake's belongings. Under normal circumstances, that would be a bad thing, but for Chessa's purposes, it was a jackpot. She dumped her suitcase on the bed and decided to explore the rest of the house while it was empty. Mandrake's stuff could wait.

She started with the room across from hers. The door opened quietly, and one look around told her immediately that it was Abi's. The dresser top was filled with cosmetics, perfumes, and a few pill bottles. There was a migraine prescription, an anxiety pill, and one other medication Chessa was unfamiliar with, all with labels bearing the name Abigail Marquis. She snapped a quick photo for later research then went about her business, finding nothing abnormal in the tidy room except the closet, which was filled with dazzling outfits far too formal for the kinds of small theater productions Abi probably frequented. Chessa smiled to herself. That pixie was going places.

The next room was a different story. She opened the door and was met with an overwhelming odor. It was like a bag of Cheetos erupted all over a pile of dirty laundry. There were piles of books, clothes, and knick-knacks all over the room, the bed was unmade, and the curtains were drawn. If Chess had ever discovered a dragon cave, she expected it would look and smell slightly better than this. Lance's comment about their missing roommate clicked in her mind. This must be Honey's room.

And sprawling in the high-back desk chair in front of a glowing screen against the wall was the pixie Chessa presumed to be Honey. She was dressed in jeans and a purple tank top, and Chessa couldn't tell if she was wearing makeup or if her elegant, butterscotch features and dark eyelashes accentuated her green eyes naturally. She was scowling.

"Who the fuck are you?" she asked, a game controller in one hand and a Mountain Dew in the other. On the screen, in a state of suspended animation, was the new release from the *Xora* game franchise. What was it called? Tears in the Fabric? Something like that. Chessa used to play *Xora* back in the day but switched over to desktop gaming once she got Gwen hooked on *Death Mob*. She found the new *Xora* releases too time-intensive, and she didn't have cash to drop on a console.

"Oh, I'm sorry, I must have the wrong room," Chessa said, thinking fast.

"That doesn't answer my question," said the other pixie, but her body language belied her words. If she truly saw Chessa as a threat, she wouldn't be so chill. Her eyes cut to her screen. It was obvious she wanted to get back to what she was doing.

"I'm Chia, the new girl. I thought this might be the bathroom. Sorry about that. Are you Honey?"

"Oh yeah. Dom said something about a new roomie. Bathroom's across the hall. Close the door on your way out." Honey returned to her game before Chessa had the chance to follow directions.

Thanking her lucky stars that Honey didn't catch her going through Abi's room, Chessa retreated back to her new room to take notes. She wasn't sure why she was surprised that Honey was also a pixie. Some fae gravitated toward their own kind, but with both murder vics being pixies, the fact that Abi, Honey, and Mandrake were cohabitating seemed noteworthy.

Once she'd jotted down the few pieces of information she'd gathered from her truncated snoop, she turned her attention to going through Mandrake's belongings under the guise of packing them up. There were tons of books on drawing and more than a few sketchbooks containing his art. Sketches of unfamiliar faces and places filled the pages. He was quite good, in Chessa's untrained opinion. There might be a clue here, but it would take hours to wade through, so she set the books on the nightstand to peruse later and got to work on everything else.

With no boxes on hand, she made neat stacks of everything. Mandrake hadn't amassed much in his room, and she made a mental note to find out how long he'd lived here. It seemed to her that he used the space as a place to sleep and that was about it. On the dresser was a framed photo of him with his family. They looked so happy—Mandrake with his arm draped over Xander's shoulders, and Xander grinning from ear to ear. She put the photo with the sketchbooks in case her client wanted to keep it.

Dom's voice made Chessa jump. "Please excuse the mess. None of us had the heart to clear it out, and Drake didn't have much of a family."

"Oh, it's no problem," answered Chessa, wondering if that was a barb directed at Xander. "Most pixies aren't hoarders."

"And you are?"

"No."

Dom raised an eyebrow. "Ok, then. Let me know if you need anything."

"Perhaps a few boxes or trash bags?" replied Chessa wondering why this interaction was so tense. Perhaps every interaction Dom was that way. It wouldn't surprise her.

"Coming right up," he said before disappearing from the doorway with a flourish.

That guy was interesting, and Chessa couldn't decide if she was drawn to him or if he creeped her out. She tried to keep any judgments at bay until time let her get a beat on people, but he seriously messed with her instincts. His vibe felt like multiple people trapped in one, flamboyant form.

He returned a moment later with a box containing two trash bags. "That's all we've got. I'll have Lance grab more at the store on his way home."

Chessa smiled. "Thanks. Where is he, anyways? And Abi?"

"Do you plan to keep tabs on everyone while you're here?"

"No. I just wanted to get everyone together to say thank you for letting me move in," said Chessa. Damn, he was touchy.

"Well, good luck with that," replied Dom. He disappeared again before Chessa could ask another question, his platform shoes sounding like hooves on the wood floor of the hall.

Once all Mandrake's possessions were packed and stacked against the far wall, Chessa stripped the bed and remade it with her own sheets. She settled in with the sketchbooks. They were dated, which was helpful because she was able to work backward, viewing the world through the dead pixie's eyes. She recognized a few locations from around town—the pocket park on Josephine, Fenway, and the columns at the IFAE campus. A few didn't look like they were from the Boston area at all, and most she had no clue about. As for the portraits, most of the faces were new to her. About halfway through the newest sketchbook, she found a sketch of Abi smiling back at her. The lines were soft, and even though the drawing was in pencil, she seemed to glow. She was quite beautiful. Chessa couldn't help but smile back at the picture. A few pages later was a portrait of Dom. He was wearing the long leopard-print jacket he'd had on when they first met and a feather boa, but the shading of his face was harsh, and his eyes almost looked cruel. Interesting. She couldn't find Honey or Lance at all.

Chessa turned each page carefully, studying Mandrake's linework, looking for anyone who seemed to bear more importance to the artist than the others. She pulled a pack of Post-its out of her messenger bag and used them to mark pages of note as she snacked on a granola bar. A knock on the door pulled her attention before she was able to make it all the way through the first book.

"Come in," she said.

It was Abi.

Her auburn hair fell around her shoulders, and she wore a sheer white robe with a feathered collar over light blue silk pajamas.

Keep it professional, thought Chessa.

"Hey there, I thought you might want some tea," said Abi. Only then did Chessa notice the mug in her hands. "You strike me as a chai girl."

Chessa gave a little laugh. "How could you tell?"

"It's a gift. I'd say you're also into beer, B-flicks, and the scent of vanilla."

Ok, that was eerie. "That's some gift you've got," said Chessa as she took the cup from Abi's hands.

"I cheated on that last one. I noticed that you smelled like vanilla when you stopped by before."

"What about you? What are you into?" asked Chessa.

"Not going through a dead stranger's sketchbooks."

Oh, shit. Chessa had forgotten that the books were spread all over the bed. She opened her mouth to respond but couldn't come up with a plausible lie. Instead, she went for the truth. "I was curious about Mandrake. I saw his death on the news, and I guess I fancy myself an amateur sleuth. Being here in his room was too tempting."

Abi squinted. Chessa realized too late that she'd underestimated the other pixie.

"You said Xander told you about the room? Why would hearing about Drake on the news be a surprise if his brother already clued you in? How do you know Xander anyhow?"

"He lives near my mom. She's been looking out for him since his parents died."

The look on Abi's face told her the jig was up. Damn. She hadn't lasted a day. She could usually read people better than this. Something about everyone in this house garbled the voice inside that she relied on to keep her safe. She would have to be careful.

"And you said you write true crime?"

"Yes."

"True crime as in *Crime Wave*, perhaps?"

Chessa took a sip of her tea to steady her nerves. She wanted to seem as unaffected as possible, but she felt everything but chill right now. "When did you figure it out?"

"Not long after you left. Dom doesn't know. I wanted to feel you out before I said anything. Is this for a story? It seems a crass way to get one if you ask me."

Chessa glanced at the open door, wondering if she should stick around or call it quits. She looked back over at Abi and decided she was up for a challenge. "No, it's not. I'll tell you everything, but I will warn you that I'm going to ask you not to share once I do."

"Why don't you ask now?"

"Because it's not a fair request before you know what you're agreeing to," said Chessa.

Abi walked across the room and shut the door before returning to sit on the edge of the bed. "I can't figure you out," she said.

"Let me clear a few things up. I'm Chessa Moon. I do run *Crime Wave*, but my primary gig at this point is private investigations focused specifically on fae cases that don't get a fair shake with the authorities."

Realization dawned on Abi's face. "Xander hired you," she said.

"Yes."

"And you're here because you think one of us was involved with Mandrake's death? Holy shit. I can't keep this from the guys! Are we suspects? The killer came forward, you know!"

"Xander didn't buy it. He says Mandrake wasn't interested in relationships of any kind." Chessa watched Abi's face to gauge her reaction. There wasn't one.

"That's true enough. Drake seemed content with the life he had. We really were like a family, you know, despite how the guys laugh it off."

"Then you must have suspected that Boros was lying too."

Abi sighed. "Honestly, I don't know what to think. The idea that someone killed Drake took us all off-guard. I guess we just wanted an explanation. When that dancer came forward, we accepted that maybe there were things that Drake kept from us, you know?"

Chessa nodded. "Did he frequently keep things from you?"

Abi hesitated before answering. "Not really. I mean, not that I know of."

Chessa's gut told her there was something there, but pushing Abi now might make her crack. She needed to turn her into an ally.

"So, now comes the part I promised," said Chessa with a hopeful smile.

"Where you ask me to keep your secret? If we're not suspects, why can't I tell the boys? It's been so hard losing Mandrake, and then, in the aftermath of it all, figuring out how to keep going."

Chessa let Abi gloss over whatever she'd been about to say. There would be plenty of time to chip away at her once they were closer. That was the hope, anyhow.

"Honestly, Abi, I try to approach cases with as little judgment as possible. I'm not the police looking for a collar. I'm just a pixie trying to get at the truth of the situation to help a grieving brother understand why he's alone in the world. I can't do that if people are acting weird, and believe me, if they know that I'm a PI, they will act weird."

Abi bit her bottom lip, the motion causing untoward thoughts to jump into Chessa's mind, then some emotion crossed her face. Chessa couldn't tell if it was resolve or defiance. "I don't know. I'm still uncomfortable with all this."

"What can I do to make you more comfortable?" Chessa asked, allowing a hint of flirtation to touch her words.

By the way Abi's eyes went wide and cheeks flushed, she could tell it wasn't in vain. "I might be able to think of a few ways," she replied, sliding close enough for the feathers at the top of her robe to graze Chessa's arm.

Chessa leaned in, only slightly, and Abi's baby blues rose to meet her gaze. When Abi gave a wicked little smile, Chessa felt the last of her reserve melt away. She was the boss, and she decided it was well within her rights to have a little fun on the job. She gave in to the smell of lavender, the softness of Abi's full lips, and the desire pulling at the center of her being.

This case was starting to get *interesting*.

8

Chessa was exhausted by the time she made it back to C&F Investigations from the house on Montello, and not just because of Abi, though the bombshell pixie had demanded a significant amount of her energy. Once both their appetites were sated, they'd spent the rest of the night running through details of Mandrake's life, the roommates' routines, and any other intel Chessa could think to gather. Until the sun rose, and she'd gone in for round two. She smiled to herself as she slipped out of the house. Abi had gone to her own room, and Chessa figured that if Dom was so secretive about everyone's comings and goings, nobody would question her about where she went in the early morning hours. If they did, she would make up a story about a day job. It wouldn't be entirely a lie, after all.

Despite the sun still being low in the sky, Norman was at his post, coffee in hand, when she arrived. He'd grown up drinking tea and had recently discovered the miracle of a steaming cup of joe. He didn't bother with a greeting. Instead, he held up his hand, an old book clutched in his fingers.

"Can you give me the Cliffs Notes?" asked Chessa. It wasn't that she minded a hefty read, but at that moment, she craved her pillow, and she was getting a bit tired of having heavy tomes thrust at her every time she flew through the door.

Norman dropped the book on the desk with a *fwap*. "In this account of

Arthur's life, Gorpus Hilldebrand talks about how the once and future king absorbed magic from Morgan and used it to heal the realm."

"Sure. All the legends agree that for a time, King Arthur brought peace to Britain."

"This confirms my theory about your magical transference. You see that, right?"

Chessa squinted. "I guess. But if that's the case, shouldn't Gwen be having an easier time of healing the Seelie Court?"

Gwen was doing great things, that fact was undeniable, but every victory was hard-won. She had a tight circle of adoring fae working to implement all of her changes The ripples were affecting fae societies across the globe, but there were plenty of wounds, both old and new, thwarting her progress. To call the work healing was a stretch.

The wizard grunted. "Perhaps." He looked like he was on edge.

"Is everything ok, Norm?" Chessa asked.

"Something about this case isn't sitting right with me," he replied. "It's not just the stuff about your magic."

Sorcha did figure eights through Chessa's legs in greeting, giving the illusion of darkness swirling around her feet. The pixie reached down and gave the shadow cat a scratch behind the ears before the shunni merged back into the shadows with a soft, gurgling sound. "The Aster case? How do you mean?"

"Nobody but the brother seems to think anything of this Mandrake guy getting offed in the back alley by his stripper ex. It's like they know something they won't share. I've been digging into his life, and he seems on the straight and narrow, so what gives?"

Chessa nodded. "Yeah, I've definitely got that same feeling. Abigail Marquis saw through me. I think she'll keep my secret from the rest, but my cover is blown as far as she's concerned."

"Bloody hell, little miss, it's only been a couple of days!"

"I know. She's sharper than she lets on. Softer too." Chessa tried not to smile, and Norman shot her a look. She cleared her throat, hoping he'd let it pass. "If you're ready to take notes, I've got a slew of information to unload. I spent hours getting as much from her as I could."

"And 'er word is good?" Norman's trust was hard-earned, but his skepticism was the perfect balance for Chessa's faith in people. It was a balance Gwen used to strike, but if there was anyone less trusting than an outcast fairy with a vendetta, it was an outcast wizard who'd been used as a political pawn for half his life.

"Yes. Abi seemed to genuinely want to help."

A rare soft smile appeared on Norman's face. "You do bring out the best in people," he said. Behind his gruff exterior, he wanted to believe in goodness in the world, even if he hadn't seen much firsthand.

They got to work documenting names, locations, routines of the victim, and known associates of the Montello housemates. Thanks to Abi, Chessa now had surnames along with information on Mandrake's art gigs and interpersonal relations. He bartended at Flit's, a beatnik bar not far from his little commune, most weekends to make ends meet, and he'd recently been talking to someone he'd met there, an ogre named Hugo, about an art commission.

None of the intel seemed like an obvious lead, but it was certainly a place to start.

"You start researching everything you can about the housemates," said Chessa. "I'm going to take a nap then run some things down about Portia Kolsch before I hit up Flit's tonight."

"Have you eaten?" asked Norman.

In a sense, thought Chessa. Instead, she replied, "I had a granola bar for linner last night."

"For the millionth time, linner isn't a thing. There's brunch, but you're supposed to have a *minimum* of two full meals per day," said Norman.

Chessa shrugged and took the pizza box Norman handed her. She really was famished, and the cold pizza breakfast washed down with Norman's special coffee blend hit the spot.

"Oh, hey," she said, "If Q comes in, tell him I want to chat with him sometime today. I'd like to bring him up to speed on the case and have him ask around about this Hugo character."

After catching a few z's, Chessa took a quick shower, freshened up, and prepared herself for a visit to the correctional facility holding Bambi Boros, the jealous not-lover not-killer of Mandrake Aster.

"Q didn't show up?" Chessa asked Norman when she emerged from the bedroom to find the wizard sitting on the threadbare couch reading yet another old book. The apartment office was beginning to smell like a library.

"No, but he called. I guess he's been spending some quality time with our client."

That was odd. Quincy always complained about the young fae invading Pub Nine from the nearby universities, and she didn't expect that he'd go out of his way to hang out with a teenage client unless he'd managed to get him to wager his trust fund in a game of poker. "Really? I wonder what he's playing at," said Chessa.

"No idea," replied Norman. "I asked 'im about Hugo, and the name didn't ring a bell. He said he'd ask around."

"Perfect. I'm heading over to the jail to talk to our patsy. You got details on her?"

Norman stood up and stretched then walked over to the desk and began to click away at the keyboard before answering. "Bambi Boros, sorceress. She was a dancer at the Painted Pony, a Tuesday afternoon girl if you catch my drift. She had a little apartment down in Hyde Park, no family, only a handful of friends. Got picked up a few years ago for shoplifting. That's it."

"Was she into the arts at all?"

"Not as far as I can tell. If so, it's not in the file Detective Wayne sent over. They got their confession, so I doubt the KPD dug too much into her social life."

Chessa nodded. "They sure do love their open and shut cases."

9

Quincy was sweating like a whore in church. Or maybe more like a half-ogre gambler in a library. Even the librarian, a human with a generally friendly demeanor, had given him the side-eye when he walked through the front doors. The glamour might cover up his ogre size, but his mohawk, scar, and biker gear still made him stick out amongst the students, mothers, and other library patrons.

"He'd better not be late," he muttered as he pretended to peruse the self-help section.

He half expected the librarian to kick him out, or worse, offer to help him find something, but thankfully, the process was mostly automated. A child who didn't look old enough to operate a phone walked up to a kiosk, navigated the touchscreen without a problem, scanned her books, took her receipt, and toddled away.

Quincy shook his head, remembering the last time he'd been in this building. His grandmother read to him in the corner. He couldn't read himself back then, and he certainly wouldn't have known what to do with an automated kiosk. Sometimes he felt like the world was passing him by.

"Cool, right?" said Xander. He must have slipped in while Quincy was distracted and seen him staring at the book-scanning robot.

"Sure."

"Why am I here?" asked Xander, skipping all pleasantries. "Did you want to talk about my brother?"

"Nah. I wanted to talk about you. Can we find a place to sit?"

Xander shrugged and walked over to an empty table. It was right in the middle of the room, the last choice Quincy would have made. He lowered himself down onto a white plastic chair that he thought might collapse under his weight.

Xander sat on the edge of the table and stared expectantly. Quincy struggled for words. With his knees nearly up to his chest, in the middle of a mortal library, he had no idea what he was trying to accomplish. He looked over at the teen. "So, uh, how's it going at school?"

"What is this?" asked Xander. "I hired your firm to help find my brother's killer, so why did you drag me here? Is there something about Mandrake you couldn't tell me last night?"

"No, nothing like that. I was just sort of, well, I just wanted to…"

"To play big brother to the lost youth of Korranthia?"

Quincy felt the blood rush to his cheeks and wondered if he might be coming down with something. It wasn't a sensation he was familiar with. "I ain't nobody's brother," he said.

"Do you suspect me of some involvement in Mandrake's death?" Xander's icy eyes bored into Quincy's dark ones. "I didn't kill my brother."

"Of course not. It's just, you remind me a bit of myself if I'm being honest. When I was your age, I could have used somebody to talk to."

"Oh, I'm a vanity project."

"The opposite actually. I don't want you turning out like me. Nobody was there for me, to tell me to go to school, to check to make sure I had food. It was just me, living day to day, taking care of myself. It ain't right."

Xander stared at Quincy. It was the most uncomfortable the half-ogre had been in his entire life, having a young pixie see a side of himself he kept hidden from the world and sit there in silent judgment. Finally, the young pixie spoke.

"Look, I appreciate you trying to reach out. It's obvious it's not a thing you do often. But I'm doing fine. Mandrake sent me enough cash to last through graduation, and after that, I'll figure something out. I'm not on the streets, and no offense, but I've got no plans to turn out like you."

That was a relief. Quincy attempted to smile. He didn't really want the responsibility of looking after a hot-headed teenager anyway.

"If it makes you feel better, we can meet up sometimes," said Xander.

"But for the love of Danu, can it not be at a library? And can we cut it down to once a week, tops?"

Quincy laughed, this time genuinely. "That would be good," he replied. "But the pub ain't exactly the most responsible location either."

"How about Viva Burrito over on Franklin? Taco Tuesdays?"

"Taco Tuesdays, I like that." He loved tacos. He actually had a tattoo of a taco with a chibi face shaking a pair of maracas on his left ass cheek, the result of a bet he'd lost a few years back, but he wasn't about to share that little nugget with this kid.

As Quincy walked away from the library, he felt like a load had been taken off his shoulders. He wasn't sure what it was about Xander that made him want to intervene, but he'd thought of little else ever since he'd shoved the pixie through the door of C&F Investigations. He didn't know the first thing about mentoring at-risk youth, but queso and beer, he could manage.

10

The Bathory Correctional Institute for Fae was a small building, not much more than an office complex, located off Southampton. On the surface, nobody would know that the concrete walls were fortified with iron particles to keep fae from breaking out. The concentration wasn't enough to be lethal, at least not on the painted-over surfaces of the walls, but every fae creature knew better than to chip away at the exterior. Nobody went so far as to drill a screw or hammer a nail to hang a picture for fear of breathing in the iron-rich dust. As a result, the walls were stark along the corridor leading to the front office. The astringent smell of cleaning products made Chessa wrinkle her nose, but the elf stationed behind a clear barrier didn't seem to mind it. She looked up briefly and motioned for Chessa to wait while she chatted on the cellphone glued to her ear.

"Horrace Grimes? No way! Well, if you want to know what I think, you should just cut him off for good. If he wants to go playing in the pig pen, he's gonna get dirty, that's what I have to say." The elf flipped her strawberry blonde hair over her shoulder and scowled in Chessa's direction. "Hang on, I've got a visitor."

After she set the phone down on the counter, Chessa flitted up to stand on the portion on her side of the partition. "Hello, I've got an appointment to speak with Bambi Boros."

The elf slid a clipboard through the slot, making Chessa have to step back to avoid being shoved off the counter. "Fill out this form. And leave any personal effects in the locker by the door. No weapons. No paraphernalia."

Chessa did as instructed. By the time she initialed and signed in all the right places, the elf was back on the phone. She didn't bother to look up as she buzzed Chessa through the heavy green door. All doors in the hallway were closed except the one at the end, which was slightly ajar. Chessa assumed that was where she was headed. The room was small and contained a table and four chairs, all bolted to the ground. A guard waiting just inside the doorway told Chessa to take one of the seats, then he disappeared down the hall. Ten long minutes later, he returned with a humanoid woman Chessa could only assume was Bambi Boros. She had stringy, light brown hair that fell to her shoulders, and big hazel eyes that regarded Chessa with suspicion. Her blue pants and shirt resembled scrubs, and Chessa could better picture her working as a nurse than dancing on a pole at the Painted Pony.

"Hello Bambi, I'm Chessa Moon. I'm a private investigator hired by Mandrake Aster's brother, and I'd like to ask you a few questions."

"I didn't know Drake had a brother," replied the woman as the guard latched her to a chair on the opposite side of the table and retreated out the door.

"Really? How long did you date?" asked Chessa.

"Oh, um, I mean to say that I didn't know his brother was in town. I don't have to talk to you, do I? Should I have my lawyer? I did it. I killed him."

It didn't take a pixie gift to know this woman didn't know the first thing about her purported boyfriend. She was clearly frightened, but Chessa wasn't sure how to get her to talk. In her experience, the only way to talk to gain the trust of someone so rattled was to be real with them.

"Bambi, I'm not here to hurt you. I've read your confession. I can tell you're scared. I'd like to help you if I can, but I don't know how long they're going to let me speak with you. I'm only here because I've got a friend at the KPD who pulled some strings."

The expression on Bambi's face nearly broke Chessa's heart. She wanted to talk, but her eyes kept darting to the door, and she was rocking back and forth as if attempting to soothe herself.

"I see you don't want to talk about Mandrake, so why don't you just tell me about you. I heard that you worked at the Painted Pony."

"Yes, I danced there on the weekdays when Glitz wanted some enticing entertainment to bring people in."

"Did you like the gig?"

Bambi stopped rocking and looked Chessa in the eye. "You know, I really did. I felt powerful up on that stage. Untouchable. They let me use my magic in my dance, to make silk scarves twirl around me and stuff like that."

"You're an air practitioner?" Sorceresses worked with elemental magic, but it was rude to ask which one unless they offered up details about their magic. Chessa was glad for the opening.

"Yeah. And when I was on stage, I wasn't just a sex object, I was an artist, and for the length of a song, I controlled the room."

Chessa smiled. "I wish I could have seen it."

A shadow passed over Bambi's face. "You won't get the chance now."

"Right. Because you killed Mandrake Aster. Did you meet him at the Painted Pony?"

"No. Drake wouldn't hang out in a place like that. He wasn't much for bars at all, except the one he worked at, of course."

"Then where did you meet him?"

"A coffee shop."

"He was an artist too," said Chessa, hoping to keep her talking. She wasn't sure how much time she had to get the answers she needed. The sorceress was sure to clam up again at any moment. "Is that what drew you to him?"

Bambi stared down at the table and nodded.

"I was told that you and Mandrake got into an argument beforehand. That there was some kind of altercation. Can you tell me about that?"

Boros glanced up before averting her eyes again. "Drake wanted to call it off, and I didn't agree. Simple as that."

"Did he hurt you? Push you away?"

The woman shook her head. "No," she said softly, "nothing like that. He wouldn't hurt me."

Chessa pressed on. "But there was some kind of physical altercation, right?"

"Oh, yes. I grabbed his arm to keep him from leaving."

It was yet another indication that Boros was lying. An air sorceress would have no need to grab a pixie's arms because she could simply manipulate the wind to hold him in place. Chessa proceeded as if she believed the story. "Both arms?"

Bambi fidgeted with her fingers. "Maybe. I don't remember. I told him to look me in the eyes and tell me he didn't love me."

There it was. A lie that could be debunked with hard evidence. "So, he was facing you while you were holding onto his arms?"

She nodded.

"Bambi, I know you didn't kill Mandrake."

"Yes, I did!" protested the sorceress, her voice cracking as she made desperate eye contact with Chessa.

"No, you didn't. I don't even think you dated him. I want to help you, but I can't if you're not going to be straight with me."

The sorceress tried to stand up, but the cuffs kept her in place. "I don't want your help," she said. "Guards!"

Chessa lowered her voice, hoping the guard wouldn't return to take Boros back to her cell before she got everything she came for. "Look, I know someone has threatened you. I just need to know who. Is it your employer?" Madam Glitz owned the Painted Pony, and it was a well-known secret that she was one of Korranthia's most powerful crime bosses. She was just too smart to ever get caught. Maybe she was the link Chessa was looking for. Her words stopped Bambi cold.

"Glitz? No. She took me in when I had nowhere else to go. She gave me a job, one that brought me peace. She has nothing to do with any of this."

In defending Glitz, Bambi admitted that someone was pulling her strings. "Then who?"

Tears filled the sorceress' eyes. Sensing that she'd gotten all she would from the woman, Chessa switched tactics. "Ok. I won't push you to say any more. Is there anything I can do to help you?"

"No. Please don't try. Nobody will miss me, and it's better this way."

"With you locked up? Why?"

Bambi shook her head.

"Ok. I'll back off," said Chessa. "Just one more thing. Do you know anything about Portia Kolsch?"

Bambi sniffed and looked perplexed. "Not much. I saw her at the Pony all the time, but we never talked about anything important."

"Did you ever see her with Drake?"

"Oh, no way. He would never be friends with someone like her. Not that she would give him the time of day anyways. She was a late-night, pop the expensive champagne for me and my girls type. I never saw her with anyone who wouldn't look good on a reel or social media feed, and that wasn't Mandrake Aster. Why are you asking?"

"She was murdered too."

"What? No way!" Bambi's surprise seemed genuine.

"The police don't think there's a connection, but I'm not so sure. Whoever it was that blackmailed you into this, I need to figure out if they had a connection to the Kolsches." Chessa knew she shouldn't say so much to someone awaiting trial for murder, but she believed Bambi's story.

"I can't help with that," replied Bambi. "I didn't know Portia well, but she didn't deserve that. I truly am sorry."

When Chessa left the prison, it was just after noon. She flitted back to C&F to plan her next move—a visit to one of the richest families in Korranthia. Despite what Bambi told her, she couldn't let go of the Kolsch case. Maybe Mandrake and Portia didn't pal around together, but that didn't mean they weren't connected in other ways.

After grabbing a peanut butter and banana sandwich, Chessa donned her best pantsuit. She tried to make herself look as businesslike as possible, which was a feat considering the intricate black tattoo work covering her iridescent wings and her hair color du jour, neon green and black. When she emerged back into the office space, Norman raised his bushy eyebrows but kept his mouth shut. Considering he was wearing his most outlandish wizard hat yet, a blue one with stars all over it, he made the right choice.

"I'm off to pay the Kolsches a little visit," she said to Norman, who was eating his own lunch, a bowl of ramen, at the kitchen table.

"You're what, now?"

"What do you think? Can I pass for a chauffeur?" Chessa did a little twirl, showing of her pants suit while he chuckled.

"I've only been in this kingdom for a few months, and even I know you ain't getting near that family. Have you considered calling in a favor?"

"From Gwen? Absolutely not." Chessa had made it clear to everyone at C&F that Gwen was a partner in name only at this point. She was now Seelie Queen, and her involvement came with strings, security, and all kinds of optics. Besides, she had more important issues to deal with than a murdered socialite.

"I'm just saying that Her Grace could open doors."

"And having her do that would close others. Nope. I'm going in alone. Did you go back to the Academy this morning?"

Norman nodded. "The magical transference theory was a dead-end, but I've found more about Arthur, Camelot, and Britain during those times. It seems that Arthur wouldn't have risen to such heights without another fairy's help, The Lady of the Lake."

"Right. She gave him Excalibur, right? Or was it in a stone? I can never keep it straight."

"The tales differ from telling to telling, but the most reliable accounts claim she was responsible for giving 'im Excalibur. But she nearly died months prior to fulfilling 'er role. She fell ill, and it was Morgan who nursed 'er back to health."

Chessa nodded. She wasn't sure where he was going with this. "We know Morgan was a skilled healer."

"Yes. But later, Nimue, that was 'er name, you know, trapped Merlin, the greatest wizard of all time, in a cave where he could no longer be at Arthur's side."

"Wow. That's some powerful fairy."

Norman grinned. "Exactly. Too powerful."

Chessa could tell by the gleam in his eye that he was building to something. "What are you getting at?" she asked.

"It would stand to reason that if Nimue had some of Morgan's power, power not known to any other fairy, she could have used it to imprison Merlin."

That *would* explain it. One superpowered fairy was stretching believability, but two in the same era? He was right. It was possible that Nimue had some kind of boost in order to accomplish what the history books claimed. "Back then, Faerie wasn't sealed off. Couldn't that mean that there was more power for the fae in the mortal realm?"

"Maybe, but there's a simpler explanation, one that shines a light on your situation."

"You think Morgan brought her back to life too?"

"Now you're spot-on."

"How is that simpler?" Chessa didn't mean to burst Norman's bubble, but she wasn't one to jump to conclusions just because they were convenient.

"Historians agree that Merlin was the most powerful wizard of his time bar none. He was appointed by Avalon to counsel the half-fairy destined to bring peace to the realm. A bloke such as 'im wouldn't let 'imself get caught by mere trickery. All the accounts agree that it were love that got its hooks into Merlin. He fell in love with Nimue. A deep love, more powerful than even his own magic."

"You're saying that Morgan le Fay left some kind of souped-up love power in Nimue when she resuscitated her." It was a bit far-fetched, and Chessa hoped Norman realized it when she verbalized her doubts.

He didn't seem to. "Precisely. Think about it. You used the power twice. You brought Gwen back, and while she doesn't seem to have gained the power to heal, she is beloved by just about all now that she's queen. You knew 'er before. Did people love 'er straight away?"

Chessa laughed.

"See! She's been using that love or loyalty or whatever it is to restructure the Seelie Court, a good use of it if I do say so. You brought Laural back, too, and 'er healing powers have flourished well beyond 'er natural abilities."

"Laural was always a skilled healer," protested Chessa.

"That may be, but she's incomparable now. Just last week, she healed a mortal of cancer with nothing but a ritual."

He did have a point. Ever since Laural, Chessa's beloved cousin by marriage, had returned to Korranthia, she'd been tirelessly putting her talents to work, far outpacing both modern medicine and known magic. Her new coven might be responsible for helping her find herself, but even their leader, the renowned healer Allison Charlesworth, wasn't able to teach the kinds of things that now seemed easy for Laural. Chessa wished Corrin was still around to see his wife flourish, finally free of the demon who'd kept her a social recluse. He'd always known she was powerful, but lately, Laural's healing was bordering on miraculous. Norman might be onto something.

"What if you didn't leave the same aspects of power in each? What if Morgan didn't either?"

He had her there. She shook her head in admiration. "Norman, you're more than a historian. You've become a true investigator."

He beamed. "I'm glad you approve. Now, could you please give that Matron West an earful and get 'er to let me into the restricted section of the Academy library? There are still so many unanswered questions, and I feel like I'm on the verge of pulling it all together."

"Sorry, buddy, I don't have that power. You'll have to ask our illustrious queen."

The smile melted from his face. "Bollocks. I was afraid you would say that."

Chessa flashed a sympathetic smile. While Gwen had allowed her to bring Norman to the States, she wasn't sure her best friend would ever forgive him for the role he played in overthrowing Avalon, and Chessa couldn't blame her. Gwen's entire family had been slaughtered, and Norman had helped to bring it about. They weren't exactly on the best of terms.

She flitted up to give Norman a quick peck on the cheek. "I've got to get downtown before business hours are over. Keep up the good work. It will be a relief to finally understand what this means." She held up her branded palm.

"Be careful, little miss. Folks like the Kolsches aren't known for their friendliness."

Chessa nodded. "Oh, and Norm, I'll talk to Gwen about the library once we close this case, ok?"

"Deal." He returned to his bowl of ramen.

Norman wasn't kidding about the Kolsches. Chessa had set her sights on the senior Mr. Walter Kolsch, patriarch of the family and grandfather of the deceased, because he was known to work out of the corporate office located downtown, but she abandoned her chauffeur plan immediately upon taking in the grandeur of the building. Tinted office windows overlooked a sprawling atrium with gleaming black marble floors and golden sconces lining the walls. If they sunk this much cash into an office building, they weren't people who would use an unknown chauffeur. They'd have private drivers.

People in suits moved briskly around her as she strode confidently up to the reception desk, hoping none of the larger fae would trample her but fully aware that flying would undermine her bravado. Her gut felt like spiders having a rave. A golden stairway led to the surface of the reception desk, another show of luxury, and she used it without batting an eye, a smile plastered on her face.

A dryad in Gucci looked up from his computer, his bark features drawn into an expression of mock friendliness. "Welcome to Wallow World headquarters. Do you have an appointment?"

Chessa rolled the dice. "No, but Walter Kolsch will want to see me. It's about his granddaughter Portia."

The dryad's already hard face seemed to petrify. "One moment please," he said as he typed something into his cell phone. A moment later, he looked back up at Chessa, his expression giving nothing away. "Please go to office 651. The elevator is just down the hall on the left. I will buzz you in."

Chessa thanked him before walking past the desk and through the doors beyond. She had no idea what she was going to say to Walter Kolsch, even if she did somehow convince him to see her. In all likelihood, she was going to get debriefed by security and tossed out. But what if she didn't? She took a deep breath and stepped into the elevator. Having a plan was overrated. Chessa always did her best work when she flew by the seat of her pants rather than by the speed of her wings.

To her surprise, Walter Kolsch himself was sitting at the head of a long table. She recognized him from the reaction pieces the tabloids ran back when Portia first hit the party scene. A young humanoid male sat beside him, probably some hotshot finance type, jotting notes in a leatherbound journal as the pixie spoke in quiet tones. At first Chessa wasn't sure if they were aware of her presence.

"Hello," she said. Neither man looked up.

Undeterred, she flitted across the chilly meeting room and pulled out the chair on the other side of Walter, directly across from the humanoid. Once she was seated, the pixie turned, his dark eyes giving her a once-over before he returned to his business.

"The margins just don't look right. If we cut the fat here and here, we should be on the right track."

The humanoid nodded without giving Chessa a second glance. "Yes, sir. I'll get right on that."

"That will be all, Martin."

The young man stood abruptly and exited the room.

Walter shuffled through some papers then extracted an envelope from the bottom of the stack.

"This should cover it," he said, handing the envelope over to Chessa. Puzzled, she reached out and took it from his hand. Inside was more money than she'd ever seen in her life, stacks and stacks of hundred-dollar bills, fresh and crisp. She could do amazing things for her community with this much dough. She could take more pro bono cases, see more justice done, fill the food pantry. As tempted as she was to slip it into her messenger bag, she handed it back.

"I'm not after your money, Mr. Kolsch."

"What do you want, then? I assume you've got some damning story about Portia to hold over my head. Why else would you be here?"

Chessa opened her mouth to speak, but Kolsch raised his hand. "No, I don't want to hear it. I will neither confirm nor deny anything you say. Portia is—was—a liability from the start. Now that she's gone, we'd like to protect our interests and let her rest in peace. What is it that you want?"

Rather than come clean, Chessa decided to let him keep thinking she had something to hold over his head. "Information."

"Ah, well, that's what brings us to this situation, isn't it? Why would I give you more leverage than you already have?"

"Because I plan to catch her killer."

Only then did Kolsch make eye contact. For the first time since she'd entered the room, he truly seemed to see her. "You don't have anything at all, do you? You're here grasping at straws, and I nearly tipped my hand. Whatever your angle, you've got gumption marching in here like this, I'll give you that."

With that, he poked his cell phone, not even bothering to set it to his ear. When a voice answered, he calmly spoke, his gaze locked with Chessa's. "I have an intruder I would like removed immediately."

That meant that Chessa only had a few short moments to say her piece. She pulled her card from her backpack and slapped it on the table. "Mr. Kolsch, I mean no harm. I'm a private investigator, and I plan to find whoever killed your granddaughter and bring them to justice."

"Nobody from my family hired you." It was a statement, but it hung in the air like a question.

"That's true. But my client's brother was killed in a similar way, and I think the cases might be related. If there's someone out there killing pixies, we've got to catch them. You must at least agree with that."

The door opened, and three fae entered, all decked out in suits. Kolsch motioned toward Chessa, and the closest one, an elf, approached with his hands thrust outward.

"No need to get rough, I'm leaving," said Chessa. She shot into the air and flew over their heads out the door.

As she walked out onto the busy street, Chessa laughed. She'd never expected to get that close to one of the Kolsches, and even though it seemed like a bust, she'd actually learned a lot from her brief interaction. Portia Kolsch had been more trouble than the tabloids let on, enough for her family to be hemorrhaging hush money. If there were secrets to keep, there were secrets to unearth. Now, she just had to get digging to figure out if any of those secrets involved a dead artist.

12

Norman was sitting at the desk when Quincy arrived at C&F Investigations, but that was nothing new. Ever since Chessa brought the ex-Unseelie spy over, he stuck close. Quincy couldn't blame him. It was tough knowing who to trust in Korranthia. They might be from different parts of the world, but Norman reminded Quincy of all the other petty criminals he'd known throughout his life, jumpy and loyal to a fault to whoever threw him a bone. Norman had a sordid past back in Glastonbury, one that he didn't talk openly about, but Quincy had him pegged the minute they'd met. If his roots weren't deeper in the muck than Chessa knew, Q would fold his hand. Because of their common ground, they'd become fast friends.

"Quincy, old chap, where did you disappear to? The boss has been asking after you." Norman flashed a smile, his manner much looser than it was around anyone else. Quincy suspected it was because he wasn't afraid of being judged.

"I've been looking out for the kid."

"What kid? Our client? Xander?"

"Yeah." Quincy slumped onto the couch. The ratty thing creaked beneath his weight.

"Is he in trouble?"

"Nothing like that. It's just not right, him having to look after himself. But I think I spooked him. He blew me off." As he said it out loud, Quincy realized that it was a little strange for Xander to dodge him, even if he wasn't in the market for a new big brother. It had only been a few days since they'd met, but Xander already seemed a far cry from the bereaved kid he'd been at Pub Nine, desperate to discover what had happened to Mandrake. In fact, it almost seemed as if he wanted Quincy to back off so he could get on with his life. It was hard to reconcile with the angry, grieving young man he'd met only a few days back.

"Hm. Well, you did drag 'im in here against his will, intimidate 'im into staying, and force 'im to hire us."

The wizard had a point. Bitching in a bar was a far cry from hiring a PI. Still, there was something about Xander that felt off.

As Quincy pondered what it could be, the door opened again. He couldn't help but smile when he saw Chessa, the green streak in her hair offset by her black and translucent tattooed wings. He'd had a soft spot for her since her days of leaning on him for stories for her crime blog. It was hard not to. She was one of the only creatures in the Kingdom who ever saw any good in him. He'd told her he'd given her the street name 'Chia' because she grew stories from nothing like one of those Chia pets, but he didn't let on that it was his grandmother who'd given him one and, for a time, he'd loved that stupid plant more than anything in the world.

"Q, I thought we'd lost you in a poker game," she said with a grin.

"Nah, my games are bigger stakes."

Chessa closed the door behind her and settled on the arm of the couch. "What's the word on our client? I heard you two have gotten close."

"Not sure I'd call it that," replied Quincy.

"Blew 'im off, today, he did," said Norman. "And he ain't the only one chumming around with key people in the case."

Quincy wondered what he meant by that, but Chessa didn't jump in to explain. Instead, she was giving Quincy one of those looks that made him want to hide. There were times where it felt like she looked right into his soul.

"It's no big deal. I'm sure he's got plenty going on in his life. We're going to get tacos later this week."

"Tacos?" Chessa's tone was a mix of concern and amusement.

"Yeah. Tacos." Quincy was ready for a change of subject. "What gives on your end? Any leads?"

Now it was Chessa's turn to look sheepish. "I don't know yet. I followed a couple hunches, but didn't get anything concrete. Norman, you ready to take some notes?"

While Chessa finished up her account of the Bambi Boros interview and the Kolsch ambush, Quincy went to the fridge for a beer. It sounded to him like they had diddly squat, but knowing Chessa, she had some gut feeling she wasn't sharing yet. Maybe that's what Norman meant when he said he hadn't signed onto this gig for the predictability. If it was going to get exciting, Quincy wished it would happen soon.

"What's next?" he asked, popping the cap off his bottle of Guinness.

"How do you feel about beatnik bars?" asked Chessa. "I think you'd fit right in."

Quincy heard Norman suppress a chuckle. He had very little appreciation for finger-snapping and craft cocktails. "I think I'll let you follow up on that one yourself."

Just then, Chessa's phone buzzed, and she pulled it out of her back pocket.

"Oh, shit," she said, causing both Norman and Quincy to snap to.

"What's up, little boss?" asked Norman.

"It's Abi. Something is going down at the apartment. She says Dom is unhinged."

"From what you just told us, dude is always unhinged," said Quincy. It was true. The guy sounded like a real prick.

"He stabbed Lance."

Now they were getting to the good shit. Quincy tried not to grin, but Chessa's next statement killed the urge.

She was out the door before he could set down his beer. "Norm, give Q the details on Flit's," she called from the hallway. "Q, you're going to have to take one for the team."

13

Chessa knew the situation was bad when Honey's was the first face she saw. Dom was pacing the downstairs, from kitchen to family room and back again, while Honey sat on a worn leather thrift store couch in the living room, her legs folded beneath her and wings pressed against the back of the couch. Chessa was envious. She was tired enough to curl up on the recliner in the corner and let this insane lot deal with their drama alone. But she might miss a scoop, and that was unacceptable.

"Will you calm down, Dom? Nobody is calling the cops," said Honey. Her pointed ears twitched as Chessa entered the room, but she didn't utter a word of greeting.

"Of course nobody's calling the cops. You know better than that! At least, I thought you did. We're all in this together, at least I thought we were, but then he goes and runs his fool mouth—"

Dom's tirade ended abruptly as his pacing brought him face to face with Chessa.

"What's she doing here?" he snarled.

"I'm pretty sure she lives here, Dom."

"Oh, right."

"What's going on?" asked Chessa. She was still standing in the foyer area at the base of the stairs, but she had a clear line of sight into the living room on the left and down the hall where Dom had been making his circles. She didn't want to tip anyone off that Abi had briefed her on the situation. Thankfully, a slamming door from upstairs drew Dom's attention.

Abi emerged at the top of the stairs. "Chia, up here," she said. "You can help me."

Dom stepped forward as if to block Chessa's path. "No outsiders!"

"Get the fuck out of the way, Dom. You lost your right to give orders," snipped Abi.

Chessa swore she saw Honey smirk as she zipped over Dom's head and up the stairwell, and she wondered why the other pixie was just sitting around rather than helping Abi care for Lance.

The goblin was sitting on the edge of the bed in the first door on the right, the one room Chessa hadn't explored, with his left hand pressed against his right side, just below the ribs. By the leopard print curtains and black feather boa hanging from what she presumed was a closet doorhandle, Chessa deduced that it must belong to Dom. Blood soaked through his flannel shirt. The guy needed a hospital, but from the sound of Dom's ranting, that didn't seem likely to happen. Still, she had to try.

"For Danu's sake, you need a doctor," Chessa said, flying over to stand on the side of the bed.

"No doctors," rasped Lance. His green flesh was paler than usual.

Abi closed the door behind them so they didn't have to hear the ruckus from downstairs.

Chessa struggled to keep a cool head. She didn't want to blow her cover, but at the same time, her medical training ended the day her sister Cora pulled her out of Sprite Scouts because the troop leader lost her on a field trip to the butterfly museum. Still, if Lance refused to go to the hospital, she had to do something. "Fine, but I'm calling my cousin. She's the best healer in Korranthia," said Chessa. She didn't give them a choice. She pulled out her phone and called Laural. Once she hung up, she assessed the situation. The blood soaking Lance's shirt and the bedspread beneath him was far too much for any creature to lose at one time. "Alright, then, I'm going to need you to take off your shirt," she said. "Abi, come put pressure on the wound. My cousin Laural is a healer, and she'll be here soon, but we need to stop the bleeding."

"Blood makes me woozy," said Abi.

Of course it does, Chessa thought. Abi was many wonderful things, but she didn't strike Chessa as the kind of pixie who got her hands dirty.

Lance didn't look like he could stand, let alone undress himself. He mumbled something in response, but even as close to him as she was standing, Chessa couldn't make it out. She pulled the flannel off his free arm revealing an undershirt that was no longer white.

"You're going to have to help out here, woozy or not."

The pixie gulped but took a few stutter-steps forward.

Chessa rolled her eyes and turned her attention back to her patient. "On the count of three, you need to let go of your side," she told Lance.

She counted, and when his arms were raised, she pulled the rest of the flannel as well as the undershirt off as quickly as she could. It wasn't quick enough. He passed out cold.

Thankfully, he was already on the bed. Blood pumped out the deep gash in his torso. Lance had a good deal of flesh around the middle, and Chessa hoped the blade had missed his vital organs as a result.

"Pressure! Now!" shouted Chessa, but Abi was just standing with wide eyes, the color draining from her face.

"For fuck's sake," growled Chessa, thrusting both hands down on the goblin's wound and applying as much pressure as she could. "Go get Honey."

Abi yipped and scurried out of the room. A moment later, she returned with Honey, who moved with the urgency of a drunk sloth. The two pixies couldn't be more unalike. Honey nearly looked bored, even amidst the chaos, and there was no hustle to her movements.

"Abi, get me a clean t-shirt and a pair of scissors," ordered Chessa, deciding that she'd be better at fetching materials than working with the patient. "Honey, come hold pressure on the wound."

She was relieved when both fae did as instructed. When Abi returned, Chessa cut the shirt into strips and tied them as tightly as she could around the goblin's torso, using wider portions of material folded over as padding. When she finished, the wound was no longer bleeding through, but there was no telling how much blood he'd already lost.

"Abi, go get some water. Honey, help me get him covered up. He's shivering. I'm sure he's in shock."

Once Lance was seen to, Honey disappeared again, leaving Chessa and Abi standing over the pale, sweat-soaked goblin.

"He's going to be ok, right?" asked Abi, her voice quivering. Chessa got the sense that she cared deeply for Lance.

"Honestly, I don't know. Abi, why can't we take him to the hospital? This is insane."

Abi chewed on her bottom lip, a move Chessa would have thought attractive if she weren't so frustrated with the situation and Abi's incompetence. "Dom would go to jail. We just can't."

"Well, let's hope Laural gets here before he dies."

The next hour passed in tense silence. Neither Honey nor Dom ventured upstairs. Abi sat on the edge of the bed, staring at Lance. Chessa paced. When the doorbell rang, she darted down the stairs to let Laural in before Dom threw her out. Thankfully, the house was quiet, Honey and Dom nowhere to be seen.

"Where is he?" asked Laural as she pushed through the door.

Chessa led the witch up the stairs and gave a cursory introduction to Abi. In a matter of minutes, Laural was getting to work setting up an altar at the foot of the bed. Once that was done, she looked Lance over. "You did good to get the bleeding stopped."

"He'll need real bandages and something to ward off infection," replied Chessa.

Laural nodded. "I brought my emergency kit, so we're covered there. But it's going to have to wait. I don't want him to lose any more blood before the ritual. He's barely holding on as is."

Abi made a sound that was more animalistic than pixie.

"Can you get her out of here?" Laural asked as if Abi were an inanimate object.

Chessa flitted up to perch on the bed next to Abi. "Sweetheart, you need to wait outside so Laural can concentrate. I promise she'll take good care of him," she said.

Abi nodded mutely, worry etched all over her face. She looked terrible. Chessa felt a pang of sympathy, but it was fleeting. She might care deeply for Lance, but if he didn't make it through the night, it would be entirely because Abi and the others refused to take him to a hospital. A spike of anger unlike anything Chessa had ever felt pierced the center of her being, and she took Abi by the arm to help her up, it was harsher than she intended. Once Abi was through the door, Chessa shut it with a thud.

"You okay, cuz?" asked Laural, peering up from Lance's bedside with a look of concern.

Chessa took a steadying breath. "Yeah. I'm just frustrated with this lot."

Whether she believed her or not, Laural let it go. "Sweetheart?" she said.

Feeling much calmer, Chessa shrugged and avoided responding to the note of accusation she detected in her cousin's voice. Instead, she focused on the task at hand. "What can I do to help?"

"Just stand back," replied Laural, stripping off her clothes. Chessa had seen her healing rituals many times, but they never failed to amaze her. First, the witch cast a circle. She called on the elements and the Danu, patron goddess of Faerie. Once her invocations were complete, light filled the room, soaking it in shades of cool blue and white. The hair on Chessa's arms stood on end as power built inside the circle. Once it peaked, Laural made a motion and spoke words in the ancient tongue, and energy burst from the dome directly at Lance's still form on the bed. As the light in the room dimmed, his body began to glow. Laural collapsed on the ground, and Chessa rushed to her side.

"Abi?" Lance sounded like he had sandpaper in his throat. He shifted in the bed as if attempting to sit up.

"Lance, stay still," said Chessa, flying to the bed after ensuring that Laural was conscious. It would take the witch a few minutes to gain the strength to stand. "I don't want you to reopen the wound before we can get it properly treated."

"Where's Abi?"

"She'll be in soon. My cousin Laural just did a healing ritual to help you through the shock. As soon as she's ready, we'll get you bandaged up and Abi can come back in."

As she spoke, Laural began to dress herself.

"Do you need anything?" Chessa asked.

"My bag," replied Laural, her words heavy and slightly slower than usual. While most healers served as funnels for magic, Laural put everything she had into healing, and it left her exhausted. It was the most unnerving part of watching her work. Chessa picked up the tote bag from the floor and brought it to the bed, where Laural rummaged through to fish out a power bar and a bottle of water. "I'll be ready to dress the wound in a few minutes. You can let the pixie in now."

Abi was waiting in the hallway and must have been listening at the door, because it burst open and she dove on the bed.

"Lance! You're awake. Are you alright?"

The goblin was still three shades paler than Chessa would have liked, but he was alive.

"I'm going to go with no."

"He will recover in due time," interjected Laural from the corner of the room where she sat on the floor.

"Don't you ever do that to me again!" yelled Abi, swatting the goblin's leg. "You scared the spark out of me!"

"Hey now, don't injure my patient. I put far too much into healing him."

Abi's head dropped at Laural's admonishment.

A quarter of an hour later, Laural dressed the wound and left Abi with extra supplies and care instructions.

"Do you need help getting home?" asked Chessa after they left the pair alone in the bedroom and made their way down the hall.

"I'll be fine," replied Laural. "My recovery time has improved from back when I was saddled with Gailan. I think he was holding me back more than I realized."

Chessa nodded, but she suspected that it was Morgan's magic, not the absence of the demon, that helped Laural recover. She planned to sit the witch down and have Norman explain everything they'd learned, but first, she needed to crack this case.

"Besides," added Laural, "I'm heading out to the island."

The island. It was where Chessa had left the baby dragon she'd rescued after the Battle of Avalon. She hadn't been to see Henrietta since before the case, but she knew Laural's coven was taking good care of her. "Give Henrietta skritches for me, and text me when you get there," she said. "Oh, and Laural? Thank you for coming so quickly. I'm not sure if he would have made it without you."

"He wouldn't have." Laural didn't bother asking any more questions. Chessa knew she would owe her an explanation later. She bid her goodbye at the door then returned to the bedroom. She didn't care who these assholes thought she was, it was time to get some answers.

14

Flit's was everything Quincy expected and then some. If he'd been out of place in the diverse patronage of the library, here he was straight-up alien. Sure, there was a lot of black clothing and funky colored hair, but color palette aside, he had nothing in common with the fae milling around the beatnik bar housed in an old church.

There wasn't a boisterous creature in the place. Everyone conversed quietly in small groups, clutching drinks with smoking sprigs of rosemary sticking out the tops or fruit garnishments on the rims as they reclined on velvet couches that contrasted with the dilapidated brick façade. Quincy had never seen so many berets in his life, and that was saying something considering he'd survived the 60s and 70s. On a small triangular stage in the corner of the room, a hobgoblin sat on a lone wooden stool, pontificating into the microphone. She was bone-thin, indicating she hadn't traveled recently, and her flesh drooped. Thick, black eyeliner was smudged around her eyes, and perched on her head was yet another black beret. Quincy snorted, earning him more than a few dirty looks.

"What is life but space and the fleeting moments between? We consume multitudes, yet we digest nothing. Not the blade of grass bent by the breeze. Not the buildings we construct to worship indifferent gods. Not the whisper between lovers stealing away from the watchful gaze of an unforgiving society bent on destroying all that is good. All that is pure in this world. In the light of day, we vomit it all up, a putrid pile of rotting memories and forsaken gifts."

When she finished, all conversation ceased, and every last patron snapped their fingers.

"Fuck me," said Quincy, shaking his head. He knew it would be bad, but nothing prepared him for this living nightmare. It was every bad television special and then some. He rolled his eyes and made his way to the bar, turning many heads as he moved through the room.

"Are you new to the community?" asked the sprite behind the bar. His eyeliner made his dark eyes look foreboding against his pale white skin, and the tips of his long, straight white hair were dyed black and red.

"Funny way to ask a guy what he wants to drink," said Quincy. "I'll take a whiskey sour, house."

The sprite looked Quincy up and down. "You're not from Dot."

"What gave it away? Can I get a drink or not?"

"Whatever." The sprite made the drink and used a jigger to measure out a precise shot of whiskey. This was definitely not Pub Nine.

"Did you know Mandrake Aster?" Quincy asked once the bartender set the drink in front of him.

The sprite paused, his eyebrows raised in an expression of surprise. "Who wants to know?"

"I work with C&F Investigations," Quincy replied, pulling one of the cards Chessa insisted he carry from the wallet in his back pocket. He set the card on the bar and slid it over. "Mandrake's brother hired us to look into his death."

"Did he now?" As the sprite examined the business card, a warlock with a guitar took the stage. For a split second, Quincy hoped it was a good sign until the warlock strummed a single chord and then launched into another existential monologue.

"What can you tell me?" asked Quincy, hoping to keep this short.

The bartender slid the card back. "Not much. He worked here from time to time. Was shit with the more involved drinks."

"Did you ever see him talking to someone named Hugo?"

"Hugo? Yeah, he's a regular. I haven't seen him tonight, but he'll probably be in at some point."

"Do you have a last name for this Hugo?"

"Considering the tab he's run up, I damn well better. Murphy. He lives nearby."

Running up an unpaid tab didn't strike Quincy as the behavior of someone who would be looking to commission art. "Did you know if Hugo was into collecting art?"

The sprite laughed. "No way. Unlike most of our customers, he's not the artistic type. More like you. He only comes in because it's the closest bar to his house, and his partner doesn't like him drinking."

This might be a lead after all. Quincy downed his drink in a single swig. "Is there anyone here who might know Mandrake better?" he asked. He knew the answer before the sprite answered.

"Not really. Drake didn't connect with anyone here. Sometimes his friends would show up. There was the hot pixie who would perform dramatic readings, the humanoid with terrible fashion sense who would read poetry, and a goblin who didn't do much of anything besides drink. He was more sociable with them than with any of the regulars."

Quincy nodded, thanked the sprite, paid his tab, and then did a quick walkabout the place so he could tell Chessa he'd been thorough. Other than a bunch of art school dropouts, he found nothing of note. He hit the can and got the hell out of Dodge.

When he stepped out onto the curb on Dot Ave, a white box truck came to a screeching halt in front of him. The back door rolled up with a great squeal, and three fae jumped out, each larger than the next, and all of them dwarfing the not-exactly-dainty Cross-Eyed Quincy.

"What the hell?" Quincy muttered as his brain raced to keep up with events. Before he had time to answer himself, two of the fae, an ogre and a cyclops flanked him.

"I heard you've been asking for me," said the ogre, a hulking creature with black, spiked hair and more piercings than teeth. The pieces clicked into place.

"You must be Hugo," said Quincy. Damn, that bartender was fast. He wondered how much they were paying him for the service.

"Let's go," growled the cyclops, roughly clasping Quincy's left arm at the bicep. The ogre went for the right, but Quincy torqued his body around and pulled the knife—the one his mother had given him to fend off the blows of dear old dad before she'd disappeared into the night so many years ago—out of the pocket of his jeans. He managed to bury it in the cyclops' forearm and wrench himself free. If they wanted to load him into the truck, they'd have to knock him out first.

He considered running, but that didn't sound like much fun. Instead, he aimed a motorcycle boot straight to Hugo's groin.

The goon collapsed on the pavement with a grunt, but the cyclops managed to get behind Quincy and grasp him in a full nelson, blood from his forearm smearing all over Quincy's neck. Quincy pulled his arms down while jerking his head back, breaking the hold. Before he could mount a follow-up attack, a cloud of sulfurous gas enveloped him. He went down hard.

When Quincy came to, his head pounded and his lungs burned. Some kind of sack covered his head, its coarse weave allowing only faint light to penetrate through. He could feel the movement of the truck lurching him this way and that, but his arms and legs were tightly bound.

"Well, ain't this some shit?"

15

D oes anyone want to tell me what happened?" asked Chessa once Lance was sitting up sipping on his water.

"It was an accident," he muttered.

Accident, my ass, thought Chessa. "Look, I should have hauled your ass to the hospital as soon as I got here, but I didn't. I'm in this with you now, whatever *this* is, whether you like it or not."

Abi sat on the bed next to Lance. "Dom can get a little—"

"Abi, shut up," interrupted Lance. "I appreciate your help, Chia, but you need to stay out of it. As far as you're concerned, it was an accident, ok?"

"Seeing as you almost bled out in front of me, not ok," replied Chessa. She needed to exploit the situation if she was going to learn anything about what was going on in this house. "I dragged my cousin into your mess, and I deserve an explanation."

"Nobody asked you to do that," quipped Lance.

"If it weren't for Laural, you wouldn't be here to piss me off like this," said Chessa. The goblin opened his mouth as if to reply and snapped it shut.

"Later, ok?" said Abi softly. "Lance needs to rest now."

Chessa hoped that Abi would follow her out when she left the room, but she had no such luck. Whatever they'd shared the night before didn't seem to change how Abi treated her, at least not where the Montello residents were concerned. Chessa saw no point in sticking around, and she figured tonight's drama would be excuse enough to bolt. She ducked into her bedroom to snag a couple of Mandrake's sketchbooks, then headed back downstairs. Dom and Honey were both gone.

By the time she arrived at C&F, it was well after midnight, but Norman was still sitting at the desk. Chessa got the impression he was waiting to hear from her.

"You had dinner?" he asked without looking up.

A pang of hunger struck at the mere suggestion of food. "No. It's been a hell of a night."

"There's a sarnie in the fridge," replied the wizard.

Thankful for something other than cold pizza, Chessa downed the Italian sub while she gave Norman a rundown of the events at the Montello house. He took notes on the computer and let out the occasional exclamation when she described Laural fixing Lance up. Despite, or perhaps because of, his sordid past, he preferred to use his magic in ways that kept the gore to a minimum, and the witch's work made him uncomfortable. Chessa had learned that about him during the clean-up efforts after the battle of Avalon.

"Did you ever figure out what Lance did to get 'imself stabbed?" he asked once she was finished with her account.

Chessa sighed. "No. I was hoping Abi would catch me up, but she made no such promise. I don't know what the deal is with that group, but something tells me it's connected to Mandrake's death."

"Do you think Dom offed him?"

Chessa had considered the possibility, but it just didn't feel right. "No. At least, not yet. I need more info before jumping to something like that. Dom is controlling and erratic, but I don't think he would intentionally kill anyone."

"Fine. Say it was an accident. It seems like that lot would have no trouble covering up for 'im."

"Maybe. I can't explain it, but none of these scenarios feel right."

Norman smiled. "Your gut?"

"Something like that. Hey, what happened to Q?"

Norman shut down the computer and pulled his wizard robe off a hook on the wall. "He went to Flit's just after you left. I haven't heard from 'im, but I figure he'll check in tomorrow morning. I'm about to head out meself."

Chessa nodded. "Have a great night, Norm."

"You too, little boss. Oh, and one last thing. I called Xander's school after you left. Seems like the lad hasn't been around for weeks."

Chessa's stomach rolled over. "What do you mean? Quincy said he's been busy with schoolwork. They even met up at the library earlier today, if you can picture that."

"According to the vice principal, Xander hasn't come back since Mandrake's funeral. She's been trying to get ahold of a guardian, but you can guess how that's gone. She's got a call in to family and social services."

"Oh boy. I'm going to call Q and make sure he knows," replied Chessa. "Was there anything else?"

"No. I had to fudge a few things to get 'er to share even that much." Norman picked up a pile of books from the desk, probably more of his research on the days of Arthur and Morgan, then headed to the door. "Goodnight, little boss."

"Goodnight, Norm, see you tomorrow."

Once she locked the apartment door behind Norman, Chessa gave Quincy a call. It went to voicemail.

"Hey, Q. About your new friend. It seems Xander's been ditching school for weeks. It might not mean anything, but I wanted to see if you knew what was up. Call me back."

Quincy had likely gone to Pub Nine to scrub off the smell of cloves and patchouli. If that was the case, she likely wouldn't hear anything until tomorrow, so she got ready to turn in for the night. After a shower, she threw on some yoga pants and a Dropkick Murphys tee and was just heading to the bedroom when there was a knock on the door. A quick peek through the peephole showed the last person she expected to see—her sister Cora.

In stark contrast to Chessa's alternative vibe, Cora wore a light pink blouse paired with navy slacks that looked smart with her transparent, untattooed wings and sharp bob brunette hairstyle.

Chessa flung open the door and tackled her big sister, eliciting an "oof" followed by weak laughter.

"What are you doing here? I thought you were in Barbados with Blade," said Chessa, batting her eyes when she mentioned Cora's latest suitor. In actuality, she liked Blade Hudson just fine. His name was the hardest thing about him, a nod to sprite culture of naming babies as if they were all born warriors. Blade certainly was not. It was just fun to poke at her big sister.

The laughter stopped abruptly, and tears filled Cora's baby blues. "I was, but I'm back now. I thought I'd stop in and visit my little sis. Is that ok with you?"

Something was wrong, and as tired as she was, Chessa was determined to figure out what. "In the middle of the night? Oh, who cares? Get in here!" She pulled Cora through the door.

16

Quincy fought against his bonds, but the zip ties were tight enough to cut into his flesh. Of all the enemies he'd made in his life, he'd never owed anyone enough money to warrant a full-scale abduction. First time for everything, he supposed.

"Oy, at least tell me who you work for," Quincy yelled. His answer was a shoe to the gut.

His captors didn't utter a word as they bumped along the street, but he could hear their breathing, and the smell of their BO was wretched. But it was nothing compared to the rotten seafood odor that followed a loud belch from off to his left.

The trip was short, thankfully. The box truck came to a stop, and Q heard the metal-on-metal screech of the back door sliding up. Thick hands grasped him by the arms, and he was hurled out into the night air. If he hadn't hit the ground so hard, he would have appreciated the break from the stench. Thuds and creaks marked his assailants' exits from the truck, and once again, he felt the viselike grips of hands under his arms. He stood and hopped briefly, just long enough to give them a false sense of security, before he went dead weight, falling to his knees in a gravel parking lot. The creatures on either side of him collapsed with yells, and he thought they might have knocked heads. He decided to believe it happened that way.

With his hands and feet bound, Quincy could do nothing but thrash.

His boots made contact with something, and Hugo let out another guttural yell followed by a string of curses. A squelching sound preceded the feeling of mud gluing Quincy's feet to the ground. He expected to sink, but the ground beneath him remained firm. Quincy felt the zip tie around his ankles snap as the material hardened into what felt like cement encasing his legs from the knees down.

The sensation was unlike anything he'd ever felt, magical or otherwise. He reached down in front of him with his bound hands, but by then, whatever it was that held him in place had hardened to the consistency of cement. "What the?"

Quincy tried to remember what the third assailant looked like, but in the shadows of the ally, all he'd managed to note was the goon's size. That's when it hit him. A golem. He'd never crossed paths with one before as they tended to avoid mortal cities, but he'd heard of them from some of his buddies at Pub Nine. They could turn into clay one moment and stone the next. There was no way he was getting his feet free until the creature decided to let him go.

An assailant grasped him under each of his arms, hoisting him into the air into the air like a rotisserie pig. Quincy could do nothing but feeble ab crunches. A few moments later, he was deposited onto a hard surface.

A male voice issued a command. "Remove his blindfold."

Thick fingers ripped the coarse fabric off his face. For a moment, Quincy blinked rapidly at the onslaught of light. Once his eyes adjusted, he realized he was in some kind of warehouse. He'd seen enough movies to know that it was a bad sign. Shelves surrounded him on two sides, filled with boxes of Danu only knew what, and hanging fluorescent lights gave off low flickers that cast shadows all around. In front of the wall to his right was a large desk, and crouched before him was the golem, its arms completely encasing his calves, ankles, and feet while its brown eyes stared blankly ahead.

"What the fuck?" yelled Q, pulling his legs toward his chest with a mighty heave. Only his upper half moved. The mud-clay-cement creature smirked at the futile gesture.

"You're not nearly as formidable as I was led to believe," said the man giving orders. Quincy tried to twist around to see who was standing behind him, but he couldn't get the leverage.

"And who might you be?" he grunted.

"Do you really think I'm about to give a villain monologue?" The man laughed, an arrogant sound that echoed off the cement floor.

Quincy didn't think much of his survival odds, but he sure as hell wanted to know what he was dying for. Maybe if he stated the facts as he saw them, his captor would decide to elucidate matters. "Great. You think you're some kind of villain. That probably doesn't bode well for me,"

"Does anyone ever truly see themselves as a villain? No, I wouldn't say I am. I'm merely a man who does what he must to protect his investments. And you've been sniffing around one of mine. So, what am I to do with you?"

"Look, man, I don't know what this is, but I'm wicked smart with investments. Maybe we can work out some kind of deal."

"Well, now we're talking. Porgis, please make my associate here more comfortable while we discuss the terms of his employment."

Maybe there was an out here after all.

The cyclops, a scowl painted on his face and a bloody rag wrapped around his arm, cut Quincy's wrists free as the material around Quincy's legs softened and retreated to reform the mud-dude's arms. Quincy tried not to shudder, but it was utterly disgusting. He climbed to his feet, careful to avoid making any sudden movement in case his new acquaintance perceived a threat, and changed his mind about having a conversation. If Q had learned anything from his time on the streets, it was that keeping people talking could be the difference between a new friendship and a broken face. He wasn't looking to make any friends here, but something told him that he had more than his face to worry about.

Once he was on his feet, he could see more of the warehouse. There were more fae here than he'd previously registered. A small group was working at the far end of the building, moving boxes and chatting, oblivious to the happenings at this end. The shelves nearest the desk held all manner of weaponry, both magical and mundane. Quincy recognized a couple of AR-15s, an assortment of wands, and a crossbow all within an arm's reach of the man who stood, gazing up at him with a look of deep interest.

The man wasn't merely humanoid. He was human. Full stop.

Quincy could all but smell it on him.

Dark hair with gray streaks was carefully coifed back, and piercing dark eyes seemed to catalog everything about Quincy. It was unnerving to be regarded so by a human who seemed to see straight through the glamour.

"You are a unique specimen, Mr. McAllen," said the man.

"How do you know that name?" asked Quincy. He felt the blood rush to his face and his vision blurred, signs he might lose control of his temper. Nobody knew his surname. He'd left it behind when his father had dumped him in the ICU all those years ago. Call him Cross-Eyed Quincy, Quincy, Q, or Asshole, he didn't give a fuck. Just never call him McAllen.

"I know a lot about you, Mr. McAllen."

Quincy focused on his breathing the way Chia had taught him after he accidentally re-killed Jarvis last month in a fit of rage when he'd caught the punk cheating at the table. The necromancer-in-training still hadn't forgiven him for that little slip, and losing his temper here would have much more permanent consequences.

"Just Quincy."

"Alright, then, Quincy. My little informant tells me that you're a well-connected half-ogre."

"If you want me to do some introductions, that's no problem." Quincy tried to make his voice sound more at ease than he felt. If this guy was just looking to recruit street toughs, he had no problem hooking him up.

"I would like that very much, Quincy. Very much indeed."

"Sure. Who do you want to know?"

"Gwendolyn Evenshine."

17

Chessa stayed up late into the night chatting with the sister who'd been more of a second mother to her. Sure, they had a loving mother, but raising young pixies alone was tough, and she'd had to work multiple jobs to keep the family afloat. It was Cora who took Chessa to school every day, who showed up for parents' night, who supported Chessa's passion for journalism, who let her cry on her shoulder after break-ups, and years later, who held her hand at their mother's funeral. It wasn't until Chessa moved out that Cora left in search of her own life. That's why Chessa couldn't blame her sister for being gone for so long. They were in contact through email, and Chessa loved seeing pictures of whatever new adventure Cora had embarked upon.

"Cora, I can tell something is wrong. Do you want to talk about it?" asked Chessa once they were settled.

Cora shook her head. "Not until after we catch up," she said, "It's been far too long. How's the PI business?"

She had a point. The last time she'd seen her sister, Chessa had been locked up. Cora took the first flight to Logan International to hound the KPD until Gwen's family connections got the murder charges dropped. She was there to help Chessa process the trauma of nearly becoming the Brain Scraper's final victim, and together, they mourned the loss of their dear cousin Corrin. If it hadn't been for her big sister, Chessa wasn't sure she would have sought the therapy she'd desperately needed to process it all. It seemed like a million years ago. There'd been an entire fae civil war between then and now.

"Lousy," replied Chessa grabbing a bottle of wine and two glasses from the kitchen. She filled them both then offered one to her sister.

When Cora reached out to take her glass, she stopped short. "Is that it? Let me see."

Chessa set both glasses on the table and held out her palm so Cora could inspect the sigil of Morgan le Fay.

"The raven, of course. It's not so much a symbol of Morgan le Fay as it is of death itself. Blade is part of the neo-pagan movement, and I hear all about the ancient deities. I'm fascinated by the ways his coven connects with earth magics, even practitioners with little to no power. They invoke Morgan le Fay as if she were a goddess and sometimes conflate her with the Morrigan. It makes sense in a way. They both have intense connections to death."

"Hence, the raven," replied Chessa.

"Exactly."

"Was Morgan named to honor the Morrigan?" Chessa suddenly wished Norman hadn't turned in for the night. She was surprised to find her sister knowledgeable on the subject. While she fully believed that Blade was part of a coven of sorts, she suspected that Cora took a special interest in the Unseelie Queen whose mark she bore.

"No. Completely different etymologies. Avalon, though, has ties to both the Morrigan, the triple Goddess over battle and bloodshed and distant relative to our dear Danu, and to Morgan le Fay, one of its first queens."

"You have got to meet Norman," replied Chessa with a grin.

"Don't be mad," said Cora, "but I might have reached out to him when I found out he was cozied up to my little sis."

Normally something like that wouldn't have upset Chessa since she knew it came from love, but for some reason at this moment, the idea that two of the people closest to her were talking about her without her knowledge felt like betrayal. She felt her cheeks flush. "If you wanted to check up on me, the least you could do is ask me directly," she fumed.

"I'm sorry, Chichi. You've been through so much, and I was worried. Don't blame Norman. He's devoted to you and only didn't tell you because I asked him not to."

The expression on Cora's face smothered Chessa's anger. She took a deep breath and released it as Cora kept babbling apologies. "Cora, stop. It's okay," she said.

Cora looked relieved, but then her face grew tight again. "I wasn't lying, though. Blade has been such a help. He's into all this new age stuff, and don't tell Gwen, but I enjoy sharing fae history with him."

Her voice held a note of sadness that seemed unrelated to her intrusion on Chessa's life, and the concern Chessa's had when she first saw her sister return. "Is everything ok?"

"Blade asked me to marry him."

Chessa let out a little squeal. "He did? Oh, my Goddess!" She was about to dive on her sister but quickly realized that Cora didn't seem excited. "What did you say?"

"I said yes." The mournful expression on her face didn't align with her announcement. Chessa thought people were supposed to be joyful when they told their family they were marrying the love of their life. Chessa knew her sister loved Blade, so she was missing something. Something big.

Chessa reached out and took her sister's hand, and Cora burst into tears. "He's been taken. I don't know who these people are, but they sent me to tell you to drop your investigation. They said they'd kill him if I didn't."

Chessa's blood went cold. Cora wasn't here for a social visit. She wasn't even here of her own free will. She was being blackmailed.

"I don't understand."

"They said they'd kill you too. Oh, Chessa, who are these people?"

"I honestly don't know. I need you to tell me everything you can."

Cora regained control. She took a shuddery breath and squeezed Chessa's hand. "I love you, Chichi. I almost lost you more than once over the past couple of years, and I just can't. Please, you have to drop whatever this case is. I need you safe. And I need my fiancé back."

"The case is about a pixie who ended up dead in an alley and nobody gives a shit. I can't just drop that. But I might be able to use whatever information you have to bring justice for my client and to bring Blade home."

"Don't you understand? I don't have any information. I came home one day, and Blade was gone. I found this." Cora dug into her handbag and pulled out a note. It read:

. . .

Blade is in Korranthia. If you ever want to see him again, tell your bitch of a sister to drop her investigation. If not, you'll be planning both their funerals. You have one week.

There was no signature, and blood was smeared across the page.

Damn. Chessa had barely scratched the surface of this case, and there were already death threats. "It's ok, Cora. We'll get him back."

"These people are dangerous, Chess. Haven't you put your life on the line enough? Please, just do what they say."

"You know I can't back down. The whole reason Gwen and I started this firm was to give a voice to those who fell between the cracks."

"Where is Gwen now? Holed up in Avalon far away from this mess, that's where! She's got bodyguards. You've got a crusty old pacifist wizard and a lowlife on a motorcycle!" Chessa waited for her sister's anger to die down, but it only morphed into desperation. "Can't you help someone else? Take a different case. One that doesn't endanger everyone I love."

"Xander deserves to know who killed his brother. Mandrake deserves justice. And so does Portia."

"Portia? As in Portia Kolsch, the dead socialite?"

Damn. That case was so big, the news made it all the way to Barbados. "That's the one."

"Doesn't her family have, like, an army of lawyers? Why in the name of Danu would they need you?"

"They don't. But Portia does. Her family wants to sweep her under the rug, to treat her like the trash they always thought she was. I won't let that happen."

Chessa didn't even know she felt that way until the words flowed out of her mouth. Portia might have been a rich party girl, but she didn't deserve to die in a hotel room at the age of twenty-two. Something about the way her grandfather spoke reminded Chessa of Gwen's family—how they always thought she was somehow lesser, the black sheep, the embarrassment of the family. Well, fuck that. Gwen turned out to be the best of the bunch. As for Portia, she would never get her chance to prove everyone wrong.

Cora had tears streaming down her face. Chessa hated to see her like this. She was the strong one, the one who was always there for everyone else.

"I promise we'll get him back, Cora," said Chessa. She hoped she was telling the truth and that she really could save Blade. There was a strong possibility that her decision here today would condemn him to death.

18

Gwendolyn Evenshine? You want me to introduce you to the fucking Seelie Queen?" Quincy felt like he'd been kicked in the head again. This was madness. No. It was a trap.

"Don't play dumb with me. It might work on your little street urchin barnacles, but I have ways of procuring information. I know she's your business partner, and I am a man of some importance around these parts. You will contact her. You will tell her you have a situation that needs her attention. And you will bring. Her. To. Me." The way he overenunciated his order made it clear he was accustomed to being obeyed.

"Look, I'm not saying no—"

"I should hope not," cut in the man. The cyclops pressed in close from behind, and Quincy could smell his rank breath.

"I'm just saying, I need to know your business with Her Grace before I can help you out. As you said, she is my partner. It's only good business."

The boss gave a small shake of the head, and the cyclops stepped back. "Here's what you need to know: your only value to me is your connections. Should you make those connections unavailable for my use, you become, how shall I put this… *not* valuable."

The implication was clear. It was an ultimatum. Either Quincy lured Gwen into a trap, or he would be killed. Quincy hated ultimatums.

"I hear you. Look, it's not as simple as you make it out. In order to get a message to Her Grace, I need two things. The first is your name. She's not going to pop over to Korranthia to visit with just anybody, even if I ask her to. You need to give me something to tell her."

"Marcus Fairburn, a businessman with a proposal that needs to be heard by the Seelie Court."

"Ok, and the other thing is Chessa Moon. I don't speak with Her Grace directly. All my communication goes through my other partner. Let me contact Chessa, and together, we can arrange the meeting you want."

Quincy knew this was a dangerous play, but it was the only one he could think of. He didn't want to endanger Chessa, but if Fairburn knew about his relationship with Gwen, there was no way he didn't also already know about their third partner. Besides, the way Q saw it, his only other option was to be killed on the spot. He wasn't about to hand Gwen over, not after everything they'd all risked to get her on the throne. Chessa was resourceful. She had gotten out of stickier situations, so he prayed to Danu she would be able to save his ass while also protecting Gwen.

"I'm supposed to believe that you don't have a direct line to your business partner?" Marcus narrowed his gaze, and the cyclops shifted restlessly.

"When my business partner is the fucking Seelie Queen, yes." Another piece of wisdom Q had picked up on the street was that when you were at the mercy of a more powerful foe, make every lie plausible.

After a moment of consideration, Fairburn gave a curt nod to Hugo, who was standing beside the desk. Without hesitation, the ogre reached in his pocket and produced a cellphone, one of those burner types you could pick up at the counter of Wallow World. He tossed it to Quincy.

Quincy tried not to react to the weight of Fairburn's laser-like gaze. "Make the call."

19

The phone rang far too early considering Chessa had barely slept. She accidentally knocked her phone on the floor reaching for it and nearly rolled off the edge of the bed to retrieve it.

"Hello?" Her voice was thick in her throat.

"Hey, Chessa, I need you to call Her Grace, and set up a meeting for us."

"Quincy? What time is it? Where are you?" Chessa's brain took a moment to catch up. She glanced at the alarm clock on her nightstand. There was no way Quincy would be calling this early after a night at the pub. Something else was off. He hadn't used Chessa's given name in years, and he always called Gwen by the street name he'd given her - Wings. Or at least her given name. What was up with this Her Grace shit? Something was very wrong.

"Where are you, Q?" she asked, this time with an alert mind.

"I'm with a potential new business associate. Marcus Fairburn. He's got a proposal for the Seelie Court, and I promised an introduction to Her Grace."

"At the ass crack of dawn? Where are you?"

Quincy kept talking as if she hadn't spoken. "I'm a partner now, too, and if I think she needs to hear this proposal, you should trust me."

It was clear that his formal wording was his way of tipping her off that something was amiss, but she was already firing on all cylinders. Even Cora was awake now, lying beside her in the bed with her head propped on her arm. Chessa shot her an alarmed glance and received a quizzical one in return. Doubtless Cora was wondering if this had anything to do with her missing fiancé. Chessa wondered the same. She needed to ask Quincy questions he obviously couldn't freely answer, so she opted for ones with answers that might seem innocuous to anyone listening in.

"Is this someone you met through Xander?"

"I believe so."

"Where are we meeting, Quincy?" she asked, hoping he'd give up his location. She had no idea what level of threat he was facing, but it must be dire.

"At Charlestown Navy Yard tomorrow at five a.m."

"I really don't think I can get *Her Grace* here by then," said Chessa, hoping that he picked up on the fact that she'd read the situation.

Quincy let out a long breath, and when he spoke, he sounded relieved. Her message hit home. "Let me confer with my associate," he replied. After a long pause, he continued. "My associate believes that four days should be enough time for her to get here. Unfortunately, the opportunity will expire if she doesn't show up on Sunday morning by five. Mr. Fairburn understands that there are time zone considerations, but he hopes that she will find a way. He assures me that she will want to hear his offer."

"Got it. And will you be in the office sometime during those four days?" she asked.

"I'm afraid not. There's business here that demands my attention."

That's what she was afraid of. Quincy was as much a hostage as Blade. Shit. Chessa wanted to make sure that his captors didn't suspect that he'd tipped her off, so she tried to keep the conversation going. "No problem. Hey, Q, while I've got you on the phone, have you picked up any other leads on the case?"

"No. Sorry, boss. All my leads were dead-ends. Well, I've got to get back to work. See you soon?"

"Yeah. In four days."

Chessa hung up and immediately flitted from the bed to dress hurriedly.

"What's going on?" asked Cora, also rising from the bed.

"I have no idea. That was Quincy. Someone had a gun to his head."

Cora gasped. "The same people who have Blade?"

"I don't know. He didn't say anything about other captives, but he couldn't talk openly. This is some kind of trap to get Gwen here. He made that clear. I need you to stay put. Can you do that for me?"

Cora nodded, and Chessa dialed Norman's number.

"Norm, I need you back in the office NOW. Quincy's in trouble."

20

Quincy had slept on a cot in a makeshift cell in the corner of the warehouse. Fairburn's goons dumped him there without so much as a snack or a sip of water for hours. The empty cell to the right of his made Quincy wonder how much need Marcus Fairburn had to imprison people and who else might get tossed in here. Somehow, this was all linked back to Xander. What little hope Quincy harbored that his abduction had been coincidental to the case flew out the window the minute Marcus had mentioned his "little informant." Was Xander trying to solve his brother's murder, or was he playing them all from the beginning? If the latter was the case, did he already know who killed Mandrake? Could he have been involved?

Quincy hated being played for a chump, but not as much as he hated unanswered questions. He was a simple half-ogre, and he liked things in life to be simple too. Dirty was fine, so long as it all made sense from beginning to end.

Where was he, anyway? At first, he thought it was a warehouse, but there was too much activity: the screeching sound of bay doors opening and closing through the early morning and voices drifting through shelves and boxes. And then there was the smell that occasionally permeated the air, at once sweet and acrid. It reminded him of when he'd accidentally burnt his arm hair off with the flame of a vanilla candle during sexy time with a kinky elf, but something told him this place was going to be a lot less fun.

"Oi," Quincy called from his cell figuring that if he could hear the bustle, then someone had to be able to hear him. "I gotta drain the lizard."

A humanoid carrying a box walked by the opening between shelves, but he didn't so much as cast a glance toward the cells. Quincy waited. Nobody else came. Eventually, a fairy driving a small forklift from atop a retrofitted seat passed along the same path.

"Oi, fairy boy! I've gotta take a whiz," he yelled.

"Not my job," called back the fairy.

At least Quincy had confirmation that he wasn't dead and doomed to haunt whatever the hell this was for the rest of his supernatural time on earth. He was so hungry, he was beginning to fear that might be his fate in any case. He tried another approach.

"It's going to be your problem when you gotta smell ogre piss for the rest of the day."

The forklift halted, but the fairy didn't fly down. "Use the bucket."

"I got a wicked huge bladder. You'd be surprised just how much rank piss it holds," said Quincy, kicking over the small pail. He wasn't lying. His bladder was the size of a large watermelon, and the bucket would certainly overflow should he choose to empty it.

"Hang on," said the fairy, flying away over the aisles of shelves and boxes. He returned a few minutes later with the mud-clay creature—the golem who had accompanied the cyclops and ogre. Once again, the creature didn't speak. He extended an arm and thrust his hand at the cell door where it oozed into the keyhole. A second later, his flesh hardened, snapping the mechanism into place, and the door swung open.

It was the fairy who instructed Quincy to follow, and the other creature followed behind.

"This guy got a name?" asked Quincy.

"I've been instructed not to speak to you beyond what is necessary," replied the fairy. "We all have, so don't bother trying someone else." He hovered around chest height as he led the little brigade.

"Fine. I'll call him Lumpy," said Quincy. "That was a handy trick back there, Lumpy. Does your hand do that even if it's separated from your body?"

Lumpy grunted, and Quincy could swear it sounded something like amusement.

They passed through a door, and sunlight momentarily blinded

Quincy. He stumbled along behind the fairy as the golem followed. At the end of the building, they hung a left and stopped before a modular unit attached to the far wall of the building. Lumpy shoved Quincy toward the door. The shitter was basically a toilet in a box. It wasn't quite porta-potty gross, but it was close. Still, it beat pissing in a bucket. Quincy took his time. He was in no hurry to return to his cell, and it gave him a moment to think about what little he'd seen of the area around the building. Other than the warehouse, there was nothing but trucks parked on gravel and beyond, trees. A barbed wire chain-link fence encircled the gravel lot. Quincy saw the gate, which was closed and secured with a thick chain. He assumed it was locked but could see no feasible way to investigate further so long as his guards were stuck to him.

A rapping on the door told Quincy the fairy was growing impatient. "Hurry it up in there, or we'll break down the door!"

Quincy forced a laugh. "Be my guest. I'm not so sure you'll enjoy what you see in here!"

On the walk back, Quincy surveyed the area. The building itself was even larger than he first estimated, and it was only one in a row of three industrial buildings, all with trucks backed up to loading bays. None of the creatures going about their business paid any mind to the half-ogre prisoner. He wondered if they all worked for Fairburn or if the inhabitants of Korranthia were so jaded, his situation didn't register as a blip on their radar. Perhaps it was a collection of illicit operations banded together to avoid detection. He shook his head, wondering how something like this could exist in Korranthia without him catching wind of it. It wasn't that he knew all the criminal comings and goings of the kingdom, but he did fraternize with enough petty criminals to pick up pieces of intel here and there. Madam Glitz was currently dealing in black-market artifacts, the hobgoblin gang had splintered, with some going straight in support of the new Seelie Queen, and Boss Briggs in the southern district was beefing with Glitz over some territorial situation. These were the kinds of things Quincy filed away should they ever be of use. But he hadn't heard the faintest rumor of Marcus Fairburn or a new player in town operating on this scale.

One of the box trucks pulled away from the docking bay and headed for the gate, the blue and yellow Wallow World logo unmistakable, and Quincy began to realize just how screwed he truly was. This wasn't just some row of warehouses. It was a Wallow World distribution center.

"So, Lumpy, what got you into this business?" he asked, swallowing the bile in his throat. If this was all happening in the open at a Wallow World property, that meant that there were powerful people involved.

"Enough questions," said the fairy, nudging him back toward the door.

Once inside, Quincy tried to catch a glimpse of Fairburn's office space, but the area from which he'd made the call to Chessa was dark.

"Any chance I can get a word with Mr. Fairburn?" asked Quincy.

"No," replied the fairy, not giving up anything. He was smarter than Quincy had given him credit for.

"I've got some information he needs."

"Nice try. Get back in your cell."

With no other plays in mind, Quincy obliged. Lumpy shut the cell door behind him and used his hand to lock it once more.

Even if it didn't spark an escape plan, his little trip to the bathroom had been educational. Quincy plopped down on the cot to try to think up a way to use the new information to his advantage. There was no way Chessa was stupid enough to bring Gwen to the shipyard to meet some stranger, especially not after confirming she understood something was up, but there was also no way he'd given her enough information to locate him. It was up to him to figure out how to get out of this mess.

A few hours later, Lumpy returned. This time, he was followed by a witch. She was tall for a human, though still short compared to Quincy, with dark hair that fell past her shoulders, and a body that made him choke on his own saliva. The bombshell walked right into the cell next to his without so much as a glance in his direction, and Lumpy locked the door behind her. He waited until they were alone before he made his move.

"How did a pretty thing like you get locked up in this joint?" he asked.

The witch sat on her cot and retrieved a book from beneath the flimsy mattress. "Save it," she said before scooching back against the wall and pulling her denim-clad knees up to her chest. She opened the book.

"You seem pretty comfortable here," said Quincy. "Do you know what this place is?"

"Yep," replied the witch.

"Care to share?" he pressed.

"Nope."

Quincy shoved a thick hand over his green mohawk causing it to flatten and then spring back up. "Can you tell me your name at least?"

"Miranda." She didn't bother looking up from her book.

"I'm Quincy," he said. "But you can call me Q."

She didn't respond. Maybe a holding cell of a Wallow World distribution center wasn't the best place to pick up chicks.

21

Chessa dialed Xander's number for what had to be the twentieth time. Whatever was going on with Quincy was linked to their client, there was no doubt about that, and she had no other leads to go on. She tried tracking down the phone number Quincy's call had come from, but it was unlisted.

"Fuck!" she screamed. She couldn't stand doing nothing. It wasn't in her genetic code.

Norman cleared his throat.

"Do you have something?" asked Chessa, darting over to the desk.

"I don't know," replied the wizard. "Miranda Xeos has been missing for a week. It's all over the news sites."

Chessa wrinkled her nose. "She's not a pixie," she replied, struggling to see a connection. Under normal circumstances, the disappearance of the CFO of one of the world's biggest online retailers would have Chessa typing up a *Crime Wave* post in record time. With Quincy in trouble, though, she wasn't motivated to work on anything else.

"No, but she is quite well-known, like Portia Kolsch. It might be nothing, but it looks like she cleaned out three of Sahara's biggest accounts before she vanished."

Now, that got Chessa's attention. Xeos was at the top of *Forbes'* "40 under 40" for her financial and business prowess, hardly the type of person who would flush her career in such a high-profile way. "How much did she get away with?"

"There's been no official statement, but speculators are saying millions."

"Holy shit."

Norman nodded. "The weird part is, it came out of nowhere. The woman had no record and was due for a substantial raise. She was poised for a long and lucrative career. Why would she toss it all in the bin?"

"That's a lot of cash," said Chessa, but her gut told her there was more to it.

"Sure, but she already had a lot of bees and honey. Cash that didn't turn 'er into a criminal. If they catch 'er, she'll rot in prison for the rest of 'er life instead of living it up in her mansion in Back Bay. It's a head-scratcher."

Chessa nodded. Norman was right, it didn't add up. A thought began to worm its way into her brain, a tenuous connection to the Kolsch case. "And another thing," she said, "Sahara is Wallow World's biggest competitor. What are the odds of the CFO of one company pulling off an epic heist on the heels of the murder of the heiress of the other?"

"Not great, I'd wager."

"I think you're onto something here, Norm. Good work."

Norman grinned at the praise. "I'll follow up with Detective Wayne and see if he can give us any more information on Xeos."

"Sounds good," Chessa replied. She knew she should be excited by a promising new lead, but it didn't get them any closer to finding Q. And time was running out. "You didn't happen to find anything else on Xander or Mandrake, did you? Anything that Q might have stumbled onto?"

"No."

"Damn it," she muttered. "I can't get ahold of Xander. I'm going to go do a fly-by this afternoon to see if I can catch him. If not, I might have to see if I can pry anything out of Abi. I see all these puzzle pieces, but I can't for the life of me click them into place. In the meantime, you follow up on Xeos. See what else you can dig up."

"Do you want to reach out to our royal friend?" asked Norman. "This feels too big for us to figure out alone, and she'll want to know about Quincy."

"Yes. Warn her that someone with powerful connections is trying to bait her into a trap. Tell her to stay away from Korranthia until we get it all sorted out."

Norman sighed. Chessa knew he wanted to call in reinforcements, but they couldn't risk putting Gwen in harm's way. Still, with a clock ticking on Quincy's life, she needed to kick this investigation into overdrive. She had so many pieces, but none of them fit together. A group of young adults mixed up in something they weren't willing to talk about, a false confession, a dead heiress, a missing executive, two hostages, and a sister begging her to drop the investigation all felt like bricks on her chest.

She retreated to her bedroom. Cora was lying in bed, scrolling her phone. "I know you're not going to stop, even if my fiancé ends up dead," she said.

Chessa sunk into the small recliner positioned by the window. "I can't."

"Not with Quincy gone, I know," said her sister without looking up from her phone. "I got to thinking. Among all the people involved in this case, who has the resources to travel all the way to Barbados to snatch a guy peripheral to your life to use as leverage? Who cares enough about your investigation to go that far?"

The answer was clear as day if only Chessa hadn't been stretched so thin. "The Kolsches."

"Exactly."

"But I still haven't established any kind of connection between Portia and Mandrake. Anyhow, they're borderline untouchable," said Chessa.

Cora nodded and set down her phone. "That may be, but the only way to get Blade back is to bring the bastards down."

Chessa looked over at her sister, and her stomach did acrobatics. The amount of strength it took Cora to have this conversation blew her away. "That's the plan. But right now, we don't have much to go on."

"If it's a connection you need, we'll find one," replied Cora. "I've gone through every one of Portia's videos, and I don't see it there. What else have you got?"

Chessa darted over to her desk, returned with a black trash bag, and dumped Mandrake Aster's sketchbooks on the bed. "It's a long shot, but maybe Mandrake drew one of them? I haven't had a chance to go through all of these, but it does seem like he captured a bunch of the people in his life. Maybe Portia's in there?"

"Even if she is, it's not very damning. Everyone knows what Portia Kolsch looked like."

She was right, of course, but that didn't stop Chessa. She divvied up the books. "We don't have anything else to go on. Maybe there will be something in here, a location, or a person, or *something*. Look for anything that feels off. When you finish one, set it over here, and we'll switch."

Under other circumstances, Chessa would love palming through a talented artist's sketches with one of her favorite people, but with missing loved ones and time slipping through their fingers, it was a tedious task. One unproductive hour in, Norman delivered coffee. Each time something stood out, Chessa and Cora would confer and mark it with a Post-it, but they found nothing incriminating, not that they recognized anyhow.

After two hours, Chessa was ready to give up and head over to Xander's. As she was about to close a hardcover sketchbook containing images of the park and patrons of Flit's, something caught her eye. Even in the shades of pencil gray, Madam Glitz's painted-up face and bedazzled outfit seemed to shine.

"Shit!"

Cora rolled over at Chessa's exclamation.

"You found a lead?" Cora looked as if her very sanity hung on the answer.

"Yes. I do believe I did. Bambi said Mandrake didn't go to the Painted Pony. If that's true, then why in the hell is he drawing detailed depictions of its proprietor?"

22

Quincy's mouth tasted like shit when he awoke to the sounds of voices approaching his cell. He stretched to make a show of nonchalance and sat up to look his captors in the eye. Lumpy's clay face was the first he made out, but there were others as well—Fairburn, an unfamiliar troll, and the little shithead who sold him out. Xander looked like he might bolt at the smallest sound. His eyes darted around the warehouse, took in the sight of Quincy behind bars, widened, and then moved on. As for Quincy's fellow prisoner, she hadn't given up any more than she had during that first conversation if you could even call it that. He had done as much probing as possible before finally settling down on the cot for a nap, defeated. Even now, she was lying with her back to the newcomers, asleep or at least pretending to be, Quincy didn't give a brownie's backside. Lumpy fashioned his hand into a key and swung the door open.

The new muscle lumbered into the cell, his massive troll body blocking the door beyond. His eyes were the color of rotten carrots, and his breath smelled worse. Quincy wondered what happened to Porgis.

"On your knees half-breed," grumbled the newcomer.

Whatever satisfaction could be gained by clocking the troll would be short-lived. Instead, Quincy flashed his most charming smile. "If you want your dick sucked, all you had to do was ask," he said, doing as he was told.

The troll kicked him in the face.

Quincy spat out a mouthful of blood, and possibly a tooth, then smiled again. After everything life had thrown at him, it would take more than a beating to rattle him.

"Enough," said Fairburn.

"I'm going to enjoy breaking you," muttered the troll before taking a step back to allow Xander to slip in.

A small vial was clutched in the pixie's left hand, a syringe in his right, and he refused to make eye contact. He said something, but his voice was so low, Quincy couldn't make out the words.

"Want to repeat that?" said Quincy, locking his gaze on the young pixie's face.

"Roll up your sleeve," said Xander, audible this time, as he drew up the liquid from the vial with the syringe.

"Make me," said Quincy.

Xander's face flushed. "Come on, just do it."

"I'll pass."

If Fairburn wanted Quincy to cooperate, he would have to use someone with more grit than this pantywaist. Quincy had opened up to this kid. He thought they had common ground. He even thought they could be friends. And this was how he was repaid. No, he wasn't about to play subservient ogre to someone who had sold him out.

"Hurry up and administer the drug," said Marcus. "I'm a very busy man."

A drug, was it? Quincy hoped it at least gave him a good buzz.

Finally, Xander met Quincy's gaze. "Please," he said. There was fear in his eyes, but at this point, Quincy didn't give a rat's ass.

"Hard pass."

Xander turned and looked back at Marcus, who shook his head before glancing over at the troll and flicking his wrist.

"A'ight twinkle toes, get out of here," said the troll. His voice was like rocks rolling around in a cavern. He held out his fat, pallid palm.

Xander placed the drug-filled syringe in his hand, then walked out of the cell with sagging shoulders and stiff legs. Quincy wondered what punishment awaited him for his ineptitude. If the fate of his brother was any indication, it wouldn't be good.

The troll wasn't nearly as polite as Xander or Fairburn. He snatched Quincy's arm in a vise grip and pulled it across his body, doubtless waiting for a fight. Quincy stared him down but kept his arm limp right up until the troll brought the syringe of translucent purple liquid in close to his bicep. Then, Quincy clocked him with his free fist.

All hell broke loose. Fae from all over the warehouse descended on the area, erecting a living barrier between Fairburn and the cell as blue blood spurted from the troll's nose all over the floor. He bellowed and grabbed at his face. Quincy rushed the door but ran straight into, nearly through, Lumpy. All too late, Quincy realized his error. The other fae's body squelched and molded around Quincy's form before Lumpy wrapped his thick arms around Q's waist in a tight hold. For a moment, Quincy was sure his ribs would crack. Lumpy's body hardened and thrust outward, sending Quincy stumbling back into the rigid metal bars of his cell. In mere seconds, Xander had secured zip ties around his ankles and wrists. Damn that pixie speed.

Once things settled down, Fairburn began to laugh. "I love when they choose the hard way," he said.

At a wave of his hand, the fae around him dissipated, heading back to whatever corners of the warehouse they came from, and he stepped forward. He walked over to the troll, who was sitting on the cell floor clutching his bleeding nose, gave him a kick to the stomach, then picked up the dropped syringe off the concrete floor.

"Hold him still," he said to Lumpy.

Lumpy stepped behind Quincy, leaving only Fairburn standing in front of the open cell door. Before Quincy could make a move, his entire back was encased in Lumpy's cool, gray flesh from shoulders to heels. He tried to pull free, but he might as well have been fighting a cement wall. Wet clay traveled down both arms and then hardened to hold him firmly in place.

"This fuckin' guy," gasped Quincy.

"Do you like my golem? A useful bit of clay indeed," said Fairburn. It took him no time at all to jab the needle into the muscle of Quincy's arm and inject him with the purple liquid. "Now, let's see if this makes you more accommodating."

Quincy was scared. Always, even in battle, he had control of himself if nothing else, but here, with an unfamiliar drug coursing through his veins and a creature that could lock him in place in seconds, he was purely at the mercy of others. His stomach roiled as childhood memories, horrible memories of feeling powerless while his father hurt him, threatened to surface. They gave way to a sensation of floating, and the hard edges of the world around him seemed to soften. He felt good. Really good. Everywhere that Lumpy's body touched tingled, and Quincy's muscles all relaxed. When the golem released him, he yearned for his touch. He fell into a heap on the ground, and the cool cement floor beneath him felt like heaven.

For the first time in his life, Quincy didn't feel like fighting.

23

The Painted Pony wouldn't open for hours, and Chessa had no way to get to Glitz until then, so she headed out to Brighton to pay Xander a visit. She was filled with trepidation as she flew up to the suburban house. The way she figured it, she was going to find one of three things: an empty house, a hostile teen, or a dead body. The lights were out, but that didn't mean much considering it was the middle of the day. By all rights, Xander should be in school, but she knew that wasn't the case. Unlike a police detective, Chessa didn't need a warrant to go snooping, so she checked one window after another. All was quiet. She decided on another approach. She kicked the door as loudly as she could while simultaneously ringing the doorbell over and over, hoping to flush out the pixie. Immediately, she took to the air to zip around the house, watching for any movement. Nada. Xander wasn't here.

The house was a typical single-family in a good school district, and it looked well cared for if you ignored the overgrown lawn and hedges. People didn't move to places like this unless they wanted to give their kids the best start in life, which meant that the Aster boys likely had a loving, supportive family before the Battle of Avalon.

"What did you get into?" she mused aloud.

However they ended up in trouble didn't change the facts. Two people Chessa cared about were missing, and two pixies were dead. After a quick survey to ensure she hadn't drawn the attention of any neighbors, Chessa pulled a lockpick set from her bag and set to work on the back door. She tripped the mechanism in less than fifteen seconds, a skill she'd developed in her teens, not that she'd ever let Cora know about how that came to pass.

The kitchen had white marble countertops and stainless-steel appliances, but the sink was full of dishes, and the trash reeked. Unsure of how much time she had, Chessa used her pixie speed to zip through the house, taking a quick survey. Other than signs of a teen boy living alone, nothing suspicious caught her eye. In the last bedroom upstairs, an iPad sat on a desk amidst stacks of soda cans and junk food wrappers. Chessa fired it up but didn't want to spend the time required to crack the passcode. After her third attempt, she decided to take it with her. Whatever was on it could be the key to finding Quincy and Blade.

With her arms full, it would be too much effort to fly, so she left on foot by the back door. From a few blocks away, she called a cab and took her stolen goods back to Norman, the most technologically savvy old man she'd ever met. He didn't bat an eye at her ill-gotten gains.

"I can crack it, but it's going to take me a bit," he said.

Chessa grinned. She was a fairly adept hacker in her own right, but Norman was a trained Unseelie spy. He might look like Merlin, but he truly was a tech wizard. "I knew you'd be up for it," she said.

Her trip to Brighton and back had taken a few hours, and the sun was beginning to set. She checked the time on her phone. A text from Abi was waiting.

You coming home today? We need to talk.

Chessa wasn't sure how to answer. It was not like she had a cover to keep up, but she also knew Abi was hiding a lot from her. It was a tiresome game. Besides, it was already pushing seven o'clock, and the Painted Pony would open soon. Chessa set the phone on her dresser without replying. Determined not to waste time while she waited on Norman, she dug a dress out of the closet, a black sparkly one with a slit that ran up to her hip, added some strappy silver heels, and prepared for a night at the club. A stop in the bathroom to put on a little makeup, and she was back in the reception area looking over Norman's shoulder.

"I'm in," said the wizard after a tense few minutes. He turned the iPad to Chessa, rose from the chair, and headed for the kitchen.

"Don't you want to see what's on here?" Chessa asked.

"It's a teenager's tablet. You'll tell me what you want me to look at, but what you won't do is remember to feed yourself, so I'll be back."

"Mmhm," replied Chessa, already lost in the information trapped in the small, glowing device. The desktop was predictable: cluttered with school documents, photos, and applications.

To make the best use of her time, Chessa went for the email. Xander's inbox was filled with unread messages from the school, the doctor's office, Seelie Court representatives, and bill collectors. She decided to focus on the correspondences that had been opened: a threaded conversation with Honey, a replied-to email from an M. Fairburn, and a message from the KPD.

The conversation with Honey was difficult to follow but seemed to provide directives to a specific location. What Xander was to do there was a mystery, but what struck Chessa as odd was the authority with which her gamer-girl housemate wrote. It was at odds with the disconnected persona she put forth. She was a key player in whatever they were all mixed up in.

"I missed it," Chessa said aloud, eliciting a grunt from Norman, who was still in the kitchen. Her gut was usually right about people, but Honey's apathetic act had her fooled. She replayed all the interactions in her mind, and it all made sense. It wasn't Dom everyone was afraid of, not at all. It was Honey. "Shit. Honey is the leader."

Beyond that tidbit, she couldn't get much else from the emails, so she moved on to the message from the KDP, just a note indicating that the Mandrake Aster case was closed.

The message from Marcus Fairburn was far more enlightening. It read:

> *Mr. Aster,*
>
> *My condolences on the death of your brother. Mandrake had high hopes for you, even if his loyalty wavered in the end. The work he accomplished will always be valued. I hope you understand that we couldn't let him make it all for naught. I expect my faith in you to be just as valuable.*
>
> *Sincerely,*
>
> *Marcus Fairburn*

"Motherfucker!" yelled Chessa.

This time, Norman poked his head back into the room.

"It was all a set-up! From the beginning, Xander was playing us. He knows who killed his brother. He works for the bastard!"

Norman walked over and set a hand around Chessa's shoulder. He put a plate with a peanut butter and banana sandwich down on the desk in front of her.

"If that's the case we all got had," he said. "Don't take it too hard."

"How else am I supposed to take it? My brother-in-law and my friend are both being held by a man who killed his own worker for going soft! What does that mean for them?"

Norman read the screen over Chessa's shoulder. "Pardon me, little miss, but it's not like you to jump to conclusions. Nothing 'ere says he has Quincy and Blade."

Chessa took a deep breath and fought to regain control of her rogue emotions. She always gave people the benefit of the doubt—it was how she was wired—and it bit her in the ass more times than she could count. She used to think that the times she was right to see the good in people more than evened the score. But now, the people close to her were paying the price for her being suckered in by a grieving teenager, and that was more than she could bear.

"You think it's a coincidence that Quincy was taken hostage after developing a relationship with Xander, the kid we just discovered hood-winked us?"

Norman stared mutely ahead. Chessa knew he was just trying to help, but she continued on. "Or that my soon-to-be brother-in-law will be killed if I don't drop this case?"

Norman shook his head. "No, little miss. I know as well as you that it's all connected to this Fairburn bloke. I just don't want you to lose yourself in all this."

Chessa stopped and looked into Norman's blue eyes, which were becoming wet. She took in the concerned wrinkles across his forehead and the genuine pain painted on his face, and she remembered that he was one of the people she'd put her neck on the line for. Gwen had wanted to lock him away, but Chessa saw something good in him and took him in. And she was right. Maybe putting her faith in Xander was misplaced, and maybe it wasn't. Maybe it put Quincy and Blade in the path of a killer, but there was nothing she could do about decisions that were already made. She sighed, and it felt like the weight of the world eased from her shoulders.

"I'm sorry, Norman," she said. "You're right. We need to focus on the way forward and getting our friends back."

The wizard's face softened. "We will."

"I need you to go through the rest of his messages and pull anything suspicious. Then see what you can dig up on this Marcus Fairburn. We know he killed Mandrake and sent Xander to us. This was a trap for Gwen from the beginning, and we played right into his hands. This email is a threat, not an expression of sympathy."

She desperately wanted Norman to tell her she was wrong, that her judgment was clouded by fear for her friends, but he didn't. He just nodded and told her to eat.

<h1 style="text-align:center">24</h1>

The Painted Pony was a bustling nightclub for fae, and Madam Glitz was the closest thing Korranthia had to a minor crime boss, not that the KPD ever had any evidence of her misadventures. She was too smart to leave a trail, but she had her hands in so many backroom dealings, even Quincy had expressed admiration for her.

Getting into the club was no problem. Chessa used the small fae door and was attractive enough to skip to the front of the line, but securing an audience with Glitz proved to be more challenging. She did a quick survey of the upstairs, which was comprised of a floating dance floor connected to the balcony overlooking the large fae dance floor below by four narrow catwalks. Small fae—pixies, brownies, sprites, fairies, gnomes, and the like—writhed rhythmically to the droning beats while others crowded around the multiple bars situated on the perimeter of the space. Glitz would be holding court in the VIP area, but Chessa knew she was kept apprised of any developments in the club through her ear comms and staff. Instead of making the obvious play by heading straight to the lush velvet ropes keeping the riffraff out of the VIP section, Chessa went to the bar on the right side of the room to order herself a beer while she waited for an invitation. Drink in hand, she found an unoccupied magenta velvet chaise and sat down. It didn't take long for a male fairy to approach.

"I love the green in your hair," he said. "Can I buy you a drink?"

Chessa smiled in response. "I've already got one."

"Oh."

"But you can keep me company if you like," she said, feeling bad for the guy. His game was weak but at least he didn't drag one of his friends along to play wingman like most males tended to do in this place. He brightened up and flitted his wings to get enough lift to land on the chaise next to her.

"I'm Alan," he said.

"Chia."

"As in Chia Pet?" he asked then immediately blushed.

"Something like that."

"I don't think I've seen you in here before. Are you meeting someone?" he asked. At least he had the sense to know that asking if she was alone would be creepy.

"No. I just needed a change of scenery." Chessa looked pointedly at the raised platforms on the floating dance floor. A sprite danced seductively on the closest one. "Do you know Bambi? She used to dance here."

"The sorceress? Yeah. She mostly stayed downstairs, but every so often they bring some of the larger fae up here to dance. She was delightful." Alan bit his bottom lip like he was afraid he'd said too much. "Not that I made a habit of hitting on the dancers. It wasn't like that."

This poor guy. Chessa wanted to let him off the hook, but it was too easy. "No? Then how was it?"

"Well, I just like to dance, and I notice a pretty girl, that's all. Bambi was nice. Too nice. She let people push her around. Sometimes security even got involved. Is she a friend of yours?"

Chessa nodded. "She was, but she went to jail for murder."

The fairy gasped. "No way!"

"Yeah. Apparently, she killed some pixie artist who broke up with her."

Chessa didn't need her pixie gift to see the doubt on Alan's face. "That's fucked up. I talked to her about a month ago, and she said she wasn't seeing anyone. And even if she was, there's no way she could have killed anyone. Like I said, she was sweet."

Chessa raised a brow. "I thought you said you weren't hitting on her."

"Oh, well, I mean, I didn't, okay, maybe I was. What of it?"

Chessa laughed to break the tension. "You should probably go find a more gullible girl to chat up."

Alan shot her a dirty look but had the sense to hold his tongue. A moment later, she was alone again, deciding on her next move. Thankfully, she didn't need to come up with a plan. A cocktail server in tights that revealed his well-muscled backside appeared with a bottle of the same Lost Druid IPA she'd been sipping on.

"Chessa Moon, Madam Glitz sends her regards and asks you to join her in the VIP section at your convenience," he said, handing her the bottle.

Chessa wasted no time heading to the back of the room where the pink velvet rope and surly looking bouncer ten times the size of any fae on this floor kept uninvited guests out of the VIP section. She knew what 'at your convenience' meant to people like Glitz, and while she did enjoy pushing buttons, she would never let her recreation jeopardize a case. The thought of her night with Abi flashed across her mind. *That was different*, she told herself.

Johnny Gross, the troll-hybrid bouncer known for keeping Glitz safe, was posted at the door. He must have been expecting her because he bent over to unlatch the rope to let her pass - a formality, really, since she could easily fly over it. Not that she would think of crossing Johnny. His reputation wasn't built on his size alone.

"Thanks," she said, flashing a grin and earning a slight smile in return. Gross probably wasn't accustomed to being treated like more than off-putting muscle.

Madam Glitz was easy to find. She stood in the center of the room, entertaining an assorted group of fae all dressed in their finest, each holding a crystal glass. She was in a shimmery golden dress tonight with matching stilettos and perfectly manicured burgundy nails with gold tips. Her makeup was divine, as always, and her burgundy lips pulled up into a smile that didn't touch her eyes when she saw Chessa.

"My dear," she called across the room, waving her hand to beckon Chessa over. "What brings Korranthia's finest reporter to my humble little corner of the city?"

As Glitz bent over to place a light kiss on her cheek, Chessa fluttered her wings to meet her halfway, a show of deference.

"I don't know about all that," Chessa replied. "But don't worry, I'm not here digging up stories for *Crime Wave*. I'm actually hoping you can help me with a case I'm working."

"I'm not sure which is more dangerous, a beautiful woman looking to make headlines or one asking questions," replied Glitz. She laughed low and deep as if her words didn't hold some truth.

"Do you have a moment to talk privately?" asked Chessa.

"For you, dear? Of course."

Glitz led Chessa to the last alcove on the left and made a hand motion to one of the servers, an elf Chessa recognized from her last visit to The Pony. He drew the curtains shut once they were seated, leaving them in relative privacy.

"I really appreciate you letting me interrupt your evening. I don't think this will take long," said Chesssa.

Glitz licked her lips. "Take as long as you need, lovely."

"I'm here to ask you about Bambi Boros."

At that, some unidentifiable emotion flashed in Glitz's eyes. "Poor dear. I tried to interfere on her behalf, you know, get the jury to go easy on her."

"She didn't do it."

"Well, of course, she didn't do it. This is Korranthia, dear."

Now, *that*, Chessa wasn't expecting. She tried not to show too much shock. "What do you know about the murder of Mandrake Aster?"

"Right for the jugular. I knew I liked you."

Chessa wasn't going to let her deflect. "Can you tell me anything?"

"I'm afraid I can't. It's bad business." Glitz batted her thick, pink false eyelashes and swirled the martini glass in her hand.

Chessa waited a moment to see if she would say more, but the witch was gazing into her drink as if lost in thought.

"How would it be bad for the Pink Pony?"

"Not that business, dear." The witch hesitated. She looked Chessa in the eye for an intense moment then turned her attention back to the olive dancing in the bottom of her drink. "Bambi's a good girl. A sweet girl. She didn't deserve this."

"Tell me something I can use to help her."

"I'm afraid my associate wouldn't like that much."

"Associate? Madam Glitz, everyone in Korranthia knows you deal magic—"

"Allegedly."

"You allegedly deal magic. Does Mandrake's death have anything to do with that?" Chessa knew she wouldn't get a straight answer, but you could tell a lot by the way people responded to direct questions.

"I couldn't say."

"What about Portia Kolsch?"

Glitz stood abruptly. "I'm afraid I must get back to my other guests. I hope you will stay and sample the hors d'oeuvres. Chef Bianca has outdone herself this evening. Excuse me."

With that, Chessa was left alone in the alcove, more confused than when she'd arrived.

Chessa considered sticking around the club to kick over a few more rocks, but she only had three days before the meeting with whoever had taken Quincy, and she felt like she had a pretty good picture of the situation with Boros. Someone had leveraged a false confession out of her. Mandrake had been here, but not for the dancing and romancing known to happen at The Painted Pony.

Instead, he was somehow mixed up in whatever business venture Glitz was currently running. But you don't unearth the darkest secrets by standing in the light yelling your questions at the sky. Nobody here would give Chessa anything, not now that she'd tipped her hand to Glitz. She'd have to find another way to piece it all together.

Her phone buzzed. Another message from Abi asking if she was coming to the house. She wasn't planning to return to her shared quarters, not after everything with Dom and Lance. With her cover already blown with Abi, she wasn't sure how much good she would do keeping up pretenses, and any normal person would be spooked by one roommate stabbing another—it was the perfect excuse to pull out of the ruse if she needed one. Besides she needed to catch a few Zs or she wouldn't be much good for Quincy or anyone, and with Abi blowing up her phone, it was clear that wouldn't happen at the Montello house.

After a few hours of sleeping on the couch in the reception room of C&F to avoid disturbing Cora, Chessa awoke with an anxiety pit in her stomach. She pulled her cell off the charger and dialed Xander's number. No answer. Again. She cleaned herself up in the bathroom and then headed out to find out why Abi was so insistent on talking. She ran by Dela's Donuts for a large latte and a cruller on the way.

Abi was in the kitchen, preparing breakfast for Lance, Honey was holed up in her bedroom, likely back to gaming, and Dom was out.

"He hasn't been back since you left," said Abi as she flipped a pancake. "I was really hoping you'd help me find him."

"Is that why you wanted me home?" Chessa asked, skeptical.

"Uh huh."

It didn't take Chessa's pixie sense to know she was lying.

"How's Lance doing?" asked Chessa, perching on the table in the bay window. She wished she knew what Abi was playing at. The pixie was brilliant, gorgeous, and, by the looks of those golden pancakes, she could cook. Chessa wanted whatever secrets were keeping them apart to vanish so she could fly over for a kiss. She fought back the urge. She needed to keep things professional, at least for now. It would suck to get into a relationship and find out that her new girlfriend was a criminal mastermind.

No, she reminded herself. *That's Honey.*

"He's doing surprisingly well, though you'd never know it. I've never heard anyone whine so much."

"He did get stabbed."

"I know, but…" Abi bit her bottom lip. "You know what? Just come up. You'll see what I mean."

Once the pancakes were loaded onto a plate, buttered, and covered with syrup, she carried the meal upstairs, having Chessa follow with orange juice in one hand and a cup of coffee in the other. Chessa heard the moaning before they reached the landing.

"Ohh, ohhhhh."

Abi looked over her shoulder at Chessa.

"Abiii, what's taking so long? I'm lonely. And hungry." Each vowel was elongated in a way that only toddlers had complete mastery over.

"Oh, boy," said Chessa.

"It's been like this all day and night," replied Abi with a sigh. That explained the dark circles under the normally flawless pixie's eyes. She'd suffered thirty hours of goblin baby drama.

Lance had been moved to his own room, though it looked like someone had tidied up, and he was propped up against an ungodly number of pillows. His blankets were pulled up to his chin. On the nightstand next to him was a monster cup of ice water, a tablet, a phone, and a television remote. When he saw Chessa, his face somehow became even more pitiful.

"Hey, there roomie, how you feeling?" she asked.

"I almost died," he replied.

"I know. I was there."

"It hurts so much. And I'm cold. And Abi took forever making breakfast."

Abi scowled and handed him the plate. "Well, here it is."

"I don't think I can eat," he replied. "I'm in too much pain."

"You just said you were hungry," said Abi through clenched teeth.

"I am, but I don't think I can eat pancakes."

"Lance, you asked for pancakes, so I made you pancakes."

Tears welled up in Lance's yellow eyes. "That was so long ago. I'm so low on energy, I need protein. Can you make me some eggs? Please?"

Abi sighed and took back the plate of pancakes. "Hungry?" she asked Chessa, who shook her head. She turned to walk out the door.

"Over medium with a side of toast and two strips of bacon," said Lance as if he were ordering a at a drive-through. Chessa thought Abi might finish the job Dom had started, but instead, she grunted something and headed downstairs.

Once she was out of sight, Lance waved Chessa over. "You've got to get me out of here," he hissed.

"Because of Dom?" asked Chessa.

"No. Dom is just panicking. You don't understand what's happening here. If I don't get out of here, I'm goblin goo."

Chessa shuddered. It wasn't that she had a problem with the goblin custom of gelatinizing their dead—Danu knew there were far weirder customs out there—but picturing Lance melting like that was beyond disconcerting.

"You've got to give me more to go on here," said Chessa as Abi's footsteps approached.

"She's coming," whispered Lance with terror in his eyes.

He sunk back into his pillows, the picture of absolute despair. Chessa was left with her head spinning. For the first time in her life, she couldn't make heads or tails of a situation. She thought she could trust Abi, but Lance obviously disagreed. She'd been wrong about Dom and Honey, could she be wrong about Abi too? One thing was certain, she needed to untangle this mess if she had any hope of figuring out what happened to Mandrake. And if Lance was to be trusted, there were more lives in the balance, and that wasn't even counting Quincy and Blade, wherever they were being held captive. This case was getting more complicated by the day.

"I've got to head into work," said Chessa.

"You just got here," replied Abi.

Chessa glanced at Lance. He looked like he wanted to say something, but his mouth remained closed. His eyes held a warning. He was either silently begging Chessa to take him with her or—

Before Chessa could complete the thought, someone grabbed her from behind. Purely on instinct, Chessa doubled over and flipped the assailant over her head. Honey hit the ground before scrambling to her feet and launching back toward Chessa.

"Abi, hold her down!" growled the other pixie. Abi stood transfixed by the bed.

As Honey closed in, Chessa flapped her wings and leveled a kick to her stomach, an unexpected move by the sound of Honey's pinched-off cry. She fell backward, and before Abi could make the decision to join the melee, Chessa zipped out the door, down the stairwell, and out into the fresh air. By the time she stopped to rest, her lungs were on fire. Her only comforting thought was that neither Honey nor Abi would be able to catch up. Pixies were only fast in short bursts, and they weren't fleeing for their lives. As soon as she could breathe again, Chessa abandoned the hiding spot in the elm and flew in a different direction. She needed to put as much space between her and the Montello house as possible.

Chessa's head was still spinning when she arrived at C&F Investigations two hours later. Samson was chatting with Norman in the reception area, and they both looked up in surprise. She must have looked a mess.

"Don't worry about me. I just escaped a house full of homicidal artists bent on making me their next exhibit," she said. She'd been able to reach a Leaf Pass station and catch a ride back to East Boston without any accidental detours.

Norman's mouth fell open.

"Who am I arresting?" asked Samson, pulling his cell from the pocket of the khakis that covered his lion legs.

"Nobody. Not yet, anyways," replied Chessa. "But I'd say my cover is definitely blown."

"If you're certain you're not about to get dusted before you close the case," said Samson. He put the phone back in his pocket.

"Why are you here, Sammy?"

"It's about your client. Norman sent over an inquiry after he realized that the kid wasn't on the level, and I went digging. Seems the junior Mr. Aster has a rap sheet."

Chessa kicked herself for not asking Samson to look Xander up in the system sooner. "Oh, really?"

"We nabbed him two years back hopped up on the dust. He did six months in juvie before being released to his parents.

Chessa couldn't help but glance at Norman. He'd told her all about his crime family back in Glastonbury, about how they dabbled in running pixie dust while also smuggling black market magical artifacts. He studied the paper in front of him intently.

"I know a lot of pixies that try it," said Chessa. She'd even considered it back in high school. So many fae had the ability to channel magic, but for pixies, the power was simply a part of their composition. Some fae were practitioners, others were simply magical in nature, and pixies were stuck in the middle—they had magical gifts, like Chessa's intuition, but they couldn't channel magic. Pixie dust changed that, and the power was seductive. The only reason Chessa hadn't dabbled in it herself was because she'd lost a childhood friend to the dust. It was highly addictive, and it turned good pixies into husks of themselves. Chessa had seen it firsthand, and it was enough to scare her off the path.

"There's more," mumbled Norman, still looking down.

"Just after his parents' funeral, he was picked up again. This time, he was carrying a lot more than a user should have on them. We booked him for intent to distribute. But Mandrake showed up with some slick lawyer and got him off."

"Where did Mandrake get the money?" asked Chessa.

"That's the thing. Nobody had seen the lawyer's mug in town, so we did some snooping. Seems like he just up and decided to take on a case out in Korranthia after living it up as a hotshot defense attorney in Hollywood. Now, why do you think he'd come to these parts for some broke pixie junkie?"

"I'm guessing it's tied to Marcus Fairburn. I'm not sure if Norman caught you up, but it seems like he's calling the shots. Xander set us up." The words were thick in her mouth. She and Gwen started the firm to seek justice for those who fell through the cracks of the fae justice system, and to think that one of her clients had tricked her for some nefarious purpose felt like a personal betrayal.

"I've scoured the internet for information on Fairburn and came up empty," added Norman. Damn. Chessa had hoped he'd found an alias, an address, or something useful

"Not even socials?" Chessa asked.

"The man doesn't appear to exist."

Suddenly, Chessa's gut clenched and the air seemed to sizzle. She darted in front of Norman just as a hobgoblin materialized beside the desk, not far from where she'd been standing. His roundness implied he'd eaten through a lot of space and had likely travelled a great distance. He flashed a wide grin before reaching down to his abdomen and digging his fingers into his flesh, wrenching it apart to expose a cavernous middle. Hobgoblin slime dripped from the opening and pooled at his feet, and a fairy guard stepped out of his innards, rank goo covering his entire body.

He didn't seem perturbed in the slightest and proceeded to survey the room before holding up a hand. Only then did the Seelie Queen step out of the new arrival, followed by another fairy guard.

"Gwendolyn Evenshine, what did I tell you about this?" Chessa demanded. "You can't just pop up in the reception area without notice! Use the back bedroom and let someone know you're coming for Danu's sake!"

Gwen put a hand on the desk to steady herself and glanced at Norman, who visibly flinched.

"Oh, I see," said Chessa, realizing Norman had known about the visit and failed to tip her off. She shot him an accusatory glare before wrapping her best friend in a hug, mess be damned.

"I didn't have time to tell ya," Norman said quietly.

Samson dropped into a bow.

"For Danu's sake, get up, Samson," snapped Gwen. "Don't be ridiculous."

The Seelie guard who'd scouted ahead seemed agitated, but that was true whenever Gwen visited Korranthia. They were trained to protect the royal family, and there were certain customs that were expected to be followed. Gwen didn't do well with expectations. Or customs.

What Chessa found strange, though, was how at-ease the other guard was. That's when she recognized Curtis Steele, notorious general of the Seelie army and, more importantly, a good friend. Chessa grinned and gave him a gooey hug too. The hobgoblin gave a curt bow then melted into the floor, and the sticky foursome headed to the bathroom to take turns cleaning up.

25

Hobgoblin wasn't the most glamorous way to traverse the globe, but it was the fastest, and these days, Gwen was short on time. Even so, she didn't waste a minute getting to Korranthia. She might be Queen of the Seelie Court, but there was one pixie she cared about more than all other fae combined, and if Norman said Chessa was in over her head, that warranted an in-person appearance, especially since Gwen had other business to see to in town as well. By the look on Chessa's face, Norman had gone behind her back when he made the call to Avalon. Not that she was surprised by the wizard's wavering loyalty.

Gwen tossed the towel she'd used to dry off to Curtis, who still had a bit of hobgoblin goo in his hair. His focus was on her safety, so he didn't take enough time cleaning up. Usually, she left him to run Avalon when she traveled, but when Norman mentioned a threat to the throne, he insisted on coming along. That meant leaving Avalon in the hands of someone she could trust. Marni, a pixie she'd relied heavily on since taking over the Seelie throne, had explicit instructions to contact her if anything unusual occurred during her absence. Marni, along with her brother Hobbes, were the heads of the newly formed Seelie Intelligence Initiative in Avalon, so she would be first to hear if anything was going down. Hobbes was on a different assignment, one not far from here.

"Quincy's been taken by who?" Gwen asked, as Curtis directed the other guard to post up in the hallway outside the apartment door. He set himself up a place by the window.

"Our client, Xander Aster, is working for a man who doesn't seem to exist, and we believe that's who has Quincy. You ever heard the name Marcus Fairburn before?"

"Nope," Gwen lied. She didn't like keeping things from Chessa, but Fairburn's name was floating around the documentation she'd received from Hobbes. This case must be linked to his assignment somehow.

"He sure seems to know you. We suspect that Xander only hired us to lay a trap for you. Norman was supposed to warn you off, so what are you doing in Korranthia?"

"He seemed to think you needed my help," Gwen replied. In truth, the wizard had warned her about the trap, but he also made it sound like Chessa could be in danger. By the look of the shiner her friend sported, he wasn't far off.

"We don't. You should call your hobgoblin and get back to where you're needed. I've got this case well in hand."

"Seems like it." Gwen smirked at the anger that flashed in Chessa's eyes. She couldn't blame her for being protective, but Gwen was sick of everyone acting like she was breakable, like she wasn't a war-tested badass who'd faced down her own brother and his army to claim the throne. She had to remind herself that Chessa wasn't just one of her subjects, she was the closest thing she had to family. "The case being the murder of a pixie in cold blood?"

As if failing to realize that she was also a pixie who could be murdered, Chessa replied, "Yes."

Gwen looked over at Samson, who was picking his feathers in the corner just like in the old days. "What do you have on the murder, Sammy?" she asked.

"Besides a jilted lover's confession and a closed file? Nada," he replied.

"If I know Chess, she thinks the confession is a misdirection," said Gwen. She plopped her Doc Marten-clad feet up on the coffee table while reclining on the old plaid couch. If her mother were still alive, she'd have a conniption over the way she dressed and acted, but Gwen was queen now, and she wasn't about to change herself to fit into stuffy traditions. Where had those traditions gotten them, anyhow?

"I'm bamboozled. The confession checked out, but Chia's gut doesn't lie."

"Chia? Really?" Gwen gave a little chuckle. Last time she checked, the only people who called Chessa by her street name were all in Quincy's pack of delinquents.

Samson pushed his round red spectacles to the top of his beak and went back to picking at the feathers of his wrist.

"It's all smoke and mirrors, trust me," piped in Chessa. "But Gwennie, you need to steer clear of this case."

"I know, I know, having Seelie royalty buzzing around spooks your clients." It stung a bit that Chessa didn't want her involved in cases anymore, but in actuality, Gwen didn't have the time to dedicate to hunting down criminals. She was busy restructuring the entire Seelie way of life, not to mention trying to track down all manner of magical misappropriation. Chessa had no idea how small her problems really were in the grand scheme of things.

"That's not it. Whoever took Quincy did it to get to *you*. We have no idea what the end game is, but you can't be here. I've spent enough of my life trying to save your ass already."

"Hey, now! Low blow!" protested Gwen, but Chessa did have a point. The last time Gwen had been captured, they'd kind of set off an Unseelie revolution.

"It's true and you know it. I love you to death, but can you please call your ride?"

"You're right. I have a lot going on right now and can't stick around. But it seems like you're in over your head. "What happened to your face?"

"Aster's friends got the jump on me," said Chessa looking down at her feet. "But I got away and they're not stupid enough to try it again."

Gwen sighed. "Can I send you some reinforcements?"

"This is messy enough without Avalon fae in the mix," replied Chessa.

"Curtis, at least?"

Chessa looked over at Curtis Steel, and he flashed a sheepish smile. "It's not that I mind having some eye candy around the office, but General Steele belongs at your side, keeping your ass out of the fire. Fairburn isn't the only one wanting to get a piece of it."

Gwen thought Curtis might turn into a tomato if he blushed any harder, but she was used to Chessa's offhanded innuendo. Technically, she could order Chessa to do whatever she wanted, but that wasn't how this relationship worked. If Chessa wanted to go it alone, that was exactly what she would do. Besides, she wasn't really alone, was she? Gwen's smile melted as she looked over at Norman, the traitor who'd helped the

Unseelie slaughter her family. She'd feel better about leaving if Quincy was around to watch Chessa's back.

"Norman, can I have a private word with you before I go?"

Chessa cocked her head to the side in curiosity, but what Gwen had to say wasn't for her ears. She'd hoped she wouldn't have to interrogate the wizard, but when she used her empathic touch to read his desk, the only sensations she discovered were the smell of old books, visions of clients, and feelings of belonging mixed with fear—none of the information she sought. She gave Chessa a big hug, promising to send a transport hobgoblin once she got word that this case was over, then she scruffled Samson's feathers and told him to be careful.

Gwen led Norman to the back room, technically a second bedroom, but used to store files and evidence for the PI firm. Curtis followed, always vigilant, and closed the door behind them.

Norman sat on a swivel desk chair in the corner while Gwen perched on a nearby shelf so she could look him in the eye. She wasted no time.

"When was the last time you spoke to anyone in your family?" she asked. Being alone with Norman made her uncomfortable, knowing that he'd been instrumental in the Unseelie revolt. It was he who made the invasion of Avalon, her home, possible, and now, most of her family was dead. The only reason she hadn't had him locked up after she took the throne was Chessa. He'd endangered himself to keep her safe, and that was worth more than anything to Gwen. Still, she wasn't sure she'd ever fully trust him, especially since his family had become a massive thorn in her side.

"Not since before coming to Korranthia," he said. "I told them I was going straight. I told them not to look for me."

Sure he did. "And did they listen?"

"Yes, Your Grace. I ain't heard word one. You can ask Ms. Moon. I've been settled in 'ere right proper like."

"Your father, he's the one who calls the shots, right?"

Norman shifted in his chair, doubtless uncomfortable. Gwen didn't give a damn. If he'd truly gone straight, he should have no problem answering her questions.

"I guess you could say that. He decides which projects the family is going to take on, if that's your meaning."

"And what projects have the family taken on?"

"Your Grace, I truly don't know nothing. At least, nothing current.

They'll do anything to make a shilling. They mostly smuggle, but you already know that."

"I'm going to level with you Norman, I've got a lot on my plate. Normally, I wouldn't concern myself with petty criminals, but your family has been stirring up trouble in Glastonbury. It seems they've gotten into the pixie dust business, and I've received word that they're working with someone here in Korranthia."

"Ah, so you ain't here for Chessa at all." It was a statement more than a question, and that irked Gwen more than anything.

"Chessa is everything to me, and if I find out you're working with your family behind her back, putting her in danger, there is nowhere on earth or Faerie you could hide from me. Is that clear?"

Norman nodded, his gaze fixed on his feet. "Your Grace, I wouldn't do anything to hurt little miss. Not ever."

Gwen took a breath to calm herself. This pathetic wizard knew better than to cross her, and threatening him was a waste of her breath. "If they're running dust from Glastonbury and distributing it globally, it becomes a problem for all fae kind. You know what that shit does to pixies."

Norman was now visually agitated. "I know that better than most! I done told little miss to steer clear of it, I did. You can ask 'er yourself!"

His words hit like a rock. It never occurred to Gwen that Chessa might try dust, but there wasn't much Chessa wouldn't do to crack a case, especially with people she cared about on the line. "She's not thinking of using, is she? I know this case she's working on is a lot, but she doesn't need magic that bad. It's not worth the risks."

"Oh, no. I mean, she would never. I mean, she'll get 'er hands dirty if she needs to, don't get me wrong, but she would never chance dust addiction. That ain't no joke."

He was right. Pixie dust might give pixies the ability to channel magic, but it also robbed them of their faculties and turned them into hungry, violent junkies who would put a knife in their own mothers if they thought they could score a hit. It was the only substance the fae world regulated, and being derived from earth magic in the soil around Avalon, the once-portal to the land of Faerie, it was potent shit. The flowers used to extract the drug, Nyxanthiums, were banned worldwide, but earth magic was wild, and the weeds occasionally popped up in Avalon. The only seeds known to the world were locked up at the palace. At least, they had been.

"I'm going to cut to the chase. When you occupied my home, did you locate the Nyxanthium seeds in the vault?"

The look on the wretched wizard's face told her everything she needed to know. His eyes were filled with tears and his hands shook.

"Norman, did you give the seeds to anyone?"

He nodded mutely.

"To your family?"

"It was when I first set up in the palace, and I was working for the Unseelie. They had me catalog everything I found, but when I found them seeds, I did what Pa said. I sent them. I didn't take them all, just a couple."

"And I assume your family has connections with pixies who would be willing to cultivate the flowers?"

Only pixies could safely extract dust. It had a suboptimal effect on other fae; specifically, the oils in the stems drove them to madness and eventually death. During the first dust epidemic, the Seelie Council had lost a number of fairy guards in their efforts to stomp out the local Nyxanthium blooms before they made that discovery, but these days, the widespread knowledge of the threat was enough to keep average fae from coming within fifty feet of a naturally occurring flower. It was how Avalon had kept control of the situation. In the event of a wildflower sighting, the citizen who discovered it would call a hotline, and a specialty task force would respond immediately. Nobody would willingly expose themselves to Nyxanthium blooms. But Norman's family weren't run-of-the-mill fae citizens.

The miserable wizard nodded again. He was openly weeping now.

Gwen knew what Chessa would say. Norman had been a victim of the world. He was trying to make amends for his past. He deserved a second chance.

Fuck that. Not only had this man broken into her home and let killers ravage Avalon, but he had stolen one of the most dangerous items from the vault and put the entire fae population, Seelie, Unseelie, and more, at risk.

He sickened her.

"Get out," she said, dismissing him from her presence.

"I'm sorry, I'm so sorry," he muttered before standing from the chair and scampering out of the room.

Once they were alone, Gwen could feel the gaze of Curtis Steele on her back. "You know he's not that man anymore," he said.

"We don't know what kind of man he is," she replied. "But I do know who he was. You can't just wish away your past. Believe me, I've tried."

"True. But people change. They grow."

"I don't need a lecture."

Curtis flitted over to stand beside her, but he didn't make a move to touch her. "No, but you do need a friend. Chessa's right, my place is by your side. You can't leave me here."

His murky green eyes were so open, so unguarded. It was off-putting to Gwen. Curtis had done well facing the Unseelie troops and leading the Seelie armies, but what right did he have to look into her soul like that? He was like a puppy.

"Your place is wherever I say it is," she quipped.

There was a slight knock on the door. Curtis shook his head and floated down to answer it. Gwen's other guard, Bobby or Jimmy or something, she could never remember, entered with a skinny, ready-to-travel hobgoblin. Without another word, Gwen returned to Avalon. Curtis followed.

26

Norman's eyes were red when he emerged from the back room.

Damn it, Gwen, thought Chessa. "I take it she's gone?" she said.

Norman nodded and swiped a sleeve across his face as he settled in behind the desk.

"Everything okay? Did you ask about the library?" Chessa pressed.

"I didn't get the chance," he replied, setting his attention to the computer on his desk. Chessa had seen that look in his eyes enough to recognize his shame. Whatever they'd talked about had brought up his old feelings of guilt and worthlessness. Yes, he'd done some terrible things in his past, but he was trying to grow past it. Gwen might be Seelie Queen, but she didn't have the right to act as administrator of his endless torment. Danu knew he tortured himself enough.

"Norm, I know the true you, and whatever Gwen said to you, she's wrong," said Chessa.

Norman didn't reply. Instead, he hid in his work, typing furiously.

"Do you have something?" she asked, thinking that talking about work might be preferable to whatever else was going on in his head.

"I ain't sure yet. Maybe," he replied. But that was it.

Samson shifted awkwardly from one lion paw to the other. Chessa motioned for him to follow her into the kitchen so that Norman could have a moment's peace to calm down. Whatever had gone down in the backroom had obviously upset him.

"What do you think Gwen said to him?" she asked once they were out of earshot.

"There's no telling. That girl is a grenade in a fireworks factory," Samson replied.

Chessa pulled a bottle of Scotch, Samson's poison of choice, from the cabinet over the microwave and handed it over while she debriefed him on the details of what went down at Montello as well as what Norman and she had learned from Xander's laptop. He was off the clock and would only use information needed for the case—the rest he would keep to himself, filed away in the recesses of his mind unless it proved useful. In return, she would get his prior approval before posting any stories involving the KPD or active cases to *Crime Wave*. It was a tenuous arrangement that was only held in place by friendship and mutual trust. Considering they didn't have a ton of leads on either end, the exchange of intel didn't take long.

When she was finished, he asked for a list of locations connected to Honey Centrella and Abigail Marquis. If she wasn't pressing charges, he at least wanted to get a bead on who they were and possibly figure out what kind of business they were mixed up in. Chessa had to admit, it was a solid plan, especially since these weren't the types who would open up to a direct call from the police.

Two hours later, Samson had left on his mission and Chessa was alone with Norman. The wizard hadn't spoken a word. After his flurry of typing, he just sat, staring at the screen in front of him. Chessa brought him a Mountain Dew, his favorite, but it went untouched on the desk. Even Sorcha made an appearance to mewl at his feet before disappearing back into the shadows. The notification sound made him jump. After a few clicks, he finally spoke.

"Chessa, I have something I need to talk to you about."

Unnerved by his use of her name, Chessa flitted over to stand on the desk, but she was careful to stay behind the screen. It was important to her that Norman knew she trusted him. He'd gone his entire life with nobody believing in him, and she refused to let that continue.

"What's going on, Norm?" she asked.

"It's my family."

Chessa waited patiently for him to be ready to continue. This was a topic she never pushed. Gwen's family issues had nothing on Norman's.

So far, she'd gathered that he came from a prominent Unseelie crime family, was one of many siblings, and had pretty much been shat on his entire life. When she'd discovered the wizard, he was holed up in a secret library in Avalon, having infiltrated the Seelie palace staff to open the doors to the usurpers. Despite all he'd done to aid in the insurrection, instead of killing her or locking her up as instructed, he'd gone up against those he worked for to save her life. Furthermore, he sacrificed himself to free her. She owed Norman a lot more than a little faith.

"Her Grace—"

"Gwen," Chessa corrected.

"Her Grace asked after my pa. I did something else terrible in Avalon. Something I never told you about."

"Whatever it is, you can tell me now, but only if you want to."

He smoothed his beard with his right hand, his eyes misty. "I took Nyxanthium seeds from the palace vault."

Chessa tried not to react, but she couldn't help but draw a shocked breath. "What did you do with them?" she asked.

"I sent them to my pa. It wasn't a part of the mission, just a side job."

Nyxanthium seeds were in the hands of a powerful crime family with ties to Glastonbury. This wasn't like the occasional wildflower that would pop up at Avalon's borders, only to be plucked by an overzealous pixie dreaming of becoming an entrepreneur. This was a situation of cultivation. It was bad news for fae everywhere. Pixie dust would flood the black market. Maybe it already had.

"I know it weren't right. Her Grace said my family is working with someone in Korranthia, so I reached out to my cousin Jerry because he ain't the brightest of the bunch, and it's true. He wouldn't give me no names, but he as good as admitted it. Pixie dust is here, and it's all my fault." Norman broke down.

Chessa tried to keep her voice level. "It had to be difficult to tell me that, Norm. It's going to take a lot of work to make this right, but I know your heart, and I'll be by your side the entire time."

That only made the wizard sob harder into the desk. Chessa still didn't see how this information tied back to the current case, but why else would Gwen be asking about it? Unless... "Wait! Do you think our vics were running dust?"

Norman sniffed and raised his head. "Mandrake, maybe, but why would Kolsch get involved in that? It ain't like she needed the money."

"Only pixies can work with Nyxanthiums, and Portia was cut off, remember? She was selling ad space and endorsements for cash."

Norman shook his head. "Maybe so, but there's no way they're sending unprocessed Nyxanthiums over. It would be too dangerous."

He was right. While it might be possible to smuggle a few blooms over on mortal ships, no fae transport would be willing to risk exposure to Nyxanthium blooms. It would be much easier to process them into dust back in the UK and smuggle the sealed bottles overseas. Still, Chessa's gut told her this was all connected somehow.

"Jerry said he could hook me up with a job. They need more people he said, and he ain't so stupid he thinks I'm a pixie. They need people for something else."

"What do you mean? What else could it be?"

"I don't rightly know, but I think I have to take 'im up on the offer."

He couldn't mean— "You want to go undercover?"

Norman's bottom lip quivered. "No, little miss. All I *want* to do is to comb through old library books. I spent so long pretending to be Seelie and then pretending to be Unseelie. I just want a quiet, honest life where I don't have to pretend no more. But I made this mess, and you're right, cleaning it up is going to be hard."

27

It didn't take Samson long to make the drug connection. His first stop was the coffee shop Dominik Perez managed since he was overdue for an everything bagel anyway. According to the barista, Dom only put himself on the schedule two days a week ever since his roommate had passed. The witch who took Samson's order told him that the few times she'd seen Dom over the past couple weeks, he didn't seem too broken up about Mandrake's death, which was odd to her. She suspected he was using it as an excuse for an extended vacation, which she didn't understand since he was still an hourly worker.

After finishing up his meal, Samson went to the next stop on his list: the Marquis home, which was located not far from the KPD precinct in Beacon Hill. Abigail came from a relatively wealthy family—wealthy enough to pony up for the Institute of Fine Art Education without going into debt, unlike most students. Samson flashed his badge to get in the door, and once they realized that Abi wasn't in imminent danger or trouble, her parents welcomed him. They'd been worried sick ever since she dropped out a semester shy of graduating at the top of her class. Her mother sobbed as her father explained that Abi was a talented actress and had no reason to be holed up with a bunch of miscreants.

"Miscreants?" asked Samson. "I was under the impression they were beatniks."

"They may have met at art school, but the only talent in that entire house belongs to my daughter," said Mrs. Marquis. "Abigail is a gifted actress who should be pursuing a promising career, not joining a sex cult or whatever is happening in that den of sin." Mr. Marquis gave her a handkerchief from his pocket. Who even carried those anymore?

"You suspect they're not on the up-and-up?" asked Samson, picking at his feathers. He hated the habit but couldn't seem to break it.

Mr. Marquis scowled. "We haven't the faintest clue. One day Abigail says to us 'I'm dropping out of school and moving in with some associates.' Just like that."

"And have you seen that mixed breed Dominik?" Mrs. Marquis shuddered. It seemed to Samson that her daughter wasn't the only dramatic one in the family.

He ignored the bigoted comment and zeroed in on something else that struck him as odd. "Associates? Not pals?"

Mrs. Marquis nodded. "That's what she said. They had some sort of business they were starting. That pixie, Sugar, was it? She knew an investor."

"I asked to see the paperwork," added Mr. Marquis. "I'm a businessman myself, and if Abigail was getting involved with these people, I wanted to understand the business. She never sent it over."

"Did she say what kind of business it was?"

"No. She claimed that she needed to find her own way in the world and that if we loved her, we would give her the space to do so."

"When was the last time you spoke to your daughter?" asked Samson.

"It's been about a year," said Mr. Marquis.

"Three hundred and twenty days," inserted Mrs. Marquis with a sniffle. "Last time we saw her, she told us to leave her alone, then she and that boy walked off.

"Which boy? Dominik?"

"No, not the mixed-breed. The pixie. At first, I thought they were an item, but Abi told me he wasn't the romantic type if you can believe that. I never met a young fae who didn't want to woo my Abigail." Mrs. Marquis began to tear up again.

Samson suspected that they didn't know about the murder, or, if they did, they were playing it off well. They certainly had cause to resent Mandrake and the rest.

"You do know that pixie boy was dusted a couple of weeks back, don't you?" he said.

"He's on drugs?" asked Mr. Marquis. "No surprise there."

"No. Well, maybe, but I mean he was offed." When they continued to stare blankly at him, Samson clarified. "Murdered. He was murdered."

Mrs. Marquis gasped.

"And Abigail? She's alright, isn't she?" asked Mr. Marquis, putting his arm around his wife's shoulders, and drawing her to him.

Samson nodded, unable to get a read on the authenticity of the reaction. He wished Chessa were here with her spot-on instincts. "I told you she wasn't in any hot water. Not yet, anyhow."

When he stepped out onto West Cedar Street, Samson was convinced that Abi's parents were right to suspect the art kids were mixed up in drugs. What other business opportunity would lure college kids away from art school? He'd seen it more times than he cared to admit during his years at the KPD. The only question was who the unnamed investor was. Could that be the mysterious Marcus Fairburn that Chessa mentioned? If Honey was the key—if Chessa said she was, Samson believed it—he figured the shipyard where Lance worked would be a dead end, so he decided to take a trip to the place where it all began next, the Institute of Fine Art Education.

The front office at IFAE was less than helpful.

"It's a shame about Mr. Aster," said a rail-thin sorcerer clad in a black turtleneck and dark jeans. Samson struggled to keep from chuckling at the walking cliché. "We will work with the KPD as much as we can, but not without a warrant. Our students pay a lot of money to attend this institution, and we can't have them, or their parents, thinking that the school is involved in any kind of illegal activity."

"I understand," Samson replied. "But I'm not here to ask about Mandrake. I'm interested in any staff who remember Abigail Marquis, Dominik Perez, Lance Gruber, or Honey Centrella."

"As I said, I can't help you without a warrant. Student records are confidential. We have a number of important families who rely on our discretion."

It was like negotiating with a brick wall. Samson stepped out of the office to call Captain O'Toole, but he knew the warrant wouldn't clear for at least a day, if at all. O'Toole hated loose ends, and as far as he was concerned, the Mandrake Aster case was closed. As Samson was pocketing his cell, a fairy exited the building and caught up with him in the parking lot. Her hair was a wreck, but otherwise, she was dazzlingly beautiful. Samson was distracted by the way the sunlight glinted off her purple, iridescent wings.

Snap out of it, you lunkhead, he thought. He was too seasoned to be distracted by a pretty dame.

"Excuse me, mister, but I heard you asking about Honey and Abi," blurted the fairy.

"Yes, ma'am. Did you know them?"

"Honey was my roommate freshman year. I'm a grad student now, and it's been a few years since I've seen her. She was a gamer girl who rarely made it to class, but she was absolutely brilliant."

"How do you mean?"

The fairy landed on the ground next to him and looked him up and down. "First, I need to know if she's in trouble or something."

"No, nothing like that. I'm investigating the death of Mandrake Aster. He lived in a commune of sorts with Honey and other former IFAE students." Samson flashed his badge. He knew Chessa would have preferred for him to stay under the radar, but he didn't have her skill with people. He needed the badge to make people sing.

The fairy's eyes widened. "You don't think Honey had anything to do with it?"

"I'm hoping I can rule that out," lied Samson. "Anything you remember could help."

"She rarely went to class, but she had straight As. Her mind is like a machine, but not like, the murderous kind, you understand. Honestly, she was always more of a scientist than an artist. She didn't really fit in here."

Samson tilted his head to the side. "What was she studying?"

"Graphic design, I think? But I think she belonged in a lab. She was great with computers, don't get me wrong, but I never saw her create a single piece of art."

"Then why was she enrolled here?"

"Her mother, I think. She was a lovely pixie who insisted that Honey's talent was worth developing. I only met her once."

"What about her father? Did you meet him?"

The fairy gave a little shudder. "Yes. He was the quiet type. Intimidating. I couldn't ever get a read on him, if you know what I mean. Honey never talked about her parents, though."

Samson took out his phone and typed a note to himself to look into Honey's folks. "What did she talk about?"

"To me? Not much. We were only roommates for a semester, and we didn't have a lot in common. Mostly, she hung out in the computer lab and talked about biochemical engineering. Not really my cup of tea. I'm more of a beer-pong fairy. Do you party?"

Samson grimaced and ignored the question, mostly because he didn't have the first clue how to answer it. "Did you also know Abigail Marquis?"

The fairy's bottom lip protruded in a pretty pout, then she shrugged. "Not as well. She was Honey's big sister."

This threw Samson. He'd just left Abi's house, and her parents didn't mention that Honey was her sister. His confusion must have shown on his face.

"Oh, not like a real big sister. It's a program run by the counseling center for when freshmen seem to be struggling. They assign an upper-classman to work with them."

That made more sense. "But you said Honey had straight As."

"She did. But she never went to class. Professors don't like it when you can ace their tests without stepping foot in the classroom. Mr. Darcie, her advisor, even stopped by here a few times to ask me about Honey. That was before he assigned her to Abi. I really hope I'm not betraying her trust by talking to you like this."

"Not at all. I promise not to rat you out. You're helping paint a picture, that's all. One that might even help Honey in the long run. Do you know where I can find Mr. Darcie? Maybe he can help me understand more about Honey and Abi's relationship."

"Let's see, what time is it?" She checked her phone. "He usually has afternoon office hours, so you might catch him over at the Mercury building. It's right through there." She pointed off in the distance.

Samson flashed his most charming smile, which just meant turning up the corners of his beak. The fairy looked put off. He gave up his rare attempt at returning her flirtation and gave a curt nod. "I appreciate your help."

"No problem. If you talk to Honey, please send her my condolences."

"10-4. I didn't catch your name."

"Marigold, but you can call me Mari." Mari fluttered into the air.

"Lovely to meet you, Mari," said Samson, turning on his lion haunches to stalk off toward the building she'd motioned to. Perhaps this Mr. Darcie could tell him more.

His phone buzzed in his coat pocket. Samson struggled to extract it with his talons. It was O'Toole.

"Sergeant Wayne, report in immediately. There's been an attack."

28

Norman lifted the receiver. "C&F Investigations, how can I help?" The wizard's face pulled into a grimace, and Chessa perked up. The one-sided conversation didn't offer any answers. "What? You sure about that? Yes. Right away."

When he hung up, he immediately got to his feet, car keys in hand.

"What's going on?" asked Chessa.

"That was Detective Wayne. We've got to get down to the precinct. They picked up Quincy on a CCTV traffic cam."

Chessa's heart leapt. "That's a good thing, right? What am I missing?"

"There was another pixie attack. It seems like our lad was driving the getaway car."

Chessa felt like she'd just been clobbered by a troll fist. There must be some mistake. Sure, Q had a rap sheet, but he would never be somebody else's henchman, and while he'd certainly thrown down in a barroom brawl on occasion or twenty, he would never assault an innocent pixie.

"Who was the victim?" Chessa asked, but Norman didn't have any more information. After changing gears from trying to convince Norman that going undercover to infiltrate his extended family was suicide to trying to process the call, Chessa had emotional whiplash. She followed the wizard down the hall and got into the beat-up old Cadillac he'd bought at a lot called "Cars! Cars! Cars!"

Samson met them in the precinct lobby. Chessa had zipped out the window and into the precinct as soon as Norman parked the car, leaving him in the wind, and he was breathing heavily when he caught up inside. Samson ushered them past Pox, through the bullpen, and down the hall to his office. Only once the door was shut did Chessa erupt.

"What is this about, Sammy? Quincy's gotten into some shit, I'll give you that, but he's gone straight! You know it as well as I do!"

"He's got you hoodwinked," replied the griffin, settling into his over-sized chair and rapping his talons along the keyboard on his desk. That spike of rage that was becoming all too familiar caused Chessa's heart to speed up, but before she could formulate a retort, the screen lit up, and a video began to play. The footage was as clear as traffic cameras get. A silver sedan pulled up to the curb in front of the Roxboro apartments, and three figures cloaked in all black, wearing troll masks emerged and entered the complex as the car pulled around. Samson paused just as the driver came into the frame. Sure as shit, Chessa could make out Quincy's green mohawk and telltale scar. The three masked assailants ran back into the frame, dove into the car, and Q floored it.

"The city doesn't have faetography lenses, so what you're seeing is glamour-altered. That makes it tough to ID the runners since we don't know if their fae forms have been obscured or if they look as they appear on camera, but that half-ogre is a hole in one."

Chessa wanted to argue that there were other large men with green mohawks in Boston, but she couldn't argue with her own eyes. Quincy wasn't exactly walking around town with a slew of doppelgangers. Even with the glamour altering his size, there was no denying it. It was him.

"There's got to be some kind of explanation," she said. "Who was the victim?"

"Hobbes Doyle."

Bile rose in Chessa's throat. "Hobbes? *My* Hobbes?"

It couldn't be. Last Chessa knew, Hobbes stayed behind in Avalon to work for the new Seelie regime. For Gwen. He and his sister Marni had been instrumental in suppressing the Unseelie insurrection, working alongside Chessa and taking her commands. What in the name of Danu was he doing stateside?

"I'm afraid so. He rented the apartment a month and a half ago. He's alive, but barely. Laural is seeing to him over at Grove General."

A month and a half? And he never came by? For that matter, Gwen didn't mention him being in town either. Chessa's pixie intuition told her

Gwen held back vital information and that she had more business in Korranthia than she'd let on. It stung.

"Have you talked to him? Found out what he has to do with any of this?"

Samson shook his head. "I've got officers standing by, but so far, he hasn't been stable enough to question. I know he's a friend, Chessa, but you need to prepare yourself for if he doesn't make it. It seems like he's caught up in something hinky. As much as it plucks my feathers to say, Quincy too."

"No! You might not have gotten to know him, but Hobbes is one of the good guys. So is Quincy, if you could see past your own beak far enough to realize it! I don't know what's going on here, but Q would never hurt Hobbes. Norman, back me up here."

The wizard was still lurking by the door. He shrugged. "I'm sure you're right, little miss. But I ain't got a clue what Quincy or Hobbes are up to. It looks bad."

"I need you to cooperate. Both of you," said Samson, leveling a weighty stare at Chessa.

She glared back at him. She couldn't believe what she was hearing. Last year, Quincy had led a group of Korranthian forces in the largest civil war the fae had ever experienced, and with nothing but one lousy video, KPD's finest were out for his blood? This made no sense.

"Cooperation with what? Stringing up Q? He's a Danu-damned hero, Sammy. So is Hobbes."

Samson broke eye contact. He looked down at his desk and picked through his feathers with idle talons. "Be that as it may, I need you to answer a few questions. I brought you here first to break the news gently."

A sudden knock on the office door made Chessa jump. Without pausing for an answer, the door flew open, making Norman jump out of the way. O'Toole strode in, followed by Pox.

"Chessa Moon, Norman Pennington, I'm going to need you to come with me."

"Oh, hell no," said Chessa. "Norman, don't say anything."

"Don't make this more difficult than it has to be. Come answer some questions, then you can be back to your little PI hole in the ground by lunch."

"Am I under arrest?"

"No."

"Then fuck off, O'Toole. I want my lawyer."

"You can cooperate, or I can make a call to my buddy over at Immigration." O'Toole turned to pin Norman with a steely gaze. "I'm sure your papers are all in order, right Mr. Pennington? I thought I heard a rumor that Scotland Yard's Fae Faction wanted a word with you."

Chessa's heart fell in her stomach. She'd brought Norman to Korranthia to start a new life, but his record was far from clean. If Immigration got involved, the Avalon Seelie Authorities would be all over him, and while being besties with the Queen had its perks, Gwen's position was tenuous at best. She'd only been ruler for a few months, and pardoning small-time criminals wouldn't be a good look. As much as she hated to say it, Gwen would have to let him go it alone. Him and everyone else too, it seemed.

"Gwen was right, you really are a snake," said Chessa. O'Toole didn't comment.

Thankfully, both she and Norman were used to covering. Once they were separated, Chessa was taken to an interrogation room for questioning. A junior detective she didn't know took Norman down the hall while O'Toole asked her about Q's known associates and recent behavior, and Chessa gave them just enough to be able to claim ignorance of anything more. Quincy hung out at Pub Nine. He associated with the regulars. He'd signed on as a partner because he wanted to give back to the community, a change brought on by the recent fae revolution. None of it was incriminating or particularly new information. As far as his recent behavior went, all Chessa could say was that he was working a case.

She could have waited for a lawyer, but she needed to get out of there fast to find Q before the KPD built a strong enough case to lock him up. That meant playing their games.

"I need details," demanded O'Toole.

"Then you need a warrant," replied Chessa. "No threats are going to make me breach client privilege."

"Look, Ms. Moon, I appreciate all Quincy did during the battle. I was there too, remember? But he was involved in an attack on a citizen of Avalon, a fellow in arms. I can't help anyone if I don't know what's going on."

O'Toole sounded genuine. He had singlehandedly taken out a legion of lutins and fought beside Quincy's forces on the battlefield. But O'Toole would put a collar on his best friend if it advanced his career. That collar wouldn't be on Quincy. Not if Chessa had anything to say about it.

"I've told you everything I thought might be helpful," she replied with a curt smile. "I'd like to get back to my case now if you have no further questions. We're on the precipice of a breakthrough."

O'Toole sighed and let her go. An hour later, she and Norman compared notes. Thankfully, Norman's crime family had taught him how to keep his mouth shut. He understood the rules—your loyalty was to your family first, and Quincy was family. The only good thing to come out of all of this was that Chessa was able to convince Norman that he couldn't go undercover now that he was under KPD scrutiny. Now, they just needed to figure out what the hell Q was mixed up in. To do that, they needed to find out how Hobbes was involved.

Chessa dialed Gwen's cell once they were in the parking lot, but there was no answer.

Typical.

29

It wasn't the first time Samson felt his loyalties divide. He watched Chessa and Norman disappear down the hall with O'Toole, and his insides curdled. The look of betrayal on the pixie's face nearly did him in, especially after all they'd been through together. Still, there was no denying that Quincy was involved in a situation that left Hobbes Doyle bleeding out in a hotel room. He clacked his beak in frustration as he puzzled over the case, struggling to understand what he was missing. It had to be related to Mandrake Aster, and if Chessa was right, to Portia Kolsch too. In the time since he'd met Chessa years ago, he'd learned one truly irritating thing. She was always right.

If he was going to look at this as one big case despite O'Toole's orders, he needed to follow every lead. He turned to walk back through his office, careful to keep his wings tightly tucked so he didn't knock anything over and sunk his haunches into the oversized chair behind his desk. A few clicks of the keyboard later, he was looking at the biography of one Glenn Darcie on the Institute of Fine Art Education website.

By all appearances, the guy was exactly what one would expect. His headshot matched his bio—a graduate of UFF with a Masters in Behavioral Science, younger than most of the IFAE faculty, a trait that probably helped him connect with students, dark hair, pointed ears, a winning smile, and translucent, rounded wings.

"Another pixie," mused Samson. "Interesting."

He switched tabs and ran the name through the KPD database. There were multiple hits. Whoever heard of a student advisor with a rap sheet?

"That's private education for you," Samson muttered, reading through the charges: solicitation of a minor, possession, assault. This guy was a piece of work. But it looked like none of the charges had stuck. He must come from money, or no school, private or not, would be willing to overlook arrests of this nature, even without convictions. That would also explain how he managed to stay out of the pen.

Samson's door flew open, and an angry Captain O'Toole entered. "Wayne, what is it with you and obstinate women?"

"Captain?"

"That pixie gave us nothing! Not even so much as an associate's name! Half the time, I felt like she was jerking me around."

Samson fought back a smile. Knowing Chessa, she probably was. "You really thought she was a rat? I'm surprised she talked to you at all without a mouthpiece."

O'Toole slumped down in the guest chair. "She did and she didn't. Her mouth was moving, but nothing useful came out. That's why I'm here. I'm going to need you to tell me everything you know about Quincy McAllen."

"I'm afraid that doesn't amount to much. He was a regular huckster, but he's gone straight, or at least that's what I was told. Used to hang around Pub Nine. And calling him McAllen will lose you a tooth or two. That's the beginning, middle, and end of all I know."

"That's about as useful as what Moon just told us."

"Oh, there's one more thing," added Samson.

"What's that?"

"He's a Danu-damned war hero."

30

Fighting felt like burning in the veins. There wasn't a voice telling him what to do, it was more like a compulsion to obey Fairburn, as if doing anything else would cause intense physical pain or worse. Quincy wasn't accustomed to obeying anyone or anything.

"What did you do to me?" he gasped between breaths.

Sweat covered his body and soaked through his ripped tee, and his entire body was convulsing. Now that he had no orders to carry out, he was filled with a desperation he couldn't name, an all-consuming need, but he didn't know for what.

"It'll pass in a few hours," said the woman in the next cell. "Don't fight it." There was a tenderness in her voice that had been lacking before as if she truly wanted to help ease his suffering.

"What is happening to me?"

"You're coming down from an epic high. The first time is the worst."

Quincy raised his head and tried to look at the woman, but his vision was blurry. He couldn't think to form another question. Instead, he crawled across the cement floor, climbed onto the cot, and rolled himself in the flimsy blanket.

He didn't know how long he'd been out when he woke up, but the lights were off in the warehouse, and there was very little activity. His head felt like someone had stuck a pickaxe in it, and his pants were soaked through with urine. "Fuck," he groaned.

The heavy breathing of the woman in the next cell was oddly comforting, and he didn't want to wake her, but he needed a change of clothes pronto. "Is anyone out there?" he called into the darkness, hoping a worker would hear and come to assist. There was no reply. "Hello?"

"Keep it down or you'll get the kind of attention you don't want," said the witch in a harsh whisper.

"Sorry. Ain't there anyone here to look after us?"

The woman shifted on her cot. "They don't care one bit about our comfort. We're tools to them. Weapons."

It was not the response Quincy expected. "How do you mean?"

"They control us with whatever's in those syringes, get us to do their bidding. I've tried listening in on their conversations, but the only thing I've gathered is that it's some kind of dust derivative. They call it Imperium."

"Dust? Pixie dust? But that shit only works on pixies. Used on anyone else, it's straight poison."

"Uh-huh. That's why you didn't just drive a getaway car while me, your pixie boy, and the golem went inside to rough up a pixie we never met."

"What the fuck are you talking about? I've been here in this cell all night long!"

"Sorry to break it to you, big fella, but you were being controlled just like me. Forget whatever you think you know about pixie dust. Sure, a sprinkle will give a pixie some magical abilities, but Imperium isn't regular dust. Whatever they've managed to turn it into makes fae obedient little soldiers."

Quincy struggled to understand. He knew about the hot drugs on the streets, but this was all news to him. Mind controlling pixie dust? Unheard of. "How do you know all this?"

"I know because they got to me first. I've got a high-pressure job, so when someone I trusted told me about a new kind of dust, made specifically for fae as a stress reliever and safe for fae of all types, I stupidly fell for it. Two days later, I landed my ass in here. I have no idea what I did for them, but I do know I walked my own happy ass into this cell."

There was a note of self-loathing in the woman's words, and Quincy found himself feeling bad for her. "Cut yourself a break. You said you weren't in control."

"I'm Miranda fucking Xeos. I'm always in control," she spat back.

Quincy bit his lip. He knew that name. Everyone in Korranthia knew this woman. If she was stuck in here being used as a living weapon and nobody was able to help her, there was no hope for a low life like him. He kept quiet for the rest of the night, sitting on the cot, drenched in his own piss.

31

Breaking into the hospital was easier than Chessa planned. Despite the KPD's interest in speaking with Hobbes, there were no guards, and it took only her cunning wit and a twenty-dollar bill to find out what floor he was on. She zipped into the room, easily avoiding notice of the nurses.

Hobbes was pale, but he was breathing steadily, and the machine by his bedside beeped rhythmically. Chessa breathed a sigh of relief. She had no idea what she was expecting, but seeing her friend alive took a weight off.

"Hey buddy, are you awake?" she asked.

"Boss G?" replied Hobbes, opening his eyes and struggling to sit up. "Is that you?" He used the codename Chessa had gone by during the Battle of Avalon, a moniker Chessa lifted from her Mob Boss gaming days.

"At ease, soldier," she joked. "I'm not sure how much time I've got before I get kicked out of here, and I have some important questions for you."

"I should have known this wasn't a social visit." His words were biting, but his tone was jovial, just the way she remembered. There was no way this guy was involved in organized crime.

"Not entirely. Though I did want to check in to see if you were ok. It looks like you'll pull through."

"They can't get rid of me that easy."

"Thank Danu. Hobbes, what are you doing in Korranthia?" Chessa wished she had time to properly visit her injured friend, but she needed answers.

"I'm on *assignment.*" The way he stressed the word told Chessa all she needed to know about the nature of his work. Gwen. Just as Chessa had suspected.

"What kind of assignment could you possibly be on?" she asked.

"I'm not sure how much I'm allowed to disclose. It's highly confidential."

"Hobbes, it's me. Whatever Gwen has you doing got you stabbed and left for dead. And it's connected to my case in some way. I need you to tell me what's going on so I can protect you."

Chessa could tell that got him. Gwen might be queen, but it was Chessa who called the shots on his team during the battle, and it was Chessa who made sure he made it through alive. He swallowed hard. "It's about Norman's family."

Dread blossomed in Chessa's gut. For Norman's sake and to keep Hobbes talking, she decided to play her cards close. "The Penningtons? What do they have to do with anything?"

"Pixie dust."

Norman's family didn't just smuggle Nyxanthium seeds out of Avalon. They'd cultivated them. If Hobbes was sent here, that meant that distribution was already wide. Global. If word got out, it would cause mass hysteria. No drug known to faekind was more addictive to pixies and more lethal to other fae. Chessa remembered how Jenny, the friend she'd lost to dust, had gradually morphed into someone she didn't recognize before she'd gone off the grid entirely. Her body was found in the woods a month later. Before Pixie dust, Jenny was kind and generous. She'd wanted to become a veterinarian. How many more were there like Jenny? Worse, how many more would there be if the Penningtons managed to secure wide distribution? This had to be stopped.

"The trail led you here?" asked Chessa, biting her lip not to give voice to her racing thoughts. *You're working in my backyard and didn't care to loop me in.* Saying it wouldn't accomplish anything. "Did you get any intel?"

"They're altering it, somehow. They're cultivating the Nyxanthium flowers, growing them in secret locations all over the world, but the drug they're selling isn't the same pixie dust we know about. It's called Imperium, and it takes pixies to synthesize it. I set myself up as a fixer, but I guess my cover was blown."

"And they tried to take you out."

Hobbes nodded. "They very nearly succeeded."

Chessa shook her head. She'd never heard of fixing pixie dust, but it made sense that only pixies could do it since they were the only fae species able to work with Nyxanthium flowers at all. "Do you know how the fixing works?" she asked.

"No. I only know it starts with dust and involves a laboratory. I met with a pixie a couple days ago, and he was going to bring me to the head fixer for training, but I must have said something wrong. Tipped him off that I wasn't who I'd said I was." Hobbes' breath was coming heavier now, and the machine's beeping sped up. It would do no good to get him worked up.

"It's okay, Hobbes. I'm going to figure this out, and I'm going to keep you safe."

He nodded. "I know you will, Boss G." The beeping returned to its steady pace.

"Did you catch any names on this side of the ocean?" asked Chessa after giving him a minute to catch his breath.

"No. They didn't use names. Everything was very clandestine. General Steele gave me a number to contact and dropped me off at a little motel. Then that lad came by."

"Lad? Was the pixie young?"

"Young, yes. Not a child, but definitely school-age. He had brown hair and light blue eyes, like ice."

Xander. Chessa nodded. "Yes, I know him. Did you get a good look at your attackers?"

"Well, he was with them, but there were others. A golem and a humanoid woman who didn't seem the type to be roughing up criminals."

"What do you mean by that?"

"She just had a way about her, I guess. And you don't see many thugs in Jimmy Choos."

"No way," said Chessa.

"No way what?"

She pulled out her phone and pulled up a picture of Miranda Xeos, flipping it around to show Hobbes.

"That's her! She's the one who stabbed me!" he exclaimed.

Chessa felt like she'd had the wind knocked out of her. How does one of the most successful CFOs in Korranthia end up working muscle for a guy like Fairburn? "I don't know what's going on here, Hobbes, but I'm going to have Sammy put some KPD officers outside your room."

Chessa had come for answers, but the more she got, the muddier the picture became. Why would the CFO of the biggest online retailer in the world be working for drug runners and stabbing pixies in shitty apartments?

3 2

The next day, Samson was sure to arrive at IFAE within Mr. Darcie's office hours, but the door was locked and the lights were out. Unsurprisingly, O'Toole had refused to issue a warrant, claiming that the KPD needed to focus on the Hobbes Doyle assault rather than spinning their wheels on an open-and-shut case. That meant Samson had to go rogue. Again.

He sighed, wondering when he became this guy. His adoptive father was also a cop, and he'd brought him up to play by the rules. It wasn't until the Brain Scraper case and Gwendolyn Evenshine came crashing into his life that he ever operated outside the box. And now, that force of nature was the Seelie Queen. Nothing in this world was what he'd expected. Still, he wasn't quite to the level of unlawful entry into the office of a person -of interest. Instead, he went back outside, pushed up from the ground, and gave a mighty flap of his wings to take to the skies and cross town to the last known address of the pixie in question.

The house wasn't noteworthy—a small suburban two-story with a picket fence. According to Samson's research, Darcie wasn't married, but a knock on the door was answered by the barking of a dog. A few moments later, the pixie Samson recognized as Darcie emerged in the air from the backside of the house.

"Waldorf isn't too fond of visitors. What can I do for you?" asked the newcomer.

Samson flashed his badge. "Sergeant Detective Samson Wayne, KPD. Are you Glenn Darcie?"

"I am. Is there something wrong officer?"

"I just have a few questions for you if you've got the time. Is there somewhere we can talk?"

Darcie scowled and landed on the front porch. Inside, the dog sounded like it was attacking the door. "What is this about?"

"I have some questions regarding a former student of yours. Honey Centrella. I heard you were close at one point."

Some expression Samson couldn't quite name crossed Darcie's face. "I wouldn't say close. I treat all the students as if they are friends, it helps me gain their trust, and Honey was no exception. Due to the nature of my job, I'm not at liberty to discuss details surrounding any of the students I counsel. So that's all I have to say about her."

"Let's talk about you then. You've been involved in a number of crimes but never sat a day in the slammer. Want to tell me about that?"

"No. I don't."

"Why are you playing hooky today? I went to your office, and the door says it's within your office hours, but here you are."

"I'm not feeling well."

"Isn't that something? You do look a little green around the gills," Samson said, making a mock show of sympathy as he pointed out how rattled the guy was. "I was at the school yesterday, and I met another student of yours. She didn't happen to tell you I was looking for you, did she?"

Darcie's brow wrinkled. "Look, detective, I have no idea what you're implying. I'm simply not feeling well today. I don't know you from Prince Liam, and I've got nothing to hide. But I'm not answering questions about the students who confide in me. Not without a lawyer."

"Mr. Darcie, I'm sure you are an upstanding citizen. I respect that. But I'm investigating the murder of a friend of Ms. Centrella's. Mandrake Aster. Your insight could clear some things up for me. You were the one who introduced her to Abigail Marquis, were you not? The two of them cohabitated with Aster."

"Shame about the kid, but unless I'm subpoenaed, I've got nothing else to say. Good day, detective." With that, Darcie flew back around the house.

Samson didn't know what to make of the interaction. Maybe he'd come at it a little hard, but he knew this guy was hiding something. The dog was still barking and scratching at the door. Samson let out a lion growl, partly in frustration, partly in annoyance. The dog yelped and then fell silent.

Frustrated, Samson flew back to the KPD. He wasn't ready to give up on the Darcie angle. While most of the charges were drug-related, the solicitation of a minor had been filed by the parents of a girl by the name of Hannah Greene. In cases like this, dropped charges usually meant angry victims, so maybe a conversation would help Samson understand Darcie's proclivities. Despite being Unseelie, the Greenes' address was recorded in the database thanks to their involvement with the Seelie court system, so long as they hadn't moved in the past ten years. They were a part of the wild fae community of Boston Commons. Samson wished Quincy was around to pay them a visit. Getting Unseelie to talk to the KPD was a near-impossible task, and he would have been glad for the help. Since going himself would be an exercise in futility, he would have to send Chessa.

When Samson arrived at C&F Investigations, Norman gave him a look.

"What's the skinny, wizard?" Samson asked. Norman held up one finger but didn't say a word. Three seconds later, the door to the bedroom burst open and Chessa entered in a flurry, words spewing from her mouth at nobody and everybody all at once.

"Two days isn't enough! Sammy, do you have guards on Hobbes? Norman, where is that file I asked you for? Who the fuck took Blade, and why hasn't anyone done a Danu damned thing about it? My sister's in there having another breakdown, two pixies are dead with a third in the ICU, and they've taken hostages! Who the fuck takes hostages?"

Norman held up a bagel in one hand and a file in the other, and Chessa snatched them both and continued zipping from one end of the room to the other in a flighted fae version of pacing. It was too much for Samson.

"You're going to need to plant those shoes on the ground before I swat you out of the air. I've got a tip, but I can't follow up on it on account of my profession."

That brought Chessa down. "You have a lead and you didn't say anything?"

"I haven't had a chance to open my beak with you buzzing all over the place. There's a student advisor from the school all your pals met at. I think he's dirty, but I can't get anyone to talk without O'Toole's support. Protocol and such."

"O'Toole needs a good kick in the head," spat Chessa. Samson had never seen her like this. She was usually the one to see the best in everyone around her, not lining up to smack them down. This case must really be itching her wings.

"Be that as it may, I think we might be able to crack the guy by talking to an Unseelie family living in the Commons."

At that, Chessa seemed to calm. She'd always had a soft spot for the wild fae of Korranthia. "I see why you want me," she said. "You wouldn't get within ten feet of them."

"Exactly. They'd be in the wind as soon as they saw me coming."

"Fine. I'll talk to them. But I need you to do something for me."

Samson felt his feathers puff slightly. He was a sergeant, not an errand boy for a PI "What?"

"I need you to question the Kolsches about my sister's fiancé, Blade. They're desperate to keep their name out of the press, and they know I'm asking questions about Portia. Maybe they're nervous enough to do something about it."

"They're a powerful family, Chessa."

"That's what makes them my prime suspect. If they don't have him, they might know who this Marcus Fairburn is."

"I can't just mosey up to people like that and ask if they kidnapped some Joe to pressure a two-bit PI into dropping an investigation. Not without a missing persons report."

"Then make the report," snapped Chessa.

Cora rushed into the room, her face flushed and her clothing disheveled. "No! You can't make a report or whoever has him will kill him!"

Samson turned to stare at Chessa. If she wanted his help, it had to be by the book, especially with people who could flick a wrist and get both Samson *and* O'Toole kicked off the force. Money was power, there was no way around it, and O'Toole was never one to challenge the powerful.

"Cora, this is the only way we can help him. I don't know what else to do," Chessa pleaded.

"You could do what they say! You could drop your investigation. I'm your sister for Danu's sake! I raised you, Chichi. You owe me this."

Chessa looked like she'd been slapped in the face, and Norman looked like he wanted to be anywhere but here. Yet Samson was inspired by the auburn-haired Chessa doppelganger in a wrinkled pantsuit.

"Cora's right," he said quietly. Chessa spun and pinned him with a glare. "It needs to look like you're complying. Pull the old hidey-ho so they still think they've got leverage."

Chessa's eyes narrowed, but she didn't say anything.

"If I go into Wallow World headquarters, they're going to clam up. That's what those types do. If you're right about them having Blade, he'd be toast. But if they think they've won, well, then they're not about to scrap their ace in the hole."

Cora was nodding as the tears streamed down her face.

Chessa looked skeptical. "But you are going to investigate?"

"Only if we're on the same page. O'Toole's got informants all over this city, but I can't make use of them without an official report. Cora, you've got to trust me. I'm on the level."

Now it was Chessa's turn to nod while her sister seemed dubious.

"I trust Samson with my life. He will not do anything to endanger Blade. You're right. You did raise me. You raised me to face life without flinching, and now it's my turn to tell you to be strong," said Chessa, putting her hand on Cora's shoulder.

"You swear you'll keep him safe?"

"I'll do everything in my power," Samson replied. He prayed to Danu he could make good on his word.

33

Quincy's throat and mouth felt like the Sahara. Miranda was still asleep on her cot, mumbling and thrashing, and the smell of vomit mixed with urine was an assault on his senses. He clambered up from the cot, causing it to squeal in protest of his weight.

"Oi, we could use some freshening up over here," he called. Nobody replied.

The sounds of workers going about their business floated in the air, but all he could see was the backside of shelves dimly lit by sparse fluorescent lighting. A bucket of water he didn't remember being brought in sat in the corner of his cell. With no idea how old it was, he chugged it down. Anything to relieve the burning in his throat.

Once he acclimated to his newest state of discomfort, he haphazardly studied the shelves. It was boring and tedious, but he had nothing better to do, and knowledge of his surroundings might come in handy at some point. Maybe he'd get lucky and locate a weapon he could pick up on one of his walks to the outhouse. Or a stick of deodorant. Most of the supplies looked to be scientific equipment. Beakers and portable burners, bottles of who-knows-what, boxes of glass tubes, and an assortment of other things that reminded him of high school chemistry class filled the only shelves remotely visible from his corner of the warehouse. None of it was packed up in the iconic Wallow World boxes like he'd expected. Instead, it was stored in crates and directly on the shelves, as if it was being used for something.

"That's fucking weird," he said aloud.

Fae were usually more interested in exploring their magical connections than in studying chemistry. Not that there weren't scientific-minded fae around, but a criminal empire running on it was borderline absurd.

"What is?" croaked Miranda.

"All this science shit. It doesn't look like it belongs to the distribution center."

"Of course it doesn't, genius. I told you they were altering the dust. That takes more than magic, I would assume." Her voice sounded like a fork dragging on sandpaper.

But she hadn't told him they were doing it here. Quincy squinted, trying to see down the aisle that ran between the shelves. If the equipment was here, maybe there was a lab or something close by. He wasn't sure what good the information would do, but it seemed worth knowing. It was no use. His cell wasn't positioned to give him a decent view of anything more than his own little corner of hell. He turned his attention to Miranda.

"I guess this don't get any easier, huh?" he said. When the drugs had begun to wear off, she'd seemed so put together, but now he could tell that she was in as rough of shape as he felt.

"You get used to coming down, but the next day still sucks ogre dick, pardon the expression."

He wasn't offended. "Seems that way."

She eventually got to her feet and retrieved her own bucket of putrid water. After a big sip, she looked back over at Quincy.

"All this nerd shit means the lab is here somewhere," he said.

Miranda shrugged. "And we're the rats."

As if on cue, the golem appeared in the gap Quincy had been staring down moments before.

"Lumpy, my man!" said Quincy, fighting back a wave of nausea as he feigned excitement at the sight of the golem. "Come to let me out for my daily constitutional?"

"He's never going to speak to you." The familiar voice came from behind the clay creature. Xander.

Quincy stuffed the emotions that rose in his chest back down where they belonged and forced a smile. "That don't mean we're not friends," he replied. "Some of my best buds don't speak to me."

Xander scoffed. "I believe it. Still desperate for connection, are you? You're pathetic."

As he spoke, Lumpy shaped his finger into a key to unlock Miranda's cage and then pointed in the direction of the door. She walked, expensive shoes clacking on the cement floor, and a moment later, Quincy was freed as well and urged to follow. After a trip to the makeshift outhouse, Xander had the prisoners stand by the wall and strip off their vomit and urine-soaked clothes. Quincy expected Miranda to protest, but she did as she was told without uttering a word, chin high and eyes staring straight ahead.

The gate opened and closed for box trucks conducting business, yet none slowed to watch the spectacle of the ogre-witch tag-team strip show. Most activity was centered around the building on the far side of the gravel lot, but even the drivers who pulled in close didn't seem to notice Quincy and Miranda with all their bits and bobs waving in the breeze. Once again, Quincy wondered how much of the complex was under the control of Marcus Fairburn. To be this blatant with his operation, the mortal had to be incredibly stupid or incredibly powerful.

Xander gathered up the pile of clothes while the clay golem looked on. Pervert. Quincy gazed across the gravel lot at the chain link fence and tree line beyond. It would take nothing to overpower the little pixie, but he didn't know how to begin to fight Lumpy. He was used to heads breaking when he smashed a fist into them, not absorbing the hit and hardening into cement handcuffs. That was a kink too far, even for him.

"What are you just standing there for?" Xander barked at the golem. The pixie's voice was overly harsh as if he were trying on a persona that didn't quite fit. "Go get the hose."

Quincy's tattooed ass puckered at the thought of cold water as Lumpy silently slogged off to obey. He was struck by an idea. He wasn't much for science, but he did know what happened when dirt got wet. How would water affect the golem? He glanced over at Miranda.

"Keep your eyes to yourself if you like them in your skull," she muttered with a growl.

"I only like happy tatas," he replied.

She scowled at him, and he realized she'd misunderstood him and taken offense. Nothing to be done about it now. He had more important things to worry about, like what his cellmate would do if he attacked their guards. Would she help, run, or remain a prisoner? She was so accustomed to following orders, he wasn't entirely positive she wouldn't fight alongside their captors.

Lumpy returned holding the end of an industrial high-pressure hose. With a flick of a knob, he turned it on and blasted Miranda. She gasped and folded in on herself. The droplets that reached Quincy's flesh were freezing. When it was his turn, he grinned at the witch.

"Don't judge a package by its size babe," he said, rubbing the dirt, piss, and puke from his green mohawk and scarred body. He knew he was well-endowed, even with freezing water turning his balls into ice cubes. It came with the ogre territory. Miranda rolled her eyes. Quincy shot her a wink, and then, without warning, charged the golem. His massive ogre dick swung with the momentum, thwacking each thigh in turn, but he didn't have time to worry about it. He cupped his outstretched hands, sending a wave of water ahead of him before Lumpy had a chance to process that a drenched, naked ogre was on him like a locomotive off its tracks.

"Stop!" yelled Xander, flying in from behind. Quincy ducked and let the stream of water slam the pixie back into the wall. He hit with a sickening crack and stuck like a mosquito on a windshield, his limbs bent in unnatural angles and eyes rolling into his head.

"What are you doing?" screamed Miranda, but Quincy was now on top of Lumpy, pummeling the wet clay with both fists, sending it splattering all over the gravel around them as the golem's body melted beneath the wet weight of the half-ogre straddling him.

"Run! Go now!" yelled Quincy, but Miranda stood, mouth open, watching the onslaught.

If she wouldn't help herself, there was nothing he could do for her. Quincy slid on the clay, and gravel dug into his flesh as he scrambled to his feet and made a break for the fence. He didn't get far. Behind him, the golem reformed in record time and roared, a terrible sound that reverberated off the buildings. Electricity buzzed through the air, making the hair on Quincy's neck stand to attention, a split second before his body collapsed in a wave of spasms. As his vision narrowed, he was aware of being surrounded by Fairburn's henchmen.

He opened his mouth to cuss, but the only sound he could make was "Phuu."

Miranda and Quincy were returned to their cells, which had been hosed out like dog kennels. Still naked, Quincy thrashed, but his muscles were too fried to be effective. He was thrown to the ground.

Once they were alone again, Miranda walked over to their shared bars. "What were you thinking? Do you have any idea how many fae he controls?"

"Obviously not," replied Quincy, not bothering to try to right himself. "Some help you were against those chuckleheads."

"Let's get one thing straight. I plan to live through this. I'm not about to get myself killed on some harebrained escape attempt when I still haven't figured out what it is they want with me. Got it?"

"They got what they wanted from you. They got the dough. Now, you're nothing to them, same as me. Welcome to gen pop, princess."

"You'll be lucky if they let you live after that little stunt. I think you killed that pixie boy. Are you proud of yourself?"

Quincy's stomach rolled over. He was only in this mess because he wanted to help Xander. "It ain't like he didn't deserve it," he replied, but he didn't truly believe it. Xander was just a kid making dumb kid choices. He was mixed up in a whack situation, but that didn't change the fact.

A while later, the cyclops Quincy recognized as Porgis appeared carrying two large black trash bags, a bandage still wrapped around his right forearm from where Quincy had stabbed him. "Don't try anything stupid," he growled.

"Oi, you still got my knife?" he asked. When Hugo didn't answer, he continued. "Where's my buddy Lumpy?" Porgis used a regular old key to open Quincy's cell and tossed one of the bags in before locking it again and doing the same for Miranda. Then, he turned and left without another word.

Inside, Quincy found a bunch of clothes in his size along with an extra pair of shoes. "Not exactly my style," he said, rummaging through the piles of polo shirts and khakis.

"Better than what you're wearing," replied Miranda as she pulled an outfit from her bag and dressed herself. It seemed the witch had a sense of humor.

The next person they saw brought food, if that's what they called the bowl of mush Quincy scarfed down. It tasted like shit, but once he'd devoured the bowl, he could feel his energy returning. After that, they didn't see another living soul for hours, so when Fairburn himself rounded the corner, Quincy knew something was up.

In one hand, Marcus clutched a garment bag, which he passed through the bars to Miranda. "I trust that I don't need to medicate you to convince you to put this on?" he said, eliciting a nod. "Good girl. You'll also find makeup in the provisions I sent over. I need for you to look your very best, understood?"

Miranda nodded again, her face stoic. Quincy stood silently in his cell. He had a feeling his treatment wouldn't be so gentle. But Fairburn didn't acknowledge him. He merely turned on his heel and strode away.

"What do you think this is about?" Quincy said once the footsteps had receded.

Miranda was already changing clothes. "I don't ask questions."

"You're just resigned to be his bitch?"

"Fuck you."

Another few hours passed in relative quiet. The prisoners were forced to piss in their water buckets, leaving them with nothing to drink. Quincy suspected it was but a fraction of the punishment his earlier antics provoked. He wondered if Xander was alive somewhere on-site or if they'd tossed his body in a Dumpster out back. He tortured himself by replaying the scene in his head over and over, but he knew he wouldn't have done anything differently if he could. He was raised on the streets where it was do or die, and his survival instincts served him well up to this point.

Still, Xander haunted him. The first time in years he ever tried to look out for somebody else, and he got the kid killed. If that wasn't a testament to the futility of his life, nothing was.

It was pushing into the evening by the time Fairburn returned. This time, he had a small army at his back, including a lumpier-looking Lumpy.

"Glad to see you in one piece, buddy," said Quincy with a grin. "No hard feelings?"

"Shut your trap, ogre," said Fairburn. He motioned for Hugo, and the larger ogre responded by following Lumpy to Miranda's cage door. In his hand was a syringe. The injection went smoothly, and in moments, Miranda Xeos was sitting on her cot, receiving instructions while Quincy made a show of lounging in his cell.

"You will accompany me to meet with an associate. You will use your charm and station to help convince her to do business. You are to act as if you are living in comfort and luxury and enjoy a prosperous business relationship with me."

To each of these instructions, Miranda simply answered "Yes." Her body writhed slightly beneath the sexy black dress cut low enough to show a sparkling diamond pendant hanging just above enticing cleavage, and her shoulders relaxed. One leg rubbed up and down the other, ever so slightly, until she crossed her legs, showing the red bottom of a shoe that likely cost more than Quincy's apartment. She seemed to be in a state of compliant ecstasy. That was some drug.

"Do I get to go to this party?" asked Quincy, suddenly feeling protective of the woman. What was it with him lately?

Ignoring the question, Fairburn stepped into Miranda's cell, offered his arm, and leisurely led her away, the perfect picture of a wealthy couple going out for a night on the town.

34

Chessa made her way through Boston Common trying to look as casual as possible. Unseelie settlements weren't known for their hospitality, but she did have a reputation for taking on cases that the Seelie had let fall through the cracks, so if anyone had a shot at getting information from this community, it was her.

"Hello!" She called into a smattering of trees. "I'm Chessa Moon from C&F Investigations. I'm looking for the Greene family."

From the base of a nearby tree, a dryad peeled himself from the bark. "Chia?"

Chessa smiled and lighted on the grass in front of him. "That's what some call me," she replied. "You know of me?"

"Everyone here knows you. The pixie with the ear of the Seelie Queen and a voice for *all* fae. What do you want with the Greenes?"

"I'm investigating a pair of murders. The KPD doesn't think they're linked, but my gut says there's more going on than they care to admit."

The dryad spit at the ground. "The KPD is a tool of the powerful. They don't give a lutin's ass about the fae they claim to serve."

Chessa thought about saying a word in Samson's defense, but she knew it would only hurt her situation. Fae didn't join the Unseelie Court because society had done right by them, and every person in this community had a lifetime of stories of being overlooked, forgotten, or used by those in power. It was a hard truth that she had tried to impart to both Gwen and Sammy, but she doubted either of them would ever fully understand the scale of it.

"And that's why I do what I do. I'm looking into a person of interest and the Greenes took him to court awhile back."

"The scumbag who works at the college? You think he's a murderer too?"

"You know about that, huh?" said Chessa, thinking this dryad might need to become a regular informant.

"We're a tight-knit community. Not all Unseelie are prowling the wilds pulling pranks on mortals for shits and giggles." The dryad's bark-like features were drawn into a scowl.

"And not all Seelie are blind to the struggles of their fellow fae," reminded Chessa. "What's your name?"

"Wayland Moss, at your service." The scowl melted, and Wayland gave a small bow in greeting. "You can find the Greenes on the north side of the frog pond if they're home and willing to talk."

"Thank you, Wayland. It's been a pleasure to meet you."

The dryad bowed once again and turned to walk back into the trees.

As she approached the frog pond, Chessa smiled at the humans feeding ducks. It wasn't so long ago it was bread crusts they were tossing, but the naiads had intervened and made signs to inform mortals of the damage they were doing, and now children laughed and tossed lettuce scraps and bits of tomato to the eager waterfowl. The humans couldn't see the naiads dancing across the surface of the pond, but Chessa thought the whole scene was indescribably beautiful.

Between her sleuth intuition and her general knowledge of the Unseelie, it didn't take her long to locate the tree the Greenes called home. The well-worn knob on the hardwood just above the leaf-line was the perfect place to hide a door. As soon as Chessa landed on it, she noticed a hole that had been sealed over with resin by the warm light glowing from within. The door itself was harder to make out as it was painted to blend in with the mottled bark, but the welcome mat affixed to the top side of a sheltered branch gave it away. She knocked three times.

A woman answered. Her hair was cut in a traditional pixie, which made Chessa smile, and it was dark with streaks of silver-gray running through it. Laugh lines at the corners of her eyes made them appear kind, as did the smile with which she greeted Chessa.

"Hello, what can I do for you?" she said.

"My name is Chessa Moon. I'm a private investigator looking into a person of interest in some recent crimes against pixies. Do you have a few minutes to talk, Mrs. Greene?"

"A private investigator? You don't work with the KPD, do you?" The kindness disappeared from the older pixie's face.

"Sometimes. But I'm part owner of C&F Investigations, and our entire purpose is to help those who have been failed by Seelie law. This person I'm looking into, you've crossed paths with him before, and from what I can tell, the system failed you."

Tears filled Mrs. Greene's eyes.

"What's going on?" asked Mr. Greene, appearing in the doorway.

"It's okay, Alfie. This young woman is trying to take down Glenn Darcie. Come in, dear, and call me Helena."

The inside of the tree was decorated in farmhouse chic with warm lights, whitewashed wooden furniture, and clean lines. "Your home is lovely," said Chessa, taking a seat on a pale green sofa. "I want to be honest with you, I don't know if I'm trying to take Darcie down. Not yet. As it stands, he's merely a background player in the life of a murder victim. I'm trying to make sure we cover all the bases."

The Greenes nodded along.

"That man is no good," said Alfie, pacing the room while Helena retrieved tea from the kitchen. "I'm not surprised he's involved."

"That much I gathered from his list of arrests. But it doesn't seem like he's ever had to pay for any of his crimes. Do you know why that is?"

"Money. At least, in our case it was. Some hotshot lawyer showed up, met with the judge, and the next day, our case was thrown out. Our attorney couldn't make heads or tails of it. How is some lowlife drug-dealing bastard that well connected?" Alfred Greene was now red in the face.

Chessa didn't have an answer for him, but she wanted to get some details about those allegations. Helena returned with three mugs and set them on the coffee table before sitting next to Chessa. "What would you like to know, dear?" she asked.

"Everything you can tell me. I think you should start from the beginning if you're okay with that," Chessa replied. "Anything about your experience with him could be helpful."

"We first started seeing problems when Hannah was a junior in high school. She acted out. Skipping school, failing tests even though she's very bright, that sort of thing," said Helena, clutching her cup of tea.

"Normal juvenile behavior," inserted Alfred.

Helena nodded. "They sent her to the school counselor. We had no idea what kind of a man Glenn Darcie was until it was too late."

"He had her selling dust to the entire school," Alfred clarified.

Chessa gasped. She knew about the solicitation of a minor charge, but there was nothing about running a high school drug ring in the file. "How did he get away with that?"

"That's a good question. The court wouldn't even let it be brought up. Hannah refused to cooperate. She claimed she was in love with that monster. All those sessions we thought he was helping her, but he was grooming her, convincing her that he loved her. He filled her head with Danu knows what. The only thing we could get him on was solicitation of a minor because there were witnesses in the school who came forward to say they'd seen them acting inappropriately together. He sent her flowers, pulled her from class for private sessions, and called her twisted little pet names." Helena's voice trailed off as the tears returned to her eyes. "I should have known something was off. I should have done something."

"Nonsense," said Alfred. "We've always been here for Hannah, and she knows it."

"But she was young, Alfie. She fell for all his bullshit, and I couldn't even see that it was happening." Mrs. Greene began to sob, and her husband walked over to place an arm over her shoulders.

"I'm so sorry," said Chessa, feeling a bit like she was intruding on a private moment. "Where is Hannah now?"

"She went to juvie for a year and a half for selling dust. She took the fall for his entire operation. When she got out, she wanted nothing to do with us, and since she was of age, there was nothing we could do about it. Last I heard, she moved down to the harbor, but we haven't heard from her in over a year now," said Alfred.

"And he just walked?" asked Chessa. "What about the witnesses?"

Helena sniffed and raised her head. "They all recanted the same day that attorney showed up. The case was thrown out. Darcie resigned from his post at the school and went about his life while our little girl paid for his crimes."

Chessa wanted to scream. This guy had wrecked a young pixie's life and went on like nothing had ever happened. Now, somehow, he was connected to the death of Mandrake Aster, she just knew it.

"I'm going to figure out his role in what happened to my client's brother," said Chessa. "And this time, he won't be able to buy his way out."

The Greenes sent Chessa off with freshly baked cookies. On the way out, Helena walked her to the door. "If your investigation leads you to Hannah, please tell her we love her. We just want her home."

35

Quincy spent the majority of the day alone. As much as he tried to pretend he didn't need anyone, he knew himself better. Alone, there was nobody to distract him from the thoughts rattling around his head. After a hellish childhood on the streets doing whatever he needed to in order to survive, he'd spent much of his adult life trying to prove something to himself. He wasn't sure what. That he was worth a shit, he supposed. But now, sitting on a cot in a cell with an overflowing bucket of his own piss, he couldn't get Xander out of his mind. Life should have proven to him that he was powerless, but for some reason, he thought he might be able to reach the kid. Maybe if he could have convinced the kid that Fairburn was bad news, he still could have. Now, he would never know.

Even though he didn't particularly like Miranda, he wished she would return, if only to make him feel less alone. He hoped she was all right. He couldn't imagine what Fairburn had in mind for her, but it couldn't be good.

After what seemed like an eternity, Quincy heard a voice. At first, he couldn't determine its origin. "Hey, shithead, you ruined my life."

"Eh? Who's there?"

"Over here, you complete waste of fae magic."

Just outside the bars, Xander was leaning against a wall. His right arm was bound in a sling, and there was a bandage around his head. His wings drooped behind him, as useless as Quincy felt.

Quincy felt his heart leap at the sight of the kid, but he tried to hide it. "You should thank Danu you're alive."

"I wish I wasn't. And if it takes my entire life, I will find a way to kill you for what you've done."

"What was that? Look out for you? Try to help you get a wing up on life?" Even as the words came out of his mouth, Quincy felt the hollowness of them. Maybe he did try to help, but he'd come along much too late. Xander was in over his head long before he'd stepped foot into Pub Nine.

"I'll never fly again."

"I'm sure your boss is real choked up about losing such a valuable asset," said Quincy, his voice thicker than he intended. "Oh, that's right, he doesn't actually give a shit about you, does he?"

Instead of fighting back the way Q expected, Xander's head dropped and his anger seemed to melt away. His shoulders shook. He was crying. Quincy didn't know what to do.

"Hey, kid. I'm sorry about your wings," he said.

"You're right. He doesn't care. I gave up everything. Everything." The pixie sunk to the floor and sobbed.

"It ain't me you hate, is it?"

"I do hate you! I hate everybody! I hate the world!" Xander looked up, and his eyes were ablaze with an anger Quincy knew only too well. This was what he had hoped to save the kid from. Xander's voice dropped to nearly a whisper. "They killed him, you know."

"Mandrake? I figured as much. Did you know that when you hired us?"

"I knew it before I went to that bar. Fairburn set you up. He told me that Drake was going to blow the whole operation, ruin all the work we'd done, and all because of me."

Quincy scowled. "Why would your brother do that?"

"To control me," replied Xander, but Quincy could hear a slight question in his answer. Suddenly, it all made sense.

"Mandrake didn't want you in this, did he? He tried to get you out. That's not control, that's love."

"You don't know shit about love," the pixie replied.

"Maybe not, but it sounds like Mandrake did."

Xander's face was contorted in grief or rage, Q couldn't tell which. "You ruined my life!"

"I learned a long time ago that your life is what you make it. Guys like Fairburn will come and go. They'll use you up until there ain't shit left. But every day you're alive, you get to choose who you are. Mandrake wasn't controlling you, but Fairburn is. You let that shithead convince you that your own flesh and blood needed to die. Maybe now that you're no good to him, you'll figure out what Mandrake knew all along. You're worth more than this."

Xander's entire body was shaking by the time Quincy finished his little monologue. In truth, Q didn't know where it came from. He simply spoke the words he so desperately needed to hear when he was young. And Xander responded in the exact way he would have back then.

"Fuck you! I hope you rot in there! You got what you deserve!"

"If you believe that, then why are you here? You look like you need a hospital."

Xander got back to his feet, but his expression didn't soften. "I just wanted to see you in that cell one more time and tell you that if you ever get out, you'd better watch your back."

"Sure, kid." Quincy turned away and sat back down on the cot. When he looked back, the pixie was gone.

36

Chessa made it to the KPD just in time to see Cora zipping through the lobby in tears. "Whoa, there," she said as she moved to intercept her sister. "What's going on?"

Cora looked stunned for a moment then she seemed to process Chessa's presence. They both drifted down to the floor. Officer Pox sat at the desk, averting his gaze.

"I just need to get out of here," Cora said.

"You filed the report." Chessa pulled her sister into a hug. "It's going to be ok. Samson is going to get Blade back."

"Promise?"

"Promise."

After walking Cora out and swearing she'd be home within an hour or two, Chessa made her way to Samson's office. The griffin wasn't alone. Sitting in the chair opposite his desk, wrapped in a long, leopard print jacket, was Dominik Perez.

Chessa stopped dead in her tracks in the open doorway. "Oh, hell no, what the fuck is he doing here?"

"He just finished giving a statement to O'Toole," said Samson, the picture of calmness. "Close the door. I've got a piano to drop on your head."

This couldn't be good. Chessa did as he instructed and flitted over to stand by the window overlooking the busy Boston street. Dominik's eyeliner was smudged and he seemed to be avoiding eye contact. Chessa stared at him, expecting her gut to tell her he was up to something, but instead, all she noticed were signs of shock and grief.

"What happened?" she asked, dreading the answer.

"Lance Gruber's body was found in the trees at IFAE this morning," Samson said. "He had a slug in his brain. Looks like he sucked the wrong end of a nine-millimeter."

Chessa felt like she might vomit on her Chucks. Lance had tried to tell her he wasn't safe, and she'd left him in that house to fend for himself. Now here was the man who'd assaulted him, sitting in Samson's office like he had no part in the death of his friend. "You do realize that your prime suspect is sitting right here," said Chessa.

"Is there cotton in your ears? The kid dusted himself."

"He did not!" screamed Dominik, leaping to his feet. "I'm trying to tell you he wouldn't do that!"

Chessa jumped into the air, startled, knocking over one of the little plants Samson had sitting on his windowsill. She hadn't been expecting the outburst. With the steam out of him, Dominik slumped back into his chair and folded in on himself. She had to admit, he wasn't behaving like a murderer.

"I've got to agree. The last time I saw Lance, he told me he was in danger, and now he's dead." She nodded her head toward Dom. "Did he tell you about the stabbing?"

The half-elf choked back a sob. "They put that shit in my veins, and I blacked out. I would never hurt Lance. He's my best damned friend."

Samson resembled an owl with the way his head swiveled from the crying humanoid to Chessa and back. "I'm afraid I don't follow."

Chessa took a steadying breath. "Catch me up first, then I'll add what I know. How did you get Dom here in the first place?"

"O'Toole had a team go by Montello after the vic was found, and he was the only one home. They hauled him in as a person of interest, but Plum's findings agree with evidence on site. Gruber shot himself."

"Shit. These guys are good," said Chessa.

"You believe me, right, Chia? It's all a big cover-up. Lance wouldn't do this. Not unless they made him."

"Right. And you wouldn't stab your best friend either." Chessa's wheels were turning. Maybe Lance wouldn't have shot himself if he were in his right mind, but there seemed to be a lot of fae doing things nobody thought they would lately. First, Quincy driving a getaway car, then Dom slicing up his roommate for no apparent reason, and now Lance putting a gun in his mouth.

"You don't understand," said Dom. He was right about that.

"This Joe needs to get out of here before O'Toole has him booked," said Samson. "He was released hours ago but wouldn't skedaddle. When I brought Cora in to file the report, he was in the lobby causing a ruckus. Pox let him camp out for a while, but O'Toole wants him gone or he's going to end up in a cell." Samson was showing his discomfort by picking his feathers again.

"Yes! Put me in a cell. I need to be taken into protective custody," squeaked Dominik, his eyes wide.

"The captain already told you that's not an option. You've provided no evidence of a credible threat to your life, and they're shutting the book on the Gruber suicide."

"Then let Captain O'Toole arrest me for making a disturbance. I can go out in the lobby and strip naked or something. The people who killed Lance will be after me as soon as they figure out I am here. They probably already know." Dom turned to Chessa, his eyes pleading. "Tell him I can't leave! If I do, it'll be my body you find next."

Chessa wanted to hate the guy, but she could tell he was genuinely afraid. He reminded her of the way Lance had begged for help. She couldn't turn her back on him, but at the same time, the KPD couldn't help him if he wasn't willing to turn over some hard evidence.

"They're not going to listen to you unless you give them something they can use. Everything points to suicide. If you know who killed Lance or why, you need to speak up."

Dom rocked back and forth in the chair, hugging himself tightly, but he didn't say another word. Chessa sighed.

"I'll take him to C&F," she told Samson "He should be safe there while we figure this thing out."

Samson pushed the glasses up his beak. "Are you sure you want to take on that risk? What if he's right? Or what if he's playing both sides of the net?"

Chessa looked Dom over once more. "He's scared shitless, and I can keep him safe. Can we go somewhere private to talk real quick first?"

Samson nodded and rose from his chair. "Don't move from that seat," he said to Dominik as he walked with Chessa out of his office.

Once they were in the relative privacy of the hallway, Chessa got right to the point. Her head was throbbing and there was bile in her throat.

"Got any leads on Blade? I'm not sure how long Cora's going to hold up now that she got the authorities involved."

"O'Toole gave me the case once she filed. I sent word to our contact within Wallow World and should have a response by sun-up. If the Kolsches are involved, I will find out," he said.

Chessa offered up a weak smile. "I know, Sammy. You're the best of the best."

"There's something I didn't want to tell you in front of Perez. The gun Gruber shot himself with? It belonged to Glenn Darcie."

A jolt of excitement caused Chessa to feel guilty. She shouldn't be celebrating the circumstances around the death of Lance, but any dirt on Darcie was a step closer to making him pay for everything he'd gotten away with. It could bring peace to the Greenes. It also explained why Lance's body was found on campus. "Are you bringing him in for questioning?"

"Sources confirmed he hadn't been in to work for days, his office showed signs of a break-in. When the boys stopped by his place, he was cooperative. He's been cleared. For now."

That last bit gave Chessa hope that Samson wouldn't allow the KPD to get in the way of justice. She still didn't forgive him for the way he talked about Quincy, but she knew he'd choose her side, the side of doing what's right, if pushed into a corner. She told him everything she'd learned about Glenn Darcie. "The man is a real creep."

"I gathered as much, and from what you're saying, he was running a dope business out of a high school. Do you think that's what this all comes down to? A pixie dust ring?"

"Think about it. If you're a drug dealer, what better place than a fine arts institute to find willing and pliable customers?"

"He got Honey and the rest hooked on dust, and it led to the killing of Mandrake Aster. A deal gone wrong?"

"I think it's a bit more complicated than that, but it definitely involves dust."

Samson nodded and pushed his round, red spectacles to the top of his beak. "And what about Gruber? If you and Perez are right, they dusted him too. Why?"

"This one, I can answer. He was breaking," Chessa replied. The excitement of the case beginning to splinter open faded, and Chessa felt a lump form in her throat. "He begged me to help him. Who else was he reaching out to?"

She left the next thought unsaid. *Who else had turned their back on him?*

"Chia," said Samson, using her street name affectionately, "You can't help anyone else if you go getting yourself snuffed trying to save everyone in a bad situation. You have to protect yourself."

Sometimes, Samson surprised her. He seemed to miss so much sub-context when it came to the fae who'd walked different paths than him, yet he saw through her like she was made of glass. She cleared her throat and changed the subject. "I'm hoping I can get intel from Dom once we get away from the precinct."

"The meeting with the people who took Quincy is coming up fast. Time is a commodity we're running out of."

"I knew it," blurted Chessa. "You don't believe that Q's gone bad any more than you believe that Lance committed suicide."

"Of course I don't. What do you take me for, a flip-flop? But he's been caught on camera driving for the thugs who roughed up Hobbes, and we can't ignore that. You've put me in a jam here. I know where to catch a wanted fugitive, but you're saying they're after Gwen and will take Quincy out the minute they sniff anyone else near the rendezvous. What am I supposed to do with that?"

"I'm sorry, Samson. I really don't know. But we can't do anything to tip them off that Gwen's not coming."

A knock on the door cut their conversation short. O'Toole didn't wait to be invited in before he thrust open the door and strode to Samson's desk. "Wayne, Miranda Xeos has been spotted at The Painted Pony. Get over there stat!"

"Spotted by who? You've got informants in Glitz's circle?" asked Chessa dubiously. Everyone in Korranthia knew Madam Glitz would sniff out a mole and hire an exterminator long before one could squeal.

"No. A patron went live on social media from the VIP room and tagged The Pony. Xeos can be seen in the background rubbing elbows with Glitz and a few other high rollers. Why are you still sitting there, Wayne? The video was posted twenty minutes ago. Get over there now!"

With that, O'Toole turned and walked back toward his office, his footsteps echoing off linoleum.

"I'm coming with you," said Chessa, trailing Samson as he returned to his office to grab his coat and tablet. Dom started at their abrupt appearance, likely taking them for assassins or some other agent of Marcus Fairburn. Samson hustled past him.

"Sorry, kid, but you've got to sit this one out. If all these cases are as connected as you say, this is a dangerous game, and I'm not about to deal you in."

Chessa flew down the halls on Samson's heels. "Please don't cut me out of this," she said.

"Q needs you to untangle this mess pronto. Get whatever you can out of Perez and we'll touch base in the morning," said the griffin.

Chessa stopped following before he made it out of the precinct. She wanted to pull out her hair. If there was one thing she hated more than anything else, it was being kept out of the action. Sitting on the sidelines wasn't in her nature, so she headed straight to O'Toole. Dominik wasn't going anywhere.

The sorcerer's office was at the end of the hall, and the blinds of the huge window were open, revealing him sitting behind his desk. Pox and Darla were seated in chairs on the other side of the desk, the former typing on a laptop while the latter poked a tablet.

Chessa gave a curt knock on the door before she opened it and flitted in.

"We're in the middle of something," snapped O'Toole without looking up from his screen.

"I signed my NDA for the Hobbes Doyle case, and I've been consulting for Sergeant Detective Wayne. If Miranda Xeos has been spotted at the Pony, I might be of some assistance. I have reason to believe she was involved with the attack."

O'Toole squinted in Chessa's direction. She thought he was about to toss her out on her ass, but instead, he sighed. "Fine. Detective Madison, show her." As Darla pulled up the video on her tablet, O'Toole barked, "Somewhere else."

Chessa followed the witch out into the hallway.

"Don't mind the captain," said the witch with a sympathetic smile.

"I never do," replied Chessa.

"This was posted a while back by a social media influencer named Gabbi Diamond. She's made a name for herself by getting into exclusive spaces and making these obnoxious videos. Glitz had her booted, of course, but she was live streaming at the time."

The video showed the VIP area of The Painted Pony just as Chessa remembered it. Groups of well-dressed fae were scattered throughout the area, drinks in hand, as they conversed in private alcoves or took hors d'oeuvres from silver plates carried by scantily clad waitstaff in black bedazzled silk uniforms. In her favored alcove sat Madam Glitz wearing a long pink sparkly robe lined with black feathers. To her left was Miranda Xeos, looking like a million bucks, and to her right was an unfamiliar man in a conservative suit.

"Who's the banker?" asked Chessa, wondering if she finally had a face to put to the name Marcus Fairburn.

"That's the interesting part," replied Darla. "Get this, he's mortal. The captain's got the Boston PD digging up anything we can on him. He's in the system as Marcus Smith, a former badge. We're trying to figure out what a mundane mortal man is doing sitting next to the most notorious crime boss in Korranthia."

Chessa felt a flush touch her face. It couldn't be a coincidence that this Smith character shared a first name with the big bad she was hunting. Fairburn must be an alias. There was nothing like the rush of a break in a case, and every fiber of her pixie sense was screaming that this man was about to bust the case wide open. All the cases.

"Do you have an address for him?"

"Not yet. But we should any minute now."

"Thank you, Darla," said Chessa, giving the witch a quick squeeze on the arm. "I've got an angle I can play with this. Tell O'Toole I'll be in touch."

37

Feet made for highly ineffective conveyance devices. Chessa's wings fluttered with frustration at how long it was taking to get to Beacon Street, the closest Leaf Pass terminal to the precinct.

"Why can't we just call a cab?" said Dominik. He was downright twitchy, jumping at every loud noise and attempting to peer into every car stuck in traffic. Friday evenings were always like this, with people trying to get to all the popular downtown spots.

"Look around, Dom," replied Chessa. "No car is going to get through this any time soon. And since you don't have wings, you're going to have to deal with hoofing it to the Commons Terminal. It's only a few blocks."

"Fine. If I get gunned down on the sidewalk, it's on you."

Chessa sighed but picked up the pace. She might not know Dom very well, but she fully believed that whoever he was in bed with was beyond dangerous. She pulled out her cell and shot a text to Norman. Hopefully, by the time they reached C&F, he would have intel on one Marcus Smith. Her phone immediately made the notification chime. The response from Norman read:

We need to talk.

That was odd. Chessa didn't have time to think about what might be going on with Norman, not if she wanted to get Dom off the street as soon as possible. Even if he didn't look like prey being run down by a wraith, he had the information she needed, and Boston Common was far too crowded for her liking. The Common Terminal was located at the George Robert White Memorial, fitting as he was the sorcerer who established Leaf Pass travel in Korranthia. Chessa zipped over to the pedestal holding the Spirit of Giving statue, a winged woman mortals assumed to be an angel, and placed her hand on the cool granite. A door formed, and a fairy emerged.

"Welcome to Common Station. What is your destination?"

"East Boston near Jeffries Point," said Chessa.

The fairy, a male with silver hair and tired eyes, looked her up and down. "Something wrong with your wings?"

It was a valid question. For shorter distances, winged fae were generally better off flying than resorting to Leaf Pass. "I've got company with me, and traffic is a bitch."

Dominik finally caught up, and realization dawned on the fairy's face. Transporting larger fae, even one the size of a human, required more than a leaf and a wind magic practitioner. "Wait here. Let me check what time we can be prepared to depart."

The fairy ducked back through the door and reemerged a moment later. "Have a seat on that bench yonder. We will depart in ten. It'll be fifty bucks."

Dom's jaw dropped. "You've got to be kidding me! Fifty bucks for a few miles?"

The fairy's lip curled. "For one your size, yes."

Chessa cringed as she pulled out her wallet and handed over a credit card, which the fairy took before disappearing back into the base of the statue. This case was racking up a lot of expenses considering how much it was bringing in—nothing. She sat with Dom on the park bench watching naiads play in the fountain. The silence was uncomfortable, but she didn't want to spook Dominik into running. He also had information she needed.

"Why did you pretend to be a writer looking for a place to crash?" he asked after a while.

"I was hired by Xander to look into Mandrake's death."

Dom laughed like she was joking. "Yeah, ok."

"Really. At that time, I had no reason to suspect there was more to the situation than what he told us. I've come to realize it was all an elaborate trap for Gwendolyn Evenshine."

Dominik jumped to his feet. "No way! What the fuck do they want with the Queen? Isn't money enough?"

Chessa looked around to see if anyone had noticed his outburst. Two humans out for a walk in the park were staring at them. Thankful that the fairy glamour hid their true natures, Chessa hushed Dom. "Don't make a scene," she said. "I was hoping you could give me more information on what they want with her, but it seems like you're as much in the dark as I am."

"I'm a walking corpse," said Dominik, his tone resentful.

Their conversation was cut short by the appearance of a woman. Chessa's innate sense told her it was a sorceress, and the bored expression tipped her off that she worked for the transit authority.

"You my parcels?" she said, tucking her dark hair behind an ear.

"If you're going to East Boston, then yes," replied Chessa with a smile.

"Strap in." The sorceress chuckled. "Sorry. Leaf Pass humor."

"Can I get my credit card back first?" asked Chessa, hoping there were no detours in the trip. Leaf Pass was valuable for the fae of Korranthia, especially those without wings or cars, but the operators weren't known for their precision.

"Oh, yeah, sure," said the sorceress before walking to the statue, sticking her hand through the door, and pulling out Chessa's card. She tossed it over, and Chessa nearly face planted snatching it up from the ground at the same moment the bench lifted into the air.

Flying on an object over the buildings and streets was unnerving to Chessa, but by the way Dominik clung to the armrest, it must have been downright terrifying for someone without wings. Looking down, Chessa could just make out the form of the fairy perched on the head of the statue, a wand pointed up at them, likely to cast a stronger glamour. The Glamour Squadron's general one could only hide so much, and a flying park bench must be outside their scope. The sorceress had jumped aboard just before takeoff and was balanced precariously on the backrest, her feet between Chessa and Dom.

"Keep your appendages onboard at all times. Magic use or sudden noises will have you ejected as will screaming, barfing, or any other action that annoys me. My name is Mika. Please give me five stars on the Leaf Pass app."

Chessa breathed a sigh of relief when the bench touched down just outside the apartment where C&F was housed. Mika didn't give so much as a "peace out" before the bench was back in the air, zipping out of sight.

"Now I remember why I never travel Leaf Pass," said Dom. His face was ghost white.

"We're here, aren't we?" said Chessa. She flashed a grin and then led him inside.

When they walked through the apartment door, Chessa knew something was off. Her pixie intuition was on high alert. It was a feeling she was all too familiar with lately, but that didn't take the dread out of it. She zipped up the stairwell of the apartment building that used to be the home of her best friend, the one she'd left her awesome pad over the industrial club to occupy in Gwen's absence, leaving Dominik to trail behind. The door was closed, but she could make out voices from within. Cora, Norman, and one other—Gwen.

"You've got to stop popping up like this," said Chessa as she pushed open the door.

"Good to see you too." The Seelie Queen was sitting on the threadbare plaid couch with Cora, who somehow looked even more frail than she had when Chessa left that morning. Norman was at his usual spot behind the desk. When he looked at Chessa, his eyes were wide, but whatever he wanted to talk about would have to wait.

"I might be more enthusiastic if you didn't leave my friends in tears every time you decided to grace us with your presence," quipped Chessa. She loved Gwen, but she would not allow her to treat good people like trash, and she was still pissed about the state she'd left poor Norman in after her last impromptu visit.

Gwen glanced at the wizard, who shifted his attention to his fingernails, then back. "Curtis said something about how hard I was on the wizard. I apologized as soon as I arrived. We don't choose our families, and I know that better than most."

"I know how you could make it up to him," said Chessa with a mischievous grin. "Put a call into the Academy and tell them to give him unrestricted access to the library."

Norman choked in surprise and tried to cover it with a cough.

"I suppose I could do that," said Gwen.

"Hey, Norm, did you get any hits on Marcus Smith?" Chessa asked, changing the subject.

If he looked uncomfortable before, he now looked like he was about to poof himself out of existence. He mumbled some non-reply and cut his eyes to the back room. Chessa got the message. He didn't want to talk in front of Gwen. She was about to pull him aside when the office door creaked open, and Dominik entered. The elf hybrid took one look around the room and dropped into a low bow at the foot of the couch. The sight of him in his eccentric outfit nearly splayed on the floor to reach a lower elevation than Gwen made Chessa snort. The Queen's choice of wardrobe, the ripped Metallica shirt she'd been coronated in paired with her beat-to-hell Doc Martens and ripped jeans with her wand poking out from the holster on her thigh, made the scene even more absurd. Gwen seemed nonplussed.

"Rise," she said, sounding bored. Dominik stood, cast a confused glance at Chessa, and then scurried off to stand by the window, where he could peek through the blinds at the street below.

"Norm, help me set up the back room for our guest," said Chessa. "He's going to be with us for a few days."

"Need any help?" asked Gwen, beginning to stand.

"Nope. You stay and visit with Cora. I'll be right back."

When they were alone, Chessa started gathering up sensitive files to bring into her bedroom. "What's going on?" she asked.

"It's that name you sent me. Marcus Smith. I know it. You know, from before."

"From your life before Korranthia? That's great! What can you tell me about him?"

Norman was tense. Chessa knew he hated talking about his past, but if he had intel on the mysterious new player in Korranthia crime, it could give them an advantage.

"He's bad news. He's an agent with the DFR, and he worked with my pa, trading favors and that sort of thing. Last I heard, he was on an intel-gathering mission, but Pa said to pay it no mind because it would only be good for business. I can't imagine anything that snake was up to was good for anyone."

Chessa had no doubt Norman was right. "Well, fuck me," she said. She'd known the guy was in law enforcement, but the FBI's Department of Fae Relations was next level. They operated in the shadows, ensuring the security of fae communities in the United States. If one of their agents was working with an overseas crime ring, it was bad, and if that work transcended the Penningtons, it was likely some traitorous shit. Like all good leads, this one left Chessa with more questions than answers. "We're going to need help on this," said Chessa.

"Please, no. She's going to think I'm keeping secrets," said Norman. He was near tears.

"I'm sorry, Norm, but this is too big for us. I need to loop Gwen in."

"Loop me in on what?" asked Gwen from behind them.

Chessa jumped. She hadn't heard the door open. "Just because you're a silent partner doesn't mean you get to sneak up on people like that!"

"Sorry, not sorry. Now what's going on?"

Norman dropped his head and busied himself moving the boxes Chessa had packed out of the room while Chessa caught Gwen up on their person of interest. If she blamed Norman for anything, Gwen at least had the sense to keep her mouth shut about it, which was something to be thankful for. Chessa could only piss on so many fires at once.

"I'll put in a call to get his records sent over from the DFR," said Gwen. It was the response Chessa was hoping for. Nobody else in Korranthia would be able to make the DFR comply, but Gwen had her own line to the top. If this guy was still one of theirs, they needed to know he was dirty, and if not, Chessa wanted everything they had on him. "And I'll have Curtis follow up to make sure it happens quickly."

"Where is Curtis anyhow? This place could use some prettying up."

By the look on her best friend's face, Chessa's attempt to lighten the mood failed. "Back in Avalon. I needed him to take care of things in my absence."

Then it sunk in. The meeting with Quincy's kidnappers was scheduled for the morning, and that's why Gwen was here. Curtis would try to stop her, so she left him behind.

"No. No way," said Chessa.

"I'm going, Chess, and you can't stop me." All the growth Gwen had done over the past few years disappeared, leaving her the picture of the obstinate, rebellious ex-fairy godmother Chessa first met what felt like a lifetime ago. Chessa didn't see a fairy imbued with some kind of power that inspired loyalty, she saw a scared woman who wanted to take on the world.

Whichever version was accurate, Chessa did love Gwen. And she wasn't about to let her put her life on the line yet again. "Absolutely not!"

"Look, as unfair as I've been to Norman, I've been even more so to Quincy. He's only in this mess because of me, and if there's a chance I can get him back after everything he's done for the Seelie Court—for me—I have to try."

For once, Chessa wasn't scared. She wasn't irritated. A cold numbness spread through her, the kind you only feel when rage takes over. "Who do you think you're talking to? That story might fly for someone else, but I know you. You're up to something. How many times do I have to explain to you that you are the fucking Seelie Queen? The last of your line! You are not some pawn to throw into the path of danger! Our entire way of life depends on your continued existence."

Gwen first looked shocked, then sad, then angry. Chessa knew she wasn't used to being yelled at by anyone, least of all her. "Don't you think I know that? I've given up my entire life for this. I never asked for it. I never wanted it. I've spent years living for everyone but myself!"

"Sacrificing yourself for Quincy isn't going to do you or anyone else a bit of good, but that's not what you're doing, is it? You don't even trust me enough to be honest."

"I'm broken, Chess."

The words hung in the air, painful and true. Chessa felt her anger melt away, and some force tugged at her, making her want to drop everything and do whatever Gwen needed. Norman was right, there was magic at work here. She wouldn't bow to Morgan's powers, not with Gwen's safety in question. "We're all broken."

"I need to do this. I do trust you. More than anyone else in my life. Please back me up," Gwen was pleading now, something Chessa had never seen her do for as long as she'd known the obstinate fairy.

"I've never done anything else," Chessa replied. "But I can't back you up if I don't know what's going on."

"Everything I do is for the people I serve. You say I don't trust you, but right now, I need *you* to trust *me*."

Chessa growled in frustration. Gwen was the most insufferably stubborn creature on the planet. She looked through the open doorway at Cora, who was standing by Norman's desk pretending to study a piece of paper, but her sister didn't meet her eye. Chessa wondered what she made of everything she'd seen—dead pixies, missing fae, a possible pixie dust cartel, and now, the Seelie Queen begging her little sister for help. It didn't matter. There was only one thing Chessa could do, the same thing she'd done since the moment Gwen's vengeful spirit swept into her life.

She dropped her shoulders and sighed.

"Always," she said.

38

Samson wasn't dressed for The Painted Pony. In truth, there was nothing in his closet that would be appropriate for the hottest fae nightclub in Korranthia, so he did his best—a pair of khakis and a navy sports coat he'd worn to his father's retirement party a few years back. He tugged at the too-tight collar as he pushed to the front of the long line of large fae, eliciting groans and rude comments from the ogres, humanoids, and cyclopses, all decked out in tight-fitting pants and shimmery dresses. He stuck out like Quincy in a library.

"KPD, move aside!" he squawked over and over until he reached the bouncer. A quick flash of the badge gained him access, but by the time he reached the second floor where the smaller fae danced and drank to the thumping sounds of whatever DJ the kids liked these days, all hope he had of surprising Glitz was gone. She stood outside the pink velvet ropes marking the entrance to the VIP lounge, waiting for him to emerge from the large fae stairwell used nearly exclusively by employees. Moving through the space to where she waited was slow going as he had to watch his step to avoid flattening non-flighted, smaller patrons.

"Sergeant Detective Samson Wayne." Glitz him with a flourish when he finally reached the back of the room. "What can I do for you this fine evening?"

"You can step aside, doll. I require access to the VIP room."

A fire touched Glitz's dramatically made-up eyes. "I'm nobody's doll, and I'm going to need to see a warrant," she said, and he realized his misstep. Chessa was always telling him to stop calling women 'doll,' and in that moment, he wished he'd taken her advice to heart.

"I beg your pardon. My bum noodle sometimes makes me come off wrong. But I still need to pass through that door," he replied, handing over his cell phone which displayed the warrant O'Toole sent over on the way.

Glitz gave it a once-over. "Hm" was all she said as she turned and walked back into the lounge. The door nearly swung shut in his face, but he was quick to catch ahold of it.

The VIP lounge was nearly empty. Only one of the many alcoves was occupied, and none of the patrons resembled Miranda Xeos or the man she'd been spotted with less than an hour earlier. One look at Glitz's impassive expression confirmed his fears—this was a dead end.

Samson wasn't about to give up so easily. They had been here, and he had proof. "I'm going to need you to come down to the station with me," he said to Glitz, hoping O'Toole wouldn't string him up for this.

She batted her false lashes. "Of course, Sergeant. I'm all yours."

Thankfully, Samson had taken the Humvee, the only vehicle large enough to accommodate his massive size, rather than flying. He couldn't imagine Glitz would have agreed to catch a ride on his back all the way to the precinct. She rode in the front seat in silence until they reached the KPD. Once they arrived, she was still tight-lipped. She answered questions in a cursory manner, giving up nothing useful about either of her associates. Samson got more and more frustrated and finally called O'Toole in for backup.

Immediately, Glitz warmed. "Captain, I'm so pleased you decided to come speak to me yourself," she said, casting a meaningful glare in Samson's direction. "The good sergeant here has been asking about some of my customers, and I'm afraid I just don't have much to tell."

O'Toole looked around the interrogation room. "This won't do at all," he said. "Wayne, this is no way to treat a guest who is here of her own will to help us out! Come, Madam Glitz, let's go to my office. Can I get you anything to drink?"

Samson tried not to roll his eyes as he followed them down the hall. He took his job seriously, but the captain's pandering to powerful fae always turned his stomach. As it turned out, the change in accommodation did little to get information out of Glitz.

"Fairburn? He's a lovely man. Miranda brought him in earlier this evening. You know Miranda, she's always associating with the most interesting people."

"You must not have heard, but Miranda Xeos is a missing person," said O'Toole.

"Oh, pish-posh. She's simply a free spirit. Something I'm sure the good sergeant here couldn't understand considering the company he keeps."

After thirty minutes of the same routine, O'Toole kissing ass while they both took potshots at Samson, Glitz bid them both farewell.

"Do you need a ride?" O'Toole asked. "I can have Pox take you back to the Pony or wherever you'd like to go.

"I can manage myself," Glitz replied, kissing the captain on both cheeks before sashaying down the hall.

Once she was gone, O'Toole slammed his fist down on the table. "What am I missing? Why did you bring her here?"

Samson turned his head to the side slightly. "She had the place cleared out when I got there. She knows something, captain."

"Be that as it may, she's got the best lawyers in Korranthia on speed dial. Do not bring her in again unless you catch her standing over a body, got that detective?"

"No, I don't got that sir," replied Samson, his feathers puffed. He was sick of tip-taloning around Glitz and anyone else with an iota of power. "She's dirty, and the whole department knows it. Why do you keep covering for her?"

"Look Wayne, I'm as frustrated as you are that we missed Xeos, but you need to cool off. Go home. Take a shower. Get some sleep. That's an order from your captain." The way he enunciated the last word held a note of warning.

Samson turned and stormed out, nearly flattening Pox in the hallway. But he didn't go home. Instead, he marched straight to his office and spent the next few hours scouring every file he could on Glitz. Eventually, he ran out of steam. She was too good at covering her tracks, and there was nothing there, just as O'Toole had spent the last few years telling him. It wasn't the way the world was supposed to work. Criminals did time. End of story.

Samson curled up in the corner of his office and had nightmares about Glitz and Darcie taking over Korranthia.

When he awoke, the morning shift had already taken over, and O'Toole was long gone. He spent the morning catching up on his paperwork documenting case notes. Sometime after lunch, his phone rang.

"Sergeant Detective Samson Wayne," he answered.

"Samson, it's Curtis. Her Grace snuck out last night, and Chessa's not picking up. I think she's going to do something monumentally…Gwen."

Samson's heart skipped a beat. Curtis might not be willing to call the Seelie Queen stupid or impulsive, but he was implying one or the other.

"I'll run by C&F in two shakes of a lion's tail."

"Thank you. Can you let me know that she's safe?"

"Affirmative." Samson wondered what Gwen could possibly be up to. He was afraid to think too much about it, especially with the Quincy rendezvous on the horizon.

"Oh, and Samson? Would you mind keeping this to yourself? She'd be royally annoyed that I went behind her back. I'm under a strict gag order about her movements, and I don't want her to think I'm disclosing sensitive information."

"Sure thing," replied Samson. He hung up the phone and was packing up his things when O'Toole popped into his office.

"Captain," said Samson, trying to sound as neutral as possible. It did no good to have O'Toole know how little respect he held for him.

"I hope you've had time to blow off steam," said O'Toole. He stood in the doorway with an expectant look painted on his detestably youthful face. He wanted an apology.

"Yes, sir," was all Samson could muster.

"I expect you'll watch your tone with me in the future if you want to remain in good standing *Sergeant*?"

Samson stared at the captain for a moment then decided to do whatever it took to get to the end of this conversation. He knew O'Toole was full of shit. He was more scared of Gwendolyn Evenshine than he was of Madam Glitz, and there was no way he'd risk pissing her off by demoting Samson. That didn't make this interaction any more pleasant. "Yes, sir. I have a question for you," he said.

"I swear to Danu if this has to do with Glitz or Aster, I'm going to demand your badge on the spot." A small flame flickered in O'Toole's palm.

Samson swallowed a retort that would likely get his feathers singed. "Did you get any word on the missing sprite?"

The flame disappeared, leaving a small puff of smoke trailing upward.

"As a matter of fact, I did. My informant over at Wallow World claims that the Kolsch family has closed ranks. Something's got them on edge. What's more, she never saw Blade Hudson in the flesh, but she did see

Walter Kolsch loading a large container onto a box truck outside the office. She would have thought nothing of it except that Kolsch got in to drive the truck himself. He never drives, and he never rides with cargo."

Samson felt a rush go through him. Maybe they would get some good news after all. He forgot his issues with O'Toole entirely.

"Is that enough to put out an APB?" he asked.

"Not officially, but I've got some guys out looking for the truck. If they find it, they'll drum up an excuse to make the stop. Whatever you might think of me, Wayne, I am the captain of the Korranthia Police Department. My duty is to serve in the best way I can, and I will not allow corruption to run free and abduct good, upstanding fae."

Samson bowed his head slightly, a sign of contrition. "I meant no disrespect, sir."

"Didn't you?" O'Toole's blue eyes blazed, and Samson felt a pang of regret. O'Toole might play at politics more than he liked, but he did try to do what was best for Korranthia. They just happened to disagree on what that was in many cases.

As Samson was about to say something along those lines, Pox burst into the office, his cheeks flushed. "Your tip was good, Captain. We've got him!"

Dominik spent the night in the back room while Cora let Gwen crash on the other side of Chessa's bed. Chessa forced herself to lie down for a few hours on the couch, waking when Norman arrived for the day. She saw him and Gwen off for their early morning trip to the Academy and had just put on the coffee when Dominik emerged from the back room. He immediately began his paranoid pacing between windows.

"Dom, if you would just tell me what's going on, we could get this case closed faster and you could return to your life," she said, watching him sit in the desk chair for approximately thirty seconds before jumping back up to check the window again.

"I told you before, they don't tell me shit."

"How did you get involved with them in the first place?" Chessa asked.

"It was Abi. I thought she was into me. We hooked up a few times, and the next thing I knew, she had me running errands for her. I thought it was weird that she lived with another dude, but then I met Drake, and well, it all kind of made sense. He was the sensitive artist type, you know? And Honey was this weird gamer chick. I thought they were into dust whenever they could score a little to help their creative processes, you know, like most pixies at school, and they were always careful to keep me clear of it. I didn't know how bad it was. By the time Lance moved in with us, I was already too far in."

Dom's cell phone notification went off, and he pulled it from his back pocket. "Speak of the devil," he muttered.

"Which one?"

"Abi. She wants to know where I am so we can meet up and talk about Lance killing himself."

Chessa grimaced and handed him a steaming cup of coffee, like he needed the caffeine. Cora must have smelled it from the bedroom because she entered the room and made a beeline for the kitchenette to pour herself a cup.

Chessa's phone dinged as Cora was settling onto the couch. She unlocked it, and her heart jumped to see a text from Abi.

I know how bad things look. I never wanted any of this to happen. I could really use a friend right now.

Chessa read it aloud and Dominik scoffed. "Yeah, I'm sure she could. And the worst part is, if you met her, she'd have you convinced she's some damsel in distress who needed saving before your feet touched down. She truly is a great actress."

"Is that how she kept you around?" asked Chessa, feeling like a chump. She glanced over to where Cora was curled up on the couch, hoping her sister didn't deduce the nature of her relationship with Abi. Thankfully, Cora was staring off into space, lost in her thoughts.

"Yep. She told me she was addicted to dust and that Honey was making her do the dirty work for her boyfriend Glenn in order to get her next fix."

"Glenn Darcie? The student advisor?" Chessa feigned surprise.

"He was offering advice of a sort, I guess," replied Dom, parting the blinds to look out the window again. "Back then, I thought he was a small-time dealer taking advantage of his place at the school. I didn't know about Fairburn. Like a fool, I stuck around and tried to get Abi clean."

"Is she actually addicted to dust?" Chessa asked.

Dom shrugged. "What does it matter? Honey might be the brains, but at least she's honest about who she is. Abi is whatever suits her at the time. The worst part is, she doesn't even need the cash. She does it all, the lying, stealing, manipulation, all of it, for the sheer joy of it. She gets off on it."

Chessa felt sick. Never before had her gut led her so astray. She blamed her overzealous libido. "Did she lure Lance too?"

Dom put his head in his hand and his voice caught. "No. That was all me."

Chessa felt for the guy. He was obviously hurting. "I can tell you cared for him. What happened the other night? If it wasn't you, then who? Honey? Tell me it wasn't Abi."

"No, she's a snake, but she doesn't like to get dirty. They told you the truth. I did it. But I wasn't in my right mind. Lance and I are the only non-pixies they brought in, and it wasn't by accident. It may have started with errands for their dealer, but it got to be so much more."

"How do you mean?"

"Honey tests out her products on us."

Now that was a curveball. "What products? Pixie dust?"

It made no sense. If they were feeding him dust, Dom would be long dead by now with his elf and who-knows-what other fae blood.

"Not dust. The shit she turns it into. Stuff that works on non-pixies." Dom's voice dropped and his eyes darted back to the window. "Imperium."

Now, even Cora was paying attention. Her face seemed to reflect Chessa's thoughts—if they were using fae as test subjects, perhaps Blade was receiving the same treatment.

"What does it do?" asked Chessa.

"She never told me what it's supposed to do. All I know is how it makes me feel. First like I'm on top of the world, then like I'm beneath it." Dom paced back and forth while he talked. "The night I hurt Lance, she injected me with batch #442, and the next thing I knew, I was covered in blood."

"You have no memory of stabbing him?" asked Chessa, attempting to keep any note of suspicion out of her voice. It was awfully convenient to forget the crimes you committed under the influence of any substance, but she knew nothing about this Imperium and its effects.

"Just flashes. At first, it's a rush. Like everything in the world is perfect. It gives you a hard-on like you wouldn't believe! Then, you black out. When you come to, you're freezing, nauseous, and empty. It's like all the good in the world was crammed into the few blissful moments, and then it's sucked out of existence."

"Oh, shit."

"The first few times, I remembered everything afterward, the things they asked me to do, but Honey kept coming home with different versions. The most recent one wiped my mind completely."

"Wait. Back up. What kinds of things did they have you do?"

"Nothing I wouldn't have done otherwise. They said it just lowered my inhibitions." Dom's cheeks grew red. Chessa got the message.

"Is this what they're doing to Blade? Drugging him with magical, fae ecstasy for some kind of sex party?" said Cora, suddenly taking an interest in their conversation, her voice terrifyingly calm. Chessa looked at her sister with concern, noting the firm set of the other pixie's jaw and distinct lack of tears.

Dominik jumped when she spoke as if he forgot she was in the room, then took a breath. "I don't know a Blade. Abi and Honey work for Fairburn, but by the end of it, Lance and I were just their pets. We never had contact with anyone else in the organization, even Darcie. Well, nobody except Xander, that little shit."

That caught Chessa's attention. "Xander works directly with Fairburn?"

"Yeah. Has done ever since they killed Drake. All my boy wanted to do was protect his little brother, and it got him killed." Dominik swiped the back of his hand over his eyes, further smearing his black eyeliner.

Chessa shook her head and glanced at Cora. How anyone could work with the bastard who killed their sibling was beyond her understanding. "Do you have any idea if there are other groups like yours? Other places where they might have kept..." She paused and glanced at her sister before continuing, "test subjects?"

Dom shook his head. "I don't think so. Honey is the pharmacist. Every morning, she packs up a case to go to a lab somewhere and returns with new drugs for us monkeys. Sometimes, she takes me or Lance into her room to shoot us up, but mostly, she spends her evenings gaming, like she's not some evil scientist playing Neit with our lives."

Chessa shivered. She suddenly understood why all her interactions with Dominik had felt so off. Despite all appearances, he was a prisoner, sometimes a heavily medicated one. She was about to ask how he got caught up in all this when Norman and Gwen returned, the former grinning and cradling a stack of old books in his arms like a precious babe. Relief washed over her. She was never sure how much torture Gwen would subject him to when they were alone. "I see your trip to the Academy was a success," she said.

"The matrons are much more accommodating when you show up with the Seelie Queen," he said as he deposited his stash on top of the desk and began sifting through books.

Dominik retreated to the back room, slinking away as if he were hoping to be forgotten. With everything he'd just divulged, that was highly unlikely, but Chessa needed to turn her attention to the Quincy meeting. Since Gwen was going come hell or high water, the only course of action was to formulate a plan together. The location was the Charlestown Navy Yard, and there were plenty of places to hide. That meant that they could enlist help, possibly even the KPD, and have backup hidden on-site, but it also meant the enemy could do the same. In fact, they could bet on it.

"What happens when our backup runs into their backup?" asked Chessa. "It will blow the whole meeting, and Q will be dead."

"Not if they know I'm coming," said Gwen. "They wouldn't scrap their only bargaining chip."

"Is he, though? What about Blade?" Chessa thought Cora might chime in, but instead, she sat quietly listening in.

"We don't know for certain that they even have him. Besides, you said this is all about me, right? If that's the case, they'll know it's Q I'm here for."

Chessa nodded. She hated that she shouldn't persuade Gwen to stay back, but she knew she'd only be wasting precious hours arguing. And she had a point. These people had done their homework, so they would know that Gwen had no relationship with Blade, even if they were the ones who'd taken him.

"It would help if we knew what they wanted with me," added Gwen.

On that point, they agreed. If these people wanted her dead, it was an entirely different situation than if they merely wanted her attention. When you walked into a trap, it helped to know what kind.

It was pushing into the evening when a knock on the door made Dominik stick his head out of the back room and then duck back inside. Chessa heard the scraping of a piece of furniture being pushed up against the door. If his account of things was true, Chessa couldn't really blame him. Fairburn had Mandrake killed simply for trying to keep Xander clear. If he suspected Dom was talking to the police, it would be the end for him as well. Lucky for them all, it was just Samson.

"Oh, we're having another little shindig, I see," he said, his eagle head swiveling to take in the assembly of fae in the C&F reception area.

Gwen flew over to hug the griffin, but he cut it short and walked over to Cora. Chessa could feel the air around him vibrating with excitement.

"I had to come in person to deliver the news. Blade is alive. We got him back."

The pixie burst into tears, and Chessa flew over to pull her into a hug. "You got Blade?"

"Your instinct was on the money. Walter Kolsch had him. Korranthia's prestigious business family didn't like you poking your nose in their business, I suppose. O'Toole acted on a hot tip and pulled his truck over on Highway 20."

"Where was he headed?" asked Chessa, her heart hammering in her chest. This was it, the break they so desperately needed.

"The only thing out there is the Wallow World property off Water Row over in Sudbury. He had some cover story about delivering goods, but it was a load of hooey, and the officers saw through it. They searched the truck and recovered our missing sprite."

"Samson, you big wonderful bird!" She zipped over and planted a big kiss on the top of his beak while ruffling the feathers on either side of his head.

Samson looked puzzled. "What did I miss?"

"If I'm right, you just discovered the lab Fairburn is using to create Imperium!"

"You say that like it should ring a bell," replied Samson as Dom poked his head out from the back room.

Chessa took a deep breath and then caught Samson up. "The reason Lance killed himself was because he was under the influence of a new drug called Imperium. I couldn't figure out the connection between Fairburn and the Kolsches, but I think this is it. Fairburn's operation is set up on Wallow World property. Think about it! Who else holds the kind of well-secured real estate needed for an illicit pharmaceutical lab?"

"Slow your roll and give a guy a chance to catch up. You think the Kolsches are responsible for the dead pixies and are involved with a drug cartel? Kid, if you're right about that, it's going to blow the Korranthia business sector to shreds. The paperwork alone is going to take the whole department."

"Where is my fiancé?" interrupted Cora, her voice barely more than a croak.

"Oh, Cora, I'm so sorry. Of course, you want to get to Blade," Chessa said, feeling guilty for her excitement over the case while her sister went through hell.

"He's been taken to Korranthia General," replied Samson. "I'm heading over now to get his statement while O'Toole works Kolsch back at the precinct. Give me a few ticks to call and let the captain in on Chessa's hunch and we can jet together."

"Thank you, Sammy," said Chessa, wrapping her arms as far around his neck as she could reach. "I knew you would come through."

"You should thank O'Toole," said Samson, giving her a look that said more than his words. "He's the hammer who knocked the screws loose."

Gwen let out a soft chuckle, and Chessa couldn't help but laugh along, feeling a mixture of relief and giddiness. She didn't realize just how much they all needed this win.

Their joy was fleeting. They still had to get Quincy back.

"Do you think they're keeping Quincy wherever they were taking Blade?" Gwen asked, giving voice to Chessa's thoughts as Samson stepped into the hall, cell phone in talon.

"Possibly, but it's not your concern. Quincy is bait to lure you into a trap—one you're hell-bent on dancing right into," replied Chessa.

"From everything you say, it sounds like their drug operation is a well-tuned machine, so why would they want to get the attention of the Seelie Court?" Something about her tone was odd. Gwen was never very good at deception. Chessa could always tell when she was holding back, and her intuition told her this was one of those times.

"I don't know," she replied, shooting her best friend a side-eye.

Samson stepped back into the room. "Your Grace, I'm glad to see you, but you need to skedaddle back to Avalon before the rendezvous tomorrow."

"Sorry, Samson. If Quincy is in trouble, I need to go to the meeting."

"Queen or not, you're thicker-headed than a troll on grog. Quincy might be at the distribution center, but an operation that big will take time to put together. The morning is too soon."

"Then you see why I can't go home. Not yet."

Samson let out a rare curse and ran his talons through his feathers. "Don't do anything until I get O'Toole caught up, capiche?"

"I'll stay right here until morning," promised Gwen. "I've got a call to make to the DFR. But come sunup, all bets are off."

"Chessa, will you please come with me to see Blade?" asked Cora, tears streaming down her face.

Gwen would have to wait. And so would the distribution center. Her sister needed her. "Of course. Norman, help Gwen go through whatever information she gets on Fairburn. I'll be back soon. And Gwen?"

"Yeah?"

"Don't do anything stupid until I get back."

40

Gwen hated to play Chessa this way, but she didn't have a choice. If the pixie knew what was at stake here, she would insist on keeping Gwen locked up. She'd probably have her hidden away on whatever island she used to house the baby dragon from Avalon until Imperium wiped out all of Korranthia. Samson's news couldn't have come at a better time. She needed to make her move tonight, before the meeting tomorrow passed and took her excuse to be here with it, and shaking Chessa would have been harder than the task she was attempting to accomplish. Norman, on the other hand, could be ordered around with no problem. She could make the wizard wet himself with a glare. Though, these days, the fae in her life seemed to bend over backward to please her, even without intimidation tactics. She wasn't used to the power. Yet.

Once they were alone, he shifted uncomfortably in his chair.

"Norman, I need your computer," she commanded.

"Yes, Your Grace," he replied, shuffling from behind the desk. "Is there anything you me to do to help prepare for tomorrow's meeting?"

"There isn't going to be a tomorrow if I don't get to Fairburn tonight," Gwen replied.

The wizard looked around as if someone else might step in, before opening his mouth and closing it again. Finally, a thought seemed to cross his mind. "You're not planning on going after him alone, are you?"

Gwen didn't bother to answer. Instead, she dialed the number stored in her phone for the DFR, a direct line to the director, and typed up an email to Curtis as it rang. Meanwhile, Norman retreated to the corner of the room, likely unsure whether he was dismissed or not. For a fleeting moment, Gwen felt bad for him. A voice came on the line. "This is Frederic Camden. Please enter the code into your cell now."

Gwen smiled. Of course, the DFR would recognize her cell number. She typed in the code her mother had taught her long ago, verification of her royal blood. 4365. Each member of the Seelie royal family had their own. They did when they were alive, anyhow. Only one code was still active now.

"Your Grace, how can I serve you?" asked Camden.

"I need you to send me everything you have on one of your agents: Marcus Smith. He goes by Fairburn these days," she said. She'd given up trying to get everyone to drop formalities, and in this case, she figured she could use her authority to get answers fast. She gave the man her private email address and a twenty-minute deadline, then ended the call.

The DFR knew better than to defy her, even if it meant turning over one of their own.

She had a response from Camden before Curtis was able to reply to her message catching him up on the facts of the case. Should she not return, he needed to know what went down.

Gwen sent the attachment to the printer so Norman would be able to work through it then began to read:

Agent Marcus Smith has been relieved of duty after complaints from his coworkers about his attitude toward the fae. Remarks about undermining the efforts of the department coupled with a series of breaks from protocol regarding investigation subjects lead senior staff to believe that he's become a liability.

"Norman, snag that off the printer and start looking for addresses and known associates of Marcus Smith," said Gwen. "He's not a fed anymore, but that doesn't mean he didn't make connections."

"Yes, Your Grace," replied Norman, jumping to follow orders.

As Gwen scrolled through the file, she noticed multiple reports of Smith abusing fae citizens while interrogating them, leveling threats against anyone who held him accountable, and speaking to his coworkers about how the fae should be eradicated for the safety of humanity.

"Holy shit," she said under her breath. She would need to discuss protocol for handling such individuals with the DFR when this was all over. "This guy never should have had this much power."

The rustling of pages as Norman scanned the document was her only response. She didn't have time to spend combing through the details of Smith's time as an agent. Every minute she spent here was one less before Chessa returned and threw a wrench in her plan. She'd hoped to find a home address for Smith, but since none of the contact information was local, she decided that her only other option was to head to Water Row and hope like hell he was at the Wallow World property. If nothing else, she might be able to locate Quincy and make tomorrow's meeting superfluous. Nothing in the file helped her think of an alternative to her harebrained scheme. She turned her attention back to Norman. "I know Chessa didn't turn in all the artifacts after the battle."

"I don't know what you—"

"Don't deny it. If you have any kind of weaponry that might give me an advantage, hand it over."

Norman set the papers he was perusing on the desk while the printer added to the stack in the tray and shuffled away into the spare room. A moment later, he returned with Chessa's wrist cuffs. "I don't know how much juice they've got left, but she couldn't part with 'em. Please don't be cross with her," he muttered.

"It's our little secret." The way Gwen saw it, she could leverage Chessa's sneakiness for forgiveness for what she was about to do. If she lived long enough to barter wrongdoings. She turned to leave, but Norman stepped in front of the door.

"I beg your pardon, Your Grace, but can't we go about this a different way? You could have the general 'ere with a word. General Steele could lead a team, go in, get Quincy, arrest Fairburn, and make 'im pay for his crimes."

Fuck. She didn't have time for this. She was hoping to hell the Wallow World lead panned out and she could end this tonight. Herself.

"No. With Kolsch in custody, Fairburn already knows he's compromised. They will be on guard, ready to pack up the whole operation if they haven't already. This needs to be a stealth mission."

"But why you? Surely you've got other people who could do this."

"Look, Norman, this is more than some drug ring. The chemical they've created, Imperium, is capable of disrupting all Seelie life. I'm the only fairy on earth who might be able to stop it. That's why I'm here. I didn't want to tell you even that much, and I'm not going to waste any more time arguing about it. Stay here and find evidence against Fairburn in this file. Chessa's going to need all the ammo she can get once we've got the bastard."

Norman's face hardened. "No."

Gwen raised her wand, but before she could act, words bubbled out of Norman's mouth. "I know I can't stop you. You're the Queen, and I'm nobody. But I'm coming with you. I'm not powerful, but I know a few spells. Maybe I could watch your back or help, or..." He trailed off.

"The element of surprise is on my side. Stay here. That's an order," snapped Gwen. Thankfully, Norman stepped aside. She really didn't want to have to blast the old guy.

Ten minutes later, Gwen's wand was tucked safely in her thigh holster and she was in the air over Boston, following the GPS on her phone. She'd spent so many hours of her life being tortured by slow, unhelpful Unseelie Wallow World employees, that she prayed to Danu she wasn't about to die there too.

41

Chessa thought Blade was faring pretty well, all things considered. Samson had tried to convince Cora to wait until he conducted his interview before seeing him, but when she insisted that she be present for the questioning, he didn't seem to have the heart to refuse. Chessa was sure poor Sammy was doing everything in his power to get through the process as fast as he could so that he could return to KPD and convince O'Toole that they needed to move on the new intel quickly.

As for Chessa, she was just glad Blade was alive. She wasn't sure how she would have been able to face her sister if it had gone another way, especially since she'd refused to give up the case to save him. She teared up just thinking about it. Now, they just needed to get Quincy back. The pit in her stomach when she thought about trusting the KPD to pull off that little miracle confirmed her next course of action: as soon as she could, she was stealing away to Sudbury.

Itching to take to the air, she decided to pay Hobbes a quick visit while she waited for Cora to resurface from Blade's hospital room.

The pixie was sucking on a milkshake and bingeing "Who's Banging the Troll" on the popular trash television network BGA.

"That sprite is the worst," said Chessa, recalling the episode about the secretary from The Covered Bridge sneaking around to hook up with the demolition expert and the sprite informant who caught it all on video.

Hobbes shot her a grin. "Hey, Boss G. I didn't take you for a reality show aficionado. Any breaks in the case?"

"Yes, actually. We've discovered a few of the key players. It seems like my roomie Honey is the scientist working on the dust, and her old student advisor was the one who recruited her and the rest. But that guy's just a cog, and the head honcho is this mortal named Marcus Smith. Goes by Fairburn these days."

"You got a name?" gasped Hobbes.

"You were looking for one?" asked Chessa. Last she'd heard, Hobbes was tracking dust distribution, not trying to uncover crime bosses. Unless he hadn't been completely honest with her about his work in Korranthia.

Hobbes turned red. Her suspicions were dead on. He did know more.

"Doyle, you never told me what led you to Korranthia in the first place," she said.

"Our team was scouring the internet for mentions of pixie dust or Nyxanthium, and we got word that someone on ArchMage was recruiting pixies to make dust, so I went undercover. Sure enough, the tip panned out."

ArchMage was all the rage with the teens of Korranthia. It allowed users to build and play their own games within a framework that many parents didn't understand. The teens were connecting with other users and barely-regulated content. In short, it was a platform Chessa wished existed back when she was getting into gaming. "Honey," said Chessa.

"Pardon?"

"Honey Centrella is a person of interest in the case. She also happens to be an avid gamer and the head scientist creating Imperium."

"Holy shit," replied Hobbes. "I need to report in."

"Report in? To Gwen? No need," said Chessa. "She's at my place, and she knows as much as I do at this point, except the gaming angle, but that's not going to change our current course of action."

"Tell me General Steele is with her," said Hobbes, a note of alarm creeping into his usually jovial countenance.

"She left him back in Avalon so he wouldn't keep her from walking into a trap tomorrow. I'm still working on how to play that one," replied Chessa. "Let me know if you have any ideas."

Hobbes was pushing back the blankets and struggling to get to his feet. "You gave her a name and left her there with no backup?"

"Whoa there, soldier. You're in no condition for field work."

Hobbes didn't break a smile. "You have no idea what's at stake here. If they get that drug into her, the Seelie Court is bloody well fucked!"

Alarms were going off in Chessa's head. "Gwen's not going anywhere. She's only here to meet their conditions for the meeting in the morning so they don't kill Quincy."

"That's bollocks! Do you really think the Seelie Queen is going to walk into a known trap?"

"It is Gwen we're talking about here." Even as she said the words, they sounded hollow. She was missing some key piece of information, and whatever it was made Hobbes think Gwen was in imminent danger. Not tomorrow. Right now.

"I know Quincy is important to you both, but even she knows that's a bad plan. If Gwendolyn Evenshine is here, she came for one purpose. The minute you gave her a name, you gave her everything she needed to fulfill that purpose. This thing is so much bigger than you know."

This time, it was Chessa's turn to snap. "Then tell me! What am I missing?"

"The drug they're making, Imperium. It isn't for recreational purposes. If it were, none of this would be registering on Avalon's radar, not while we're working to restructure Seelie governance."

"If it's not for recreation, what is it for, Hobbes?" Chessa fought to keep her voice steady. She was damn good at her job, but if the people she was trying to keep safe weren't telling her everything, how could they expect her to be effective?

Hobbes pulled the tube from the port in his wrist and the sensors from his chest, and headed for the door, dressed only in his hospital gown. He didn't seem to notice the loud, steady beeping originating from the machine next to the bed. "Mind control."

Chessa froze. "Excuse me?"

Even as she tried to process the gravity of what Hobbes said, her mind snapped the final piece into the puzzle. Quincy driving a getaway car. Dom stabbing Lance. Lance killing himself. Oh, Danu, this wasn't just some substance that lowered inhibitions, it was powerful enough to make a creature stick a gun in his mouth and pull the trigger. As the thumping of feet in the hall approached, nurses responding to the monitor alarms, she was vaguely aware that Hobbes was still speaking.

"It's for mind control. They're not in this to make a buck. They're in it for power. And you just sent them the fucking Seelie Queen."

"Sir, you need to lie back down," barked a newcomer, a sprite dressed in scrubs.

Hobbes pushed past her, but two more nurses were in the hall, blocking his path. Chessa decided to intervene before things got physical.

"I will fix this," she said. "You're in no shape to fly."

"Get out of my way," Hobbes said to the nurses. He fluttered his wings as if to attempt to outpace them but could barely get off the ground.

"Hobbes Doyle, get back into bed now. That is an order," Chessa barked. "You might be head of some task force back in Avalon, but you're injured, and every minute you fight me on this is another one wasted."

The sprite nurse was looking at Chessa with admiration while the other two stood between Hobbes and the path to the exit, both wearing expressions of uncertainty. As for Hobbes, his wings sagged. His face was so pale, he looked like he might hit the ground. "These people are danger-ous, Boss G. You can't face them alone."

The nurses stepped back to allow Chessa through. Just before she began to jog down the hall, she looked back at Hobbes. "Who said I was going alone?"

42

The trees were thick beneath her as Gwen flew alone through the night sky. She knew her plan was reckless, but she didn't have much of a choice. Asking her army to raid a Wallow World facility would make too much noise, and with the power of mind control at his fingertips, Fairburn/Smith would take her troops in no time.

Why don't you send in a stealth team? Norman's question echoed in her mind. Chessa was right, he was far more astute than he seemed. Still, she didn't trust him with the whole story. She couldn't afford to. The theory that her empathic touch might be able to disrupt the mind-control properties of Imperium was the only glimmer of hope her team had discovered against the new drug. Curtis was fully against using her in the field, which was why she'd ordered him to stay put in Avalon. He might be her friend, but he was also her general, and he was forbidden to go against her orders. As for the wizard, she was glad he had the sense to get out of her way. When she'd left C&F, he was back at his computer, hopefully digging up shit to put Fairburn away for a long time.

Hobbes had followed the breadcrumbs to Korranthia under her orders, to attempt to infiltrate the operation and gain intel. In a roundabout way, it had worked. She might not have confirmation on the way to neutralize the drug, but she had something better. A name. And a general location.

She flew above Water Row, slowing over any industrial-looking complexes that could be the fae distribution center. She considered stopping to use her phone to search out Wallow World properties, but the stretch of road Samson mentioned wasn't long, and she was already in go mode. Every delay further impeded her chances at success.

"Where are you?" she growled, pushing onward.

Marcus Fairburn and Honey Centrella. The mastermind ex-DFR agent and the mad scientist, a formidable duo who would use every weakness against her if given half a chance. That's why she couldn't give it to them. All she had to do was take the two of them out, and she would deal a major blow to those looking to utilize this dangerous new weapon. According to Hobbes' notes, pixies were being recruited from all across Korranthia through some computer game and trained in the manufacturing process of Imperium, but without Marcus and Honey, Gwen's teams would have the time they needed to break up the organization and seize the drugs for analysis. This Honey might be a prodigy, but Gwen was the Seelie Queen. She had the best fae minds in the world at her disposal. They would find a way to destroy Imperium. They had to.

First things first, she needed to take the enemy by surprise.

The dark trees below gave way to fluorescent lights illuminating a gravel lot around a complex of large warehouses. This must be it. Most of the buildings were quiet at this time of night, but the farthest one on the end had vehicles parked in the lot and a door propped open. A quick survey assured Gwen that nobody would notice a lone fairy dropping in from directly above. She flapped her wings to gain altitude as she approached, a maneuver designed to keep her out of sight of any surveillance equipment. Just when she was beginning to feel light-headed, she dropped, landing on the roof of the suspicious building with a soft thud of boots on shingles.

At first, Gwen simply crouched, listening for any alarms or other signs that she'd been spotted. When none came, she crept along the roof until she was positioned above the ajar door, held open by a brick. With a quick drop and duck, she was positioned on the ground and free to peer inside. Again, she paused to listen. Still no alarms. Gwen took a deep breath and turned sideways to squeeze through the crack. Now, she just had to locate her targets: Quincy, and the evil duo, if they were even on-site. She didn't know what Fairburn looked like, but she doubted there were a bunch of mortals hanging around a pixie dust lab. Was this even the lab? All she could see were lines of shelves filled with boxes, exactly what she would expect inside a Wallow World distribution center. The first order of business was to find a hidden vantage point to do a bit of guerilla surveillance. She was about to fly to the top of a nearby unit when she heard footsteps behind her. In a moment of panic, she pushed off the ground and flapped her wings, but she was too late. Something held her by the ankles.

"A visit from the Queen. I must be moving up in the world," said a man emerging from around the corner of one of the industrial shelving units.

Gwen twisted around to glance back at the door. A troll blocked her exit, and a pile of clay with dark, expressionless eyes flashed a sickly grin from a few feet away, his arms extended to wrap around her ankles. A golem. She hadn't seen one of them since her childhood days in Avalon before the last of them left the Seelie Court. Gwen turned back to face the man who had spoken. He was an unassuming mortal with slicked-back salt and pepper hair and an ill-fitted gray suit.

"Marcus Smith, I presume," said Gwen, deciding to keep her weaponry hidden under the sleeves of her leather jacket until the right moment. If she could conjure a mortal with hubris enough to attempt to mind-control fae creatures that dwarfed him in power, it would be a specimen of mediocrity such as this.

"And she knows my birth name. What an honor." Fairburn dropped into a mock-bow. "I can't say I'm surprised to see you, *Your Grace.* I've heard of your recklessness and had no doubt you'd show yourself here. Still, to come alone in the night like a commonplace thug? That was certainly unexpected. Not unwelcome, mind you, but unexpected. Please relieve our esteemed guest of her wand." He made a motion, and the clay around her ankles softened just enough to hoist her into the air. The troll came forward, snatched the wand from her thigh-holster, and snapped it in half before dropping it on the ground.

For a moment, Gwen's insides turned to jelly. She was sure she was about to be locked in a box again. The cold fist of claustrophobia clenched her heart. Right moment or not, she would blast anyone who tried to smithereens. But there wasn't a box. Fairburn turned his back and walked through the rows of shelves, and the golem followed, with Gwen dangling upside down by her boots. She caught sight of some cages in the back corner of the warehouse just before they made a left-hand turn into a makeshift office space, partitioned off by yet more shelving.

She didn't see evidence of drug manufacturing, but just beyond the shelves, fluorescent lights illuminated an open area easily large enough to contain a laboratory. Gwen wondered if Honey was lurking back there somewhere, working to transform pixie dust into Imperium. Both targets in the same location could come in handy, even if Gwen did have to avoid breathing in the dust. That is, if she could figure out how to lose the mud pit first. She must have wriggled because the golem clenched down harder, nearly cutting off circulation to her toes.

If I get out of this, I need to get one of these guys on staff, she thought.

Fairburn collapsed in a chair and made a motion as if graciously inviting Gwen to do the same. The golem grunted and dropped Gwen on the floor. She hit her head hard, and her wings were caked with clay, making them heavy and unusable. She would have complained, but she was too shell-shocked to think of a biting remark. Standing next to Fairburn's desk was Quincy.

A rush of excitement renewed Gwen's hopes of surviving the night. "Q! You're alive!"

Quincy didn't so much as flinch. His thick hand was wrapped tightly around something, and he stared at Fairburn with a look of expectation.

Marcus smiled. "Inject her," he said.

A troll, a golem, a mortal, and Quincy—all against one grounded fairy with little control over her magic. The odds were not in Gwen's favor. But she couldn't let them inject her with a mind-controlling drug. She was the Seelie Queen, and the power they would gain by controlling her was immeasurable. It was why they lured her here in the first place. She knew it from the moment she got Norman's call, but there was never a choice. She had to come. She palmed her wand in her right hand and raised her left, sending a pulse of energy from her borrowed wrist cuff straight at Fairburn. He crumbled, but the golem was back on her in an instant. His soft, clay body was everywhere, pinning her arms to her side as Quincy advanced with the syringe. Even if she could raise her arm, she didn't think she'd have the nerve to blast her business partner, colleague, and friend. No, she had to get her hand on him to create an empathic connection. It was her only choice of getting them both out of there alive. But her hand was as immobilized as the rest of her.

Maybe if Marcus died, the bond would be severed. If nothing else, at least he wouldn't be able to give her directives once the Imperium took her over.

The troll had gone to help his boss, a small favor.

Gwen took a deep breath. She let her mental defenses fall away and imagined the sun warming her skin, powering her very center. If she couldn't get to Quincy, maybe she could influence the golem. She leaned into the feeling of falling, and a series of sensations unlike any she'd ever experienced flowed through her.

Images of Fairburn, Xeos, Quincy, and a thousand other faces she didn't recognize, a pervasive cold followed by the rush of something warm and bubbly, like a mother's hug but more euphoric, the sounds of commands hitting like thunder, and beneath it all, a kind of connectedness as if all her cells were one and the same, millions of nerves all feeling the same thing simultaneously.

The golem might look indestructible, but he was one big homogenous center of nerves.

With the golem's body fully wrapped around hers, Gwen let loose a second energy blast from the wrist cuff.

Searing pain made her sever her connection to the creature, and his entire body exploded outward with a loud splat. As soon as she was free, Gwen flapped her wings, only to feel Quincy's fat hand wrap around her waist.

"Q, snap out of it!" she screamed, but it was too late. The needle was already buried in the muscle of her leg.

With no idea if Fairburn was alive or dead, Gwen was acutely aware that she was still in enemy territory. This drug would strip her of her own free will. She would be a puppet for whoever knew how to pull her strings. She couldn't let that happen. She couldn't let them take control of the Seelie Court through her. Without another thought, Gwen reached down and pressed her palm against Quincy's hand, which was still clenched around her waist. She opened the empathic connection.

Euphoria washed over her followed by something else, a kind of overwhelming expectant need. The image of Xander smashed into a wall, the sickly smell of urine and vomit, and pain. Unlike the many other beings she'd read, she felt a presence, an otherness tethered to Quincy's brain. Fairburn. She focused on the connection and enveloped it in her magic. As she gave a mighty tug, she sent her own command:

Kill me.

Quincy had completed the final task sent by Fairburn. He had injected the Queen with Imperium. Without a clear follow-up, his brain was murky, as if he were lost in a mire of half-thoughts and incomplete ideas. He was vaguely aware that he was still holding Gwen, and the place where she pressed her hand to his was warmer than the small point of contact warranted. He tried to focus on her, but his vision was cloudy. That's when he heard her voice, clear as if she were sitting on his shoulder. Kill me.

It was his new order, and she his new master. For a moment, he hesitated and looked over to the desk where he'd seen Fairburn go down. Neither his original master nor the troll bodyguard were anywhere to be seen.

The command echoed in his skull.

Kill me, now.

This time, there was no choice to be made. It was a biological imperative that he follow orders. He raised the fairy into the air, and with tears streaming down his face, he smashed her into the cold, cement floor.

Someone screamed. Quincy felt his grip loosen, his fist forced apart by a thousand spider webs. The strings of energy were all over him, pulling him away from the mangled fairy, even as blood dripped from his fingers. He stumbled backward as darkness crept from his periphery inward, and the brain fog took him.

44

When Chessa got back to C&F, everything Hobbes said was confirmed. The place was deserted. On the desk was a crumpled piece of paper with nothing but an address for the Wallow World distribution center scrawled in Norman's shaky hand. By the look of it, he must have been in a hurry. She wondered how things played out after she'd left for the hospital. If she knew her best friend, Gwen would have steamrolled poor Norman, and she certainly wouldn't have let him tag along. That meant he must have followed her into danger. How very like them both.

Chessa cussed under her breath, fighting the bile rising in her throat, snatched the paper, and flew out the door. She was already in the hallway when her cell phone vibrated in her pocket with a text from Laural. Her ride was here.

She made her way up the emergency stairwell to the rooftop, where Laural was sitting astride Henrietta, the young dragon from Avalon. Henrietta whined and clicked in excitement as she approached. It had only been a few weeks, but the dragon had grown at least a foot since she last saw her; she was now twice the size she'd been when they first met, but she still acted like a hatchling. The coven of healer witches who'd been looking after her didn't help matters. They spoiled her rotten.

"Whoa, baby," cooed Laural, and the dragon dropped into a low crouch, twitching her tail back and forth like an oversized dog, her black scales gleaming in the moonlight.

Chessa put her hand on Henrietta's snout. "How did you get here so fast?" she asked Laural.

"I was with the coven when you called," Laural explained. "Allison has everyone standing by in case we need support when this is over."

"I very much hope we don't," Chessa replied, but still, she was thankful to have the support of such a talented group of healers.

She flew up to sit at the base of Henrietta's neck in front of Laural, and they took off into the night. It didn't take the dragon long to cover the distance to Sudbury. The air whipped Chessa's hair and clothes as she scanned the trees and roads below. As they neared the address Norman left, a smattering of large warehouses became visible in the middle of a gravel parking lot. A chain link fence topped with barbed wire surrounded the perimeter, and lights mounted on poles illuminated the surrounding area. Swarms of fae moved in and out of the doors, some diving into vehicles, some wielding weapons as they flooded in. Something was going down inside.

That's when Chessa saw him: Norman running for the front gate, cradling something in his arms, but Chessa couldn't make out details from this distance.

"Henrietta, down!" she ordered. The dragon's dark wings stretched outward, allowing them to glide to the ground.

Henrietta landed between the wizard and the gate, and Chessa darted through the air to meet him. Blood soaked through Norman's shirt and coated the tips of his beard, and his eyes were wild and puffy. When he saw Chessa, a great sob wracked his body. He stumbled to his knees and opened his arms enough to reveal a small, mangled body.

A mop of dark hair, matted with blood, covered much of her face, but there was no mistaking the broken form of Gwendolyn Evenshine.

"I tried to stop 'er, I did. She wouldn't listen. It were Quincy. He smashed 'er like she was a rag doll."

Laural clambered down from the dragon and ran to see to Gwen, but Chessa could tell from one look that it would take more than Laural and her entire coven to revive the Seelie Queen. Her best friend, her Gwennie, was dead. Instead of grief or even anger, Chessa felt a cold nothing, an abyss inside that expanded to encompass everything around her.

She looked toward the cluster of buildings. None of the fae swarming the place paid them any mind. She knew she was still missing a major piece of the puzzle. Despite being a hothead, Gwen wasn't an idiot. She came here alone for a reason, and she died for it. Chessa could only hope Gwen had accomplished whatever it was she believed that she was solely capable of doing. And she hoped it was worth it.

Chessa needed to make sure Gwen's death counted for something. She zipped back to Henrietta, who was standing stock-still, violet eyes fixed ahead. Chessa didn't need to speak a word. As soon as she touched down on the dragon's back, Henrietta flapped her great wings and rose into the air. This wasn't the first time they flew together into battle united in heart.

"Little miss, please," cried Norman, but Chessa barely registered his voice.

Laural didn't say a word—if anyone could understand what Chessa was about to do, it was the witch who had once been possessed by a vengeance demon. Instead, she stood over Gwen and bore witness.

Once in the air, Chessa turned the dragon away from Gwen, Norman, and Laural. She emptied her mind of all thoughts of those she loved and the life she had waiting for her. She didn't scream. She didn't cry. She didn't mourn. A great stillness settled over her as she flew the dragon over the warehouse, and when they were close to the roofline, Chessa gave the command. Flames erupted from the dragon, bathing the night in red-hot death.

45

When he opened his eyes, the darkness gave way to smoke. The air was thick with it. No commands echoed in his skull, and he wasn't sure what had transpired. Quincy climbed to his hands and knees before vomiting all over the floor, his stomach spasming and head throbbing. When he tried to pull air into his lungs, he coughed violently. Images flashed through his brain: Lumpy exploding, Gwen's mangled body.

He struggled to make sense of it all. He remembered being woken in his cage by a troll he didn't know injecting Imperium into his thigh without warning. He remembered fighting against Fairburn's commands and the agonizing pain that resulted. And he remembered Gwen's voice in his skull, but her words were garbled. Three facts clicked into place in quick succession. The first, he had killed the Seelie Queen. The second, the building around him was ablaze. And the third, Xander was standing next to him screaming.

"Get up! Get up now!"

"Wha—" Quincy tried to speak, but the words wouldn't form.

"Now, Quincy! I know a way out, but you've got to follow me right now!" Xander was on the verge of full-blown panic.

Quincy crawled toward a dark spot on the cement floor and reached out to touch the puddle of thick blood. "Gwen?" he whispered. There was no body. Maybe the images in his head were lying to him. He didn't kill her. She was ok. She probably wasn't even here. In fact, that probably wasn't even blood.

"Now, Quincy!"

Xander darted off beneath the smoke, and as Quincy climbed to his feet. He had to stoop to make out the small form of the pixie, a bag strapped to his back, breaking to the right. Not knowing what else to do, he followed clumsily, tripping and coughing, until he reached a doorway. The pixie must have already blown through it.

"Don't stop," Xander screamed from somewhere outside. "We've got to get the hell out of here!"

The moon was high in the sky, and the air felt raw in Quincy's scorched throat. As he tried to get his thoughts in order, a dark shape swooped from overhead. A stream of fire burst from the shape, illuminating a dragon and blanketing more of the warehouse in flame.

Xander doubled back. "You just killed the fucking queen. Get your ass moving, or that dragon's going to roast you alive!" The words came out in a torrent, and the young, flightless pixie grabbed Quincy's hand and pulled hard.

The Queen. Gwen. Those flashes of memory were true. An anguished scream surrounded him before he realized it was coming from within. The dragon must have heard it too. It was heading straight for him.

Henrietta looked more like a beast of war than the baby Chessa had saved from Avalon. Chessa was likely riding on her back at this moment, on a warpath to avenge the fallen queen. Xander was right, he had to get the hell out of there. Friend or not, Chessa would kill him for what he had done.

For the first time in his adult life, Quincy felt tears pool in his eyes. Maybe it was just the smoke. He ducked his head and ran across the gravel parking lot toward the fence. By the time he reached it, Xander had already cut a hole through the chain link. Quincy ducked through and disappeared into the night.

46

I thought you hated me. Why are you helping me?" Quincy's voice came out as a soft growl as he sat propped himself up against a tree not far from the conflagration. The woods seemed to glow, and the blaring sound of sirens floated on the smoke-filled air.

Xander stared straight ahead. "You were right. He doesn't give a shit about me."

Quincy didn't say anything. He didn't have it in him to cast judgment or gloat. Instead, he nodded. "You wanted me dead."

The pixie's voice cracked as he turned to look Quincy in the eye. "I never meant for any of this to happen. I thought it would be different."

Quincy's body felt like it had been run over by Samson's Humvee, he was covered in soot, blood, and vomit, and the kid who'd lured him into the situation in the first place was telling him what? That he thought joining a drug ring intent on world domination and luring innocent fae in order to trap the Seelie Queen was going to turn out sunshine and rainbows? "You never meant for what? For a cult to control the fae? For the downfall of the Seelie Court? For the death of the Queen?"

"Hey, man, you did that last bit yourself."

"I was under mind control. What's your excuse?" he retorted. But the truth was that the knowledge that he wasn't in control of his actions did little to ease the anguish inside. He didn't remember anything beyond the few flashes, but the image of her pulverized little body tore him apart.

215

Despite his bravado, he retched again, but nothing came up. "All I wanted was to help you," he said in barely more than a whisper.

"And all I wanted was a family," said Xander, dropping his book bag to the ground and slumping against the other side of the tree.

"You had one. You had a brother who loved you, who died trying to protect you." Quincy immediately regretted his words.

The pixie buried his face in his hands. His shoulders shook, and Quincy scooted close enough to put a hand on his back. He let Xander cry for a few minutes before speaking again. "All we can do is learn and move forward," he said at last.

Xander sniffed, swallowed, and then raised his head. "I looked up to Drake. Once Mom and Pa died, he just seemed to have the coolest life, you know? He lived with his friends and did whatever the hell he wanted. But he didn't want that for me. I thought he was keeping it all for himself. He made me stay at home and go to school while he lived this exciting life of adventure. While I was alone, he had it all. He had a family, and it didn't include me. That's what I thought, anyhow."

Quincy sighed. He understood the weight of loneliness better than most. "Then what happened?"

"I didn't know about Fairburn at first. It was Honey who said she saw something special in me, but Drake didn't want me involved in the business. When he found out she took me to Fairburn behind his back, he said he was done with it all. He was going to move out of the house and come home with me. He said we were going to start over."

"So Fairburn popped him."

"He couldn't risk Drake exposing him. He said Drake was jealous of my ambition, and he offered to be a sort of father to me in the way that Drake wouldn't. He made me believe that I was special, and Drake was a threat to our family." He began to cry again. "I'm so stupid."

Quincy rubbed the pixie's back, feeling like shit for acting superior when he'd done much worse than the pixie. "No, you're not. You're a kid who was grieving the loss of his parents. You were lonely, and that bastard manipulated you."

"He murdered my brother, and I was his little bitch."

Quincy didn't know what to say, so he let Xander sit in his feelings. Soon, they would need to get moving if they didn't want the KPD to find them, but for now, the authorities were occupied with the inferno. They had time. Eventually, the pixie took a shuddering breath and wiped a sleeve across his face. He reached over to rifle through his bag and pulled something out.

"Here. I swiped this from Fairburn's desk," he said, handing over a small knife that didn't seem so small in his pixie hands.

A wave of emotion swept over Quincy when he recognized the pocket knife his mother had given him so long ago. He didn't trust his voice to offer thanks. Instead, he took the knife and gave a pointed nod before changing the subject.

"Was it Honey who aimed you at C&F?" As much as he wanted to put miles between himself and the warehouse, he needed to get as much information as he could while Xander was in a generous mood.

"No. Fairburn. He knew you were tight with the Queen. He made it sound like this was my chance to prove myself worthy of being his son." This time, his voice was colder, filled with the resentment of someone who had just figured out how badly he got played. Good. If they were going to survive life on the run, he would need that anger.

Quincy fought through another wave of vertigo as he pushed up from the ground and used a tree to steady himself. "We ain't so different. He got in your head better than any drug," he said.

"And now I've got nothing." Xander took the hand Quincy offered, his small grip wrapped around Q's finger, to climb to his feet, and they both looked back to where lights flickered in the trees from the emergency vehicle lights and dancing flames. Then, they turned and walked deeper into the woods, away from the life they used to know.

"You and me both, kid."

47

Gwen was back on the tor of Avalon, walking soundlessly through the grass. The sun kissed her face and soaked the field in golden radiance. Everything here felt somehow more real, from the gentle breeze caressing her skin to the heady scent of grass, flowers, and earth. Even the soft trilling of birds in the distance made her feel more alive than ever before. She filled her lungs with the sweet, crisp air. Her mind was clear—no muddled thoughts and whispers of commands from an unseen would-be tyrant, no smoke, no heat, no anger. She'd been here before, in this realm between life and death. And just like before, Chessa stood squinting in the sunlight. Only this time, blood-red tears streaked her face, and she clutched the hand of another. Gwen ran across the field to them. She immediately recognized Laural, the healer-witch with whom Gwen had a turbulent past. She suspected that Laural still blamed her for the death of her husband Corrin at the hands of the serial killer who'd taken everything from so many. If so, there was no sign of resentment on Laural's face now, only awe. The witch was bathed in soft blue light.

"Chessa. Laural. How are you here?" asked Gwen, struggling to make sense of everything around her. Chessa merely stared into the empty space before her, her eyes unfocused. The purple bruise around her eye had faded to a sickly yellow that complimented the washed-out green streak in her tangled hair.

It was Laural who spoke. "Norman. He told me about his research, about the magic of Morgan le Fay and how we each hold a piece of it."

"Chessa mentioned something about that to me, but it doesn't make any sense." Gwen spoke to Laural, but her eyes were locked onto Chessa, searching her face for answers to questions she hadn't yet formulated. There was no sign that her best friend was even listening.

Laural smiled serenely as if everything was fine.

"There are three aspects. Healing, which lives in me. Loyalty, an aspect of love that has been helping you. And something else, something that overtook my dear cousin the moment she saw your lifeless body." A flash of sadness touched Laural's eyes, but it passed quickly.

"I'm dead?"

The healer nodded but remained quiet. The knowledge of her own death was more comforting than upsetting—until an unthinkable idea caused fear to creep into her heart. "Is Chessa dead too?" That would explain the blood.

"Not yet. What you see is a physical manifestation of her internal state, only visible, I suspect, in this place you've created. But if we don't help her, she will be."

Gwen didn't understand, but looking at the shell of Chessa caused the old feelings to bubble inside of her. Shame. Terror. Anger. Instead of facing them, she did what she always did and stuffed them back down. "If I'm dead, then how can I help her? How is any of this happening?"

Some unidentifiable emotion flashed over Laural's face but quickly vanished. When she spoke, her voice was measured and calm. "The law of conservation of magic. The power flowing through you is ancient, from far before even Morgan's time." She motioned with her hand to indicate the field around them. "This place lives inside of you. It is your home, free of all the turbulence and grief that plagued your life, and it's where you go as you slip away from the mortal coil."

"How do you know all this?" asked Gwen.

"Some, I learned from Norman, but much of it, I believe, is from the gift Chessa left in me. I found you here with the healing power of Morgan le Fay. Like the love which binds you to your people, my healing transcends life and death, and with it, I brought the three aspects of her power together as they were always meant to be. Powers gifted not by Chessa or even Morgan, but by the goddess of death herself."

None of this made a damn bit of sense, and Gwen was losing patience. She desperately wanted Chessa to say something, anything, but the pixie stood mute. "Ok, Yoda, if you know so much, tell me what's wrong with Chess."

When Laural turned to look at Chessa, her eyes filled with tears. "Tonight, my dear cousin became the destroyer, the polar opposite of her true nature, and she will need us more than ever to help her come to terms with what she has wrought."

Even in this divine, warm place, a chill sunk deep into Gwen's bones. Chessa was the one who brought people together, the one who saw the good in others even when they didn't see it in themselves. The destroyer? What in the name of Danu was Laural talking about? "I'm dead, Laural. I don't see how I can possibly help her."

"Norman discovered a ritual to recombine our powers. He's setting it up now, even as we speak."

"This ritual will pull the powers from us and do what with them? Resurrect me? Heal Chessa? Bring back Morgan?"

Laural shook her head. "We don't know. It might do any one of those things, all of them, or none of them. But we have to try."

Chessa didn't look to be in any condition to perform any rituals. Her head turned slowly toward Gwen, and as her eyes finally seemed to focus, a fresh wave of bloody tears fell.

"How did this happen?" asked Gwen, fighting back the urge to cry. "How did it happen to any of us?"

"When Arthur was on his deathbed, Morgan prayed for the power to heal him. He was supposed to unite the world, and if he died, so did her hopes that fae and mortals would live in harmony."

"Harmony? She founded the Unseelie Court, and you think she wanted to live in harmony?"

"We only know what we were taught and what Norman has been able to dig out of dusty old books. You of all people should be able to understand that the situation isn't always as clear as we are led to believe," replied Laural, anger flashing in her eyes.

She was right. Gwen had already made herself unlearn many "facts" she'd been brought up to believe before she ever took the throne. "Ok, fine. I'll play along. Morgan le Fay wasn't just a powerful fairy. Her powers came from Danu. Is this going somewhere?"

"Though she is patron to the fae, Danu is not the only deity in the realms. Someone answered Morgan's prayer that night. At least, that's what the texts seem to imply. Morgan became a vessel of power that far surpassed any known by the fae. Powers that could be transferred. When

Chessa brought you back, she did so out of love. Into you, she poured Morgan's loyalty, born of love, a power you need to bring all fae together. And when she resurrected me, she did so with intention, accessing the healing powers granted to Morgan."

"And this is what she kept for herself?" asked Gwen, motioning to the mute pixie silently crying tears of blood. Gone was her mischievous friend who was quick with a grin or a saucy joke. Finally, Gwen understood Laural's profound sense of sadness hiding just beyond the calm. Her heart shattered.

"The Morgan of legend, the vengeful one used to scare young Seelie children, wasn't born that way. She became so because she was left with nothing but rage. For now, the same is true of our Chessa," replied Laural, taking Gwen's hand with her free one. "That's why you need to come back to us, so we can figure out how to save her from the power that is eating her alive."

"Gwennie?" said Chessa. Her voice sounded like shards of glass, frail yet sharp. "Is that you?"

Gwen's heart fell into her stomach. Chessa was fucked up. "Yes, I'm here, Chess."

"Take her hand to complete the circle," said Laural. "Norman is ready."

Gwen did as instructed, and the three of them stood for what felt simultaneously like a moment and a lifetime, forming a sacred circle on the tor of Avalon.

Blue light flowed from Laural's palms into both Gwen and Chessa. Gwen looked down and realized that golden sunlight was pouring from her own hands, flowing and dancing with the blue. From Chessa, red energy sparked and subsided like flames in a chaotic dance.

A moment later, Gwen felt a pulling in the very center of her being that grew until it felt like her soul was being ripped free. She screamed as golden light burst through, into the center of the circle, where it merged with energy emanating from both the other women. It all combined into a deep, sparkling purple light that built and built until it exploded outward, and everything went black.

4 8

Gwen woke up in a small room with off-white walls. Samson was crushing a nearby couch, sleeping in the sitting position, and Curtis was standing on the window sill, peering out, ever vigilant. If the adjustable bed with a handrail didn't tell her she was in the hospital, the smell of rubbing alcohol and the beeping of a heart monitor did. She groaned, not with pain, but with exhaustion. She didn't have so much as a headache.

Samson startled awake at the sound. "Thank Danu," he breathed, his voice touched with awe.

"Sammy?"

"That healer is some witch. When I found you, your own mother would've struggled to ID you." His eyes widened at his own words. "Oh, sorry kid," he muttered.

"It's okay, Sammy. I get the point." Her mother had been killed by her brother during the uprising, but with everything they'd all been through, she wasn't about to fault Samson for misspeaking.

He babbled on, his tone excited. "Laural had you and Chia by the wrists. Norman wouldn't let anyone touch you. He tied up anyone who tried with those wizard threads of his." Samson's feathers puffed in a way Gwen knew meant that there was more to the story he wasn't willing to share. She deduced that he and Norman had come to blows and he'd ended up dangling. Under normal circumstances, the mental image would have given her a good chuckle, but she was still trying to remember what had happened. Her mind was calm but disorganized, memories of what transpired blending and blurring together.

"But then you took a breath. There you were, bloody and broken, and you started to breathe." Samson stopped speaking abruptly, and Gwen realized he was openly crying. Big tears ran down the feathers of his face. "Don't ever do that to me again, do you hear me!"

Gwen opened her mouth to comfort him, but then she remembered how Laural brought her back from the dead. "Chessa!" she said, pushing herself into the sitting position.

"I'm doing everything I can for her," replied Samson. "Maybe now that you're awake, you can step in. She slaughtered everyone in that warehouse, Gwen."

"No." Gwen spoke the word low and quiet, but she knew he was telling the truth. Chessa, her Chessa, had killed dozens, maybe hundreds. "What about Quincy?"

Samson dropped his head and gave it a sad shake. "No sign of him."

She remembered the half-ogre wrapping his fist around her, raising her in the air, and then…It didn't matter. He was only following orders, her orders. He probably didn't know that he was protecting all fae-kind. If he was alive, she would have to find him. Right now, Chessa needed her more.

"Where did they take Chess?"

Samson cleared his throat and did a little shake, his feathers fluffing up before falling into place as he slipped back into the role of sergeant detective. "She's at Bathory. She's not aces, if you know what I mean. She was arrested just after you were brought here. Eighteen fae died in the fire and another twelve are unaccounted for."

Gwen struggled to stand but couldn't find the energy. She collapsed back onto the pillow. Curtis zipped over to stand on the mattress by her side. "I convinced O'Toole to allow Laural to take Henrietta back to wherever Chessa's been stashing her, but that was the extent of his generosity. I tried to get him to let me take Chessa to Avalon. He was quick to remind me that even the general for the Seelie army doesn't have the power to meddle in KPD business."

"We've got to get her out of there." Gwen's voice came out as a growl. She reached down for her wand but came up empty.

"I've already got a dryad crafting you a new wand from the grove in Avalon," said Curtis. He picked up a folder from the nightstand. "And I agree. We need to help Chessa. She's not doing well, and we can't do anything for her from the outside. I've got Avalon's best lawyers on the case, but without your backing, O'Toole is shutting us out at every turn."

"Get me up. Now."

Captain O'Toole wouldn't stand in the way of the Seelie Queen, even if she was dressed haphazardly in the pair of leggings and oversized Gojira shirt Curtis snagged from her dresser at the Palace of Avalon in his haste to get to the hospital. Her Docs still smelled like smoke.

Curtis tossed the folder to Samson and then helped Gwen out of bed. "I already had the pardon papers drawn up. They need your signature. But, Gwen, you have to understand, you can't just let her go free. She's in no shape to walk the streets. I think you should go see her before you sign."

Once she was dressed, Gwen tucked the papers under her arm. Curtis stuck his head out into the hallway and said something to one of the guards standing watch. Moments later, a pair of nurses brought in a lightweight, padded chair sized for the two fairies to sit side-by-side.

"What's this?" asked Gwen.

"I had it made for you while you were out," said Curtis. "I knew nothing would keep you from Chessa once you awoke, so I figured it was better to plan safe travel. You don't have the energy to make the flight, and I know better than to tell you to wait. I'll sit with you and cast a cloaking glamour while they fly us to Bathory."

Gwen felt some kind of warm emotion build in her chest. Curtis was more than merely her general. He was her friend, and she was more thankful for him than she knew how to express. She sat in the chair next to him and let the guards hoist them into the air and out the window.

As soon as the first prison guard caught sight of her, everyone at Bathory was accommodating.

"Your Grace, Captain O'Toole requested that he be notified of your arrival so he could escort you in to see the prisoner," said the nymph at the reception desk. He looked everywhere but directly at Gwen and fidgeted.

"Captain O'Toole has no authority over me. I want to see Chessa Moon. Now."

"Yes, Your Grace. Right away." The nymph buzzed her in while picking up the phone. He quickly dialed a number, muttered something, and slammed it back down. The thick green door swung open and a sprite emerged to walk Gwen down to an empty interrogation room.

"Ms. Moon will be brought in shortly. Can I offer you a cup of coffee?" asked the sprite with a cheerful smile, her red lipstick a striking contrast to her white hair and pale complexion.

"Get Chessa," growled Gwen, sending the sprite skittering off down the hall.

Five minutes later, Gwen was about to go royal on their asses when the door opened, and O'Toole stepped in. He immediately dropped into a low bow. "I apologize for the delay, Your Grace, but I wanted to be here for this meeting. Seeing Ms. Moon might be a bit of a shock."

"Stop fucking with me, Tool," snapped Gwen, slipping into her old ways. Something about the captain brought out the worst in her. "Where is my best friend?"

The blood drained from O'Toole's cheeks, but he was saved from answering by the door creaking open again. This time, it was the sprite accompanied by an ogre carrying a box. Gwen felt panic rising in her chest and her breath quickened. It was the same kind of plexiglass prison that haunted her flashbacks. She fought back the unbidden memories of the serial killer who'd taken so much from her and set off a chain of events the fae world was still struggling through. Somehow, it felt like it just happened while also seeming like a lifetime ago. It had been Chessa who saved her ass. Gwen's blood turned to red-hot rage. Screw decorum. "Get her out of there now!"

With O'Toole sitting to her right, the ogre set the box on the table before them and the sprite closed and locked the door. The ogre unsnapped the latches keeping the top of the plexiglass box in place and lifted it straight up. In the center of the table sat a pixie. Her legs were folded beneath her, and her head was dropped as if she were in deep meditation. The green streak in her black hair was brassy and faded, and it seemed like a comb hadn't come near her head in days.

Gwen's voice caught in her throat. "Chess?"

The pixie raised her head. Aside from the missing bloody tear tracks and remnants of a black eye, her face was exactly as it had been in Gwen's vision, eyes staring at nothing. Gwen moved forward, intending to wrap her friend in a hug, but O'Toole put his hand out, blocking her path.

"Your Grace, she's dangerous," he said.

"That's fucking ridiculous. She's Chessa Moon! You've worked with her for years. She's my best friend and the best fucking person I know," said Gwen, fluttering her wings to give her enough loft to get over his hand. She sunk down to where Chessa sat and wrapped her arms around her friend. The sprite scaled the table and stood uncomfortably close, her red lips pursed tight, while the ogre held the top of the box up, ready to snap it down at a moment's notice as if Chessa were an unpredictable beast poised to rip out all their throats. His breath made the whole room smell like salt and vinegar chips.

"I'm getting you out of here," murmured Gwen.

"Out," said Chessa, her voice flat.

"Before you do that, Your Grace, you need to see something," said O'Toole. He pulled a file out of his briefcase and set it on the table.

Gwen didn't let go. "I don't need to see anything. We're going home."

"Please." O'Toole was nearly begging. "Look at the photos of her cell. She needs help."

"Out," echoed Chessa.

None of this made any sense to Gwen. Chessa might have acted in the moment, doing horrible things for the sake of Korranthia, but she was still *Chessa*. She made a difficult call that would haunt her forever, but that didn't change her heart. Gwen finally released her friend and walked over to the photo O'Toole pulled out of the file. They depicted a standard-looking prison cell with painted cinder block walls. On those walls, from top to bottom, in some kind of reddish-brown ink, was writing. It was a list of names.

Abigail Marquis
Dominik Perez
Honey Centrella
Lance Gruber
Xander Aster
Jack Pennington
Madam Glitz
Glenn Darcie
Hobbes Doyle
Miranda Xeos
Quincy McAllen
Gwendolyn Evenshine
Marcus Fairburn

Some of the names were barely legible because they were smeared. It was as if Chessa had taken her pinky and struck through them.

"Chessa, what is this?" asked Gwen, knowing full well she wouldn't get an answer.

"It's blood," replied O'Toole. She cut her hand open to do this and won't tell anyone why. The prison walls are flecked with lead, so using her fingers to write this must have been excruciating. She's highly disturbed, Your Grace. Now do you see why you can't just take her home?"

Gwen walked back to Chessa, and both the sprite and the ogre tensed.

"They're all names of people involved in the case, right Chess?" She dropped to her knees and took Chessa's face in her hands. She looked deep into her friend's eyes. Chessa's face softened, and Gwen saw a spark of the pixie she knew.

"Gwennie? I didn't mean to." Chessa gave a dry sob, and Gwen pulled her close.

"It's going to be ok."

For a moment, they simply embraced. Gwen tried not to access her magic, but she was too exhausted to keep the barrier down. The sensations she got from Chessa were unlike anything she'd experienced before. Instead of a series of images, smells, sounds, and emotions, all she sensed was emptiness, like a dark, silent pit with no end. Gwen's heart raced, and she felt like she'd never be warm again. Chessa wedged her palms between them and shoved, sending Gwen careening backward across the table. She landed uncomfortably close to the edge. She tried to flit her wings, but they were frozen stiff, and her entire body was shivering. O'Toole yelled something, and the sprite leapt into action, grabbing Chessa from behind and wrestling her arms behind her.

Chessa struggled against restraints the sprite snapped onto her wrists and lurched toward Gwen only to be pulled back. "It will never be ok," she said. "Not until every last one of those motherfuckers pays for what they did. For what they made me do."

Gwen finally got her wits about her and was able to climb to her feet as Chessa thrashed and raved. She didn't dare speak her racing thoughts out loud because they would only give O'Toole ammunition. She glanced back at the photograph of the prison cell to confirm what she already knew— the names that were smeared through belonged to fae who were either already dead or were inside the warehouse when Chessa had set it on fire. This wasn't a list of people involved in the case. It was Chessa's hit list. She planned to hunt down the rest, including Gwen. O'Toole was right, this was not the pixie that Gwen knew and loved. Suddenly, she felt like she was the one trapped in the box, like the walls were closing in around her. She had to get out of the room or she'd burst into tears in front of everyone. In the hall, she nearly ran into Curtis. She half expected an "I told you so," but instead, he wrapped her in a tight hug as she broke down.

Later that night, Gwen sat in the living room of Laural's bungalow cottage with Curtis, Samson, and Norman while Laural passed around cups of tea and Norman gave a report on everything he'd learned about the properties of magical transference. The stack of books he'd retrieved during their trip to the Academy was piled on the coffee table.

"It's not her, you understand," he said. "When she left the healer and the heart in the two of you, she was left with only the raw rage of Morgan le Fay for 'erself. It must have been lurking under the surface ever since."

"She had been more on edge," said Laural. "But I thought it was the case getting to her."

"Me too. It weren't though. It was the magic, and only someone as generous of spirit and heart could have held it at bay for so long. It was only when 'er own emotions got too much to bear that it fully took over."

Guilt felt like a yoke on Gwen's shoulders. When she'd gone in all half-cocked, she'd been sure she was the only one who could stop Fairburn, and when she'd ordered Quincy to kill her, she thought she was saving all fae. In doing so, she'd sacrificed the only one who truly mattered to her. "You mean when she saw me pulverized?"

"By Quincy, no less. It broke 'er heart and enraged her in a way she'd probably never felt before. She's still in there, somewhere though. We've just got to figure out how to bring 'er back to us."

"Or cleanse her of the cursed magic," mused Laural.

"Perhaps," Norman replied. "But I fear that's beyond even your capabilities, Miss Laural."

"I felt her when we were all together in the in-between," said Laural. "It's not just the darkness of Morgan's magic. It's like she's crossed over or morphed or something, almost like when Gailan took over my body." She gave a shiver. If Chessa were here, she would have sat next to her, given her a comforting squeeze or some shit, but Gwen wasn't Chessa. Instead, she scowled.

Curtis took Gwen's hand as he spoke. "As horrific as her actions were, she did what was necessary to protect the fae world from Imperium. If the drug got out, the entire Seelie Court would fall."

"Sammy, has there been any progress on the case?" asked Gwen, eager to change the subject. She snatched her hand back.

"We were able to get the jump on Abigail Marquis. Honey must have been tipped off. She and Darcie are on the lam, but we've got the best dicks at the KPD hunting them down. Dominik turned himself in, and the DA is working up a plea deal in case Fairburn surfaces."

"And Glitz? She was on Chessa's list too."

"She's a tough nut to crack. We got nothing on her unless someone implicates her down the line. Perez claims he never heard her name before. As far as we know, Glitz has done nothing but get cozy with known members of a crime ring."

"You think Fairburn escaped?" asked Norman. He'd had his head so buried in the books, he wasn't caught up.

"We haven't IDed his body yet, so it's possible. Of the names on the list, we've only IDed Xeos."

Gwen flinched. Miranda Xeos had been found burned alive in one of the cells at the distribution center. The other was empty. "Still nothing on Q?" she asked.

Samson shook his head. "We got a couple of John Does in the fridge, but none the size of Quincy. We found a cut in the fence that might have been used by some of the henchmen escaping the fire. Maybe he made it out."

Norman shook his head, and when he spoke, his voice shook with emotion. "I left 'im bound with wizard thread. I don't see how he could have gotten free in time. I want to talk to little miss. I want to tell her that I'm as much to blame as she is."

The wizard's head dropped, and Laural touched his shoulder. "You did what you had to do to save the Seelie Queen. Norman, you're a hero."

He looked at Gwen, and she met his gaze. "I don't feel like no bloody hero."

Gwen realized that everyone in the room was now looking at her. She'd been so hard on Norman, it was no wonder he didn't see himself as anything but the Unseelie spy who'd helped bring down the Seelie Court. A lump formed in her throat when she wondered what perfect words Chessa would have for the wizard. "You have atoned for your part in the insurrection," she said. "I will never doubt your loyalty again."

It might not have been perfect, but it did the trick. Norman's shoulders relaxed and he offered up a weak smile.

"What are we going to do about Chessa?" asked Laural. She addressed the room, but she was looking expectantly at Gwen. "We can't leave her at Bathory."

"I agree. I'm planning to take her back to Avalon with me," said Gwen. Her voice sounded more confident than she felt. "The paperwork is being processed, and we will leave in the morning."

"I spoke with Cora before she and Blade left this morning, and I promised her that I would go with you to watch over her. It was the only way I could convince them to leave. They've both been through a lot and need some time to heal."

Gwen opened her mouth to protest, but Laural cut her off.

"I know I'm not strong enough to cure what ails my cousin, but I hold a piece of the power that has corrupted her, and I want to be with her. To help in any way I can."

The desperation in her voice shut down all Gwen's arguments. She nodded. In truth, she had no idea how to begin to help Chessa on her own and was glad for the support. "What about the dragon?"

"My coven will care for Henrietta."

"Can we trust them?" asked Gwen. She still struggled with relying on others, even though she was rapidly having to get used to it as queen.

"They healed the fae who survived the fire. They even healed Hobbes. At this point, they're as much a part of our deranged little family as I am," said Laural.

A wave of gratitude for the group of healer witches washed over Gwen. She was the reason Hobbes was stabbed, and she hadn't even thought to ask about him. Knowing he'd been healed helped assuage her guilt.

Curtis shifted on the couch next to her. "I have something I need to discuss with you about Avalon," he said. "Can we go somewhere private?"

"After everything we've been through, there's nothing you can't say in this room," Gwen replied, apprehension prickling her skin. Curtis wasn't one for dramatics, so whatever he was about to say must be important.

Curtis' muddy green eyes flashed in anger, but he didn't insist. "Fine. There's been a breach."

He was just telling her now? They'd been sitting around for over an hour! "What kind of breach?" she asked, working to keep her voice even.

"The grove. The morning after the… incident… while I was at the hospital waiting for you to awaken, our guards were taken by surprise. Marni sent a report. A small faction of Unseelie, all fairies, flew into the grove and dispatched our guards. It seems like they conducted some kind of ritual. They left a dead fairy and vanished."

"They didn't take anything?" Gwen knew the answer before she asked the question. During the Battle of Avalon, the Unseelie had been attempting to open the gateway to Faerie with some ritual involving the spilling of royal blood. It's why they'd massacred her family and how some legendary creatures from Faerie had slipped into the mortal realm. Gwen thought her heart might burst through her chest as she processed the information. There was no Seelie royal blood left to spill except her own and one other—one the world wasn't supposed to know existed.

She couldn't risk anyone learning that Gracie, the true Seelie Queen, had survived, not even those gathered around her. Not even Curtis. The girl needed to be protected until she was old enough to take the throne. It was why Gwen worked so hard to fix the Seelie way of life, so that when the time came, Gracie could be crowned Queen of a balanced, fair, and thriving fae society. As for Gwen, once she handed over the throne, she would disappear and finally figure out what she wanted from life free of expectations and vows of vengeance. All she wanted was a chance to find herself.

"Did you identify the dead?" asked Gwen, her mouth dry.

"Yes. It was Talia Eviscera."

Gwen felt guilty for the relief that washed over her. The Unseelie Queen was dead, but sweet baby Gracie was still alive.

"And King Oberon?"

"Our agents haven't picked up any intel regarding his whereabouts, so we must assume that he's still in play," replied Curtis.

Gwen nodded, unsure what this all meant for Avalon. "Am I to also assume that Moliana Eviscera managed to pass into Faerie using the blood of her own mother?"

"I believe so," Curtis replied grimly.

"Was she alone?"

The unspoken question, of whether Grimore, the traitor who'd played them all and cost Gwen her brother, was with her, hung in the air.

"Our guards are well-trained. They didn't have time to raise the alarm, which indicates that the princess was not acting alone. Whether she took an army through or simply an ally remains uncertain."

Uncertain. That was the perfect word to describe the future of the mortal realm.

Detective Darla Madison was the best sleuth Samson knew, next to Chessa, of course. So when she called his cell with a tip about the location of Honey Centrella and Glenn Darcie, he was in the air before you could say "Roscoe's rats."

The address she texted belonged to one of those workspaces for rent places, the kind of joint with a coffee stand at one end of a large space subdivided into rentable cubicles. It didn't feel much different than the bullpen, truth be told, but with a more bohemian vibe—exposed brick walls, butcher block desktops, and couches that looked like they came from IKEA. The tip had indicated that Darcie rented out a small office space just off the main room and that a pixie matching Honey's description had been seen taking meetings with various unidentified pixies for the past few days.

It made Samson think that Darcie might be attempting to gather another team to turn pixie dust into Imperium. Over his dead body. He strode through the open area, which was filled with mortals who didn't give him the time of day. Thankful for the powerful fairy glamour covering all public spaces in Korranthia disguising his true nature, he approached the office registered to Darcie. The blinds were drawn, so he stood by the door and listened. Nothing. He took a deep breath, turned around so his back was to the door, and thrust out his enormous back paw.

The door crashed open with a splintering sound. A handful of mortals jumped, gasped, and gawked. Samson flashed his badge, and they scattered. To them, this would look like a police raid, which is exactly what it was.

"KPD!" he yelled as he dove into the office.

Honey was sitting on a cushion on the desk with a laptop open in front of her, cool and collected as if the door hadn't just exploded into matchsticks.

"I'm not resisting," she said. There were dark circles under her eyes, and her flesh was pale.

"Lay on the desk with your hands behind your back," instructed Samson, taking the room in two strides once she complied and using his talons to deftly fasten zip ties around her wrists. Once she was secure and he'd read her rights, he began to ask questions.

"Where is Darcie?"

"Gone. And so is the dust."

Samson realized the pixie was shaking, despite her cool demeanor. At once, the truth dawned on him. "You're a junkie."

Honey began to laugh as she struggled to sit up. "You're a regular Sherlock, aren't you?"

Samson glanced at her laptop screen. She was logged into that game he'd heard Madison complaining about her teenage son wasting his life on, ArchMage, and the chat window was open.

> SweetBee: $ opp for pixies, PU
>
> PixiePunk: handle?
>
> BB_fly: no pr0n
>
> SweetBee: nyx. D4L_Chemist

It only took a moment for him to realize that Hobbes was right on the money. Honey was using the game to recruit pixies. If Samson was making sense of the shorthand, she wanted them to make dust, not Imperium. That must mean she still had access to Nyxanthiums, but perhaps Fairburn had left her not-so-high and dry.

"Where are the flowers?"

"Unless you've got some dust on hand to trade for intel, I'm not saying shit."

Samson clucked. "Is that all this was ever about to you? Imperium is a threat to fae existence as we know it, and all you can think about is your next fix?"

"Oh, you poor sheltered cop," Honey spat. "Of course it is. It's all any of us care about. That's how this works."

Samson cocked his head to the side. "Care to elaborate?"

"Imperium doesn't work on pixies, you idiot, I made sure of that. But Fairburn needs us to make it since dust kills every other creature. That's where Darcie came in with his pretty words and endless supply, to keep us compliant."

Damn. That was diabolical. "Why don't you just make it for yourself?"

"Do you really think the supplier is going to hand over Nyxanthiums for one lone pixie to feed her habit? No. They've got their goals, and we've got ours."

"You make Imperium for Fairburn in exchange for dust." It was so simple, but somehow the truth had eluded him until that very moment. "And now you're trying to start all over again."

"Bingo. Cop's got a brain after all."

Samson couldn't believe that she'd sell out the entire fae community in exchange for a fix. "Don't you understand? Dust distribution alone would kill thousands, and Imperium could do so much more. It could topple governments. It could end fae society as we know it!"

Honey's voice was steel. "Fae society has never done shit for me."

"So you want to end it all? You want to make people like Xander suffer? People like Lance, Dom, and Abi? They're your friends. Make this make sense!"

Honey's expression softened slightly. "I don't have a choice."

"There's always a choice," said Samson. But even he knew his words were superficial. Honey was right. He was sheltered from the harsh world of addiction and desperation. He did know one thing though—once a pixie was hooked on dust, it took an act of Danu to get them clean. By the looks of her, Honey had been using for some time.

"You're the brains of the operation. Are you telling me that you discovered how to turn dust into Imperium while high out of your mind?"

The kind of intelligence she must possess was beyond anything he could comprehend, yet she was reduced to this. It was unbelievable.

Honey leveled a steely stare at Samson. "I want my lawyer."

Finally, he was beginning to see a glimmer of the smart pixie he knew she must be, but she'd already given away so much. She had to know that any leverage she had for her own defense would be lost if she admitted her part now, and she'd freely admitted to being a junkie. The only other thing she'd confessed to so far was working for Fairburn under duress. At once, Samson saw her play. Imperium was more than just a drug, and she knew it. It was chemical warfare of a kind the realm had never seen, and the sentencing for its creation would not be light. She was setting Fairburn up to take the fall and casting herself in a sympathetic light, just a smart pixie with a dust addiction who'd fallen victim to his evil schemes. Still, he had to get everything he could from her. "When did you last see Darcie?"

Honey glared at him and spoke in an exaggerated, slow manner. "Lawyer."

The message was clear. Honey had calculated exactly how much to say, and she'd said her piece. He wouldn't get anything else from her today, not until there was a plea deal or a pinch of dust on the table. At the moment, the pixie needed medical attention. She was going through withdrawal, and by the looks of her, she wasn't going to last much longer without help. Samson wondered if she'd called in the tip herself, bringing him here to play the part she'd already cast, but it didn't matter. He needed her alive and talking.

As Samson loaded Honey into a small fae containment box, he heard the cavalry arriving. Detectives Madison and Adamu were first on the scene. Samson handed over the box.

"No Darcie?" asked Darla.

"He must have slipped through my talons," replied Samson. "And this one is lawyering up. Hopefully, O'Toole can get her to sing."

"He can be very persuasive."

Samson hoped the detective was right, but everything he observed indicated that Fairburn had left Honey to fend for herself. "I'll catch you back at the precinct. Good work Madison. We might not have nabbed Darcie, but this one is the brains of the operation. Darcie is just a two-bit hustler. It's Fairburn I want, but you've done the Seelie Court a greater service than you will ever know by catching this one. Without her, they've got nothing but dust."

He directed his attention to Adamu. "Make sure you bag her hardware. Don't damage the computer. We're going to need it."

5 O

Just when Gwen thought the stakes couldn't be raised, Moliana Eviscera threw her a curveball. Faerie had been sealed away since the end of the reign of King Arthur, and opening the gateway could have devastating effects. At least, that's what historians seemed to believe.

"Norman, I need you to go to the Academy and see if you can find a definitive text relating to the gateway between Faerie and Avalon. Take this." She handed him an envelope bearing the royal seal. He shouldn't have any trouble accessing the restricted parts of the library now, but just in case, she wanted to make sure nobody got in his way.

Norman bowed in deference. "Yes, Your Grace. What am I to learn?"

"Last year, we were convinced that opening the portal would cause the realms to converge. Unless Faerie looks a hell of a lot like Boston, it doesn't seem like that happened when Moliana passed through. Maybe they didn't fully open the gateway, or maybe we're missing something. Either way, we have to be prepared for whatever they're planning."

As far as the plans of the Unseelie went, Gwen had spies across the world working to gain information. Now that Hobbes had recovered, he joined his sister Marni back in Avalon, sifting through all correspondence her agents had sent over the past year, and the DFR was compiling information on all known active Unseelie insurrectionists. Still, she had little faith they would find anything now that the Unseelie Princess had crossed over.

"Aye," replied Norman. "And what about little miss?"

"I've had a secure chamber prepared for Chessa in Avalon. She'll have everything she needs."

"You mean you're locking 'er up."

Gwen didn't care for the note of judgment in the wizard's voice, but she understood it. Chessa was the first person to ever believe in him, and Danu knew, that meant a lot. "Laural and I will bring her back if it's the last thing we do," she promised.

"Please don't say that, Your Grace," Norman replied. His voice was low, and he was misty-eyed.

"Why not?"

He paused before responding, then he tilted his head downward to look Gwen directly in the eye. "Because ever since you and Chessa came into my life, it seems like everything you do could be the last. I'd like to think that you will bring 'er back and be here to celebrate with us too."

Gwen smiled, finally seeing in the man what had taken Chessa only moments. "I'll do my best."

Curtis escorted Gwen out of C&F Investigations onto the bustling Boston street. They had one more stop to make before they could head home to Avalon.

"Do you want me to summon a hobgoblin?" he asked.

Gwen shook her head. "Save them for the longer trips. My wings could use the exercise." She was feeling stronger every day and was sick of lying around. The flight to the island owned by the Charlesworths was only a few miles over open water.

To her surprise, Gwen immediately liked Allison Charlesworth, the head of Laural's coven of healers. For starters, the witch didn't bow to her. Instead, she met her on the beach with a smile.

"Laural told me you were stopping by," said Allison. Her red-kissed, dark blond hair blew into her face, but she didn't seem to notice.

"I wanted to make sure you have everything you need for Henrietta," said Gwen.

"You mean you wanted to make sure we're not going to use her like a weapon," replied Allison.

Laural had warned Gwen that Allison didn't take any bullshit, but she was still surprised at her candor. "Yes, that. Also, I heard your coven helped clean-up my mess, and I wanted to say thank you."

"We don't consider healing fae in need clean-up, but I'm glad we could help."

Curtis stood silent, as usual, as Gwen and Allison got acquainted, then the three of them went to visit Henrietta. The structure the witches had constructed in the center of the island was more than she expected. There was a courtyard with a large pond in the center, sleeping quarters for on-site caretakers, and a large space enclosed on three sides, where the dragon could take shelter.

"How do you keep her here?" Gwen asked.

"Oh, that's easy. We don't! She's free to come and go as she pleases."

Oh hell no. "We can't have a dragon flying over the Boston harbor," said Gwen, glad she'd come to check out the situation.

Allison had the gall to laugh. "Chessa has it all arranged with the Glamour Squadron. We've got a fairy on staff just to keep Henrietta hidden from mortal eyes. As for the fae, well, they know better than to mess with a dragon."

Gwen didn't like it. Most fae believed that dragons were long extinct in the mortal realm, and she didn't see how any good could come from proving otherwise. But she didn't have a better suggestion, so she decided to trust the system Chessa had set up.

Henrietta was in the shelter, making more noise than Gwen thought possible, but as soon as she caught sight of Gwen, she quieted down. She walked out of the enclosure to circle Gwen, stretching her wings and looking off into the distance as if she were searching for something. Or someone.

"Chessa's not here," said Gwen, a bit taken aback by how large the dragon had grown since she saw her in Avalon. "But she's going to be alright." She had no idea if Henrietta understood, and she felt silly talking to a dragon, but Allison gave her an encouraging nod, so she continued. "I'm going to take her to Avalon. I'm going to help her."

At that, Henrietta stopped her pacing. She approached Gwen and lowered her head to the ground. Unsure of herself, Gwen reached up and put her palm on the dragon's snout the way she'd seen Chessa do. They stood like that for a long moment. When Gwen left a half-hour later, Allison stooped to hug her goodbye and promised to take good care of Henrietta in Laural's absence. Gwen felt like she'd also made a promise, and she hoped she was able to see it through.

51

Sergeant Detective Samson Wayne charged down the hall, hung a right, and flung open the door to O'Toole's office. The captain was sitting across from the Korranthia District Attorney, an elf Samson wouldn't want to cross. Not that he was ever allowed to speak with her directly.

Upon his abrupt entrance, Adela Cruz jumped.

"What is this about?" asked O'Toole, clenching his hand to keep the flame from igniting. Samson didn't care. He was beyond pissed.

"You gave Centrella a deal without getting her dust sources! What kind of criminal-supporting anarchy are you running here, captain?"

Before O'Toole erupted, Ms. Cruz stood. "It wasn't his call. Take a seat Detective Wayne, and I will explain everything to you."

The captain glared in a way that told Samson there would be hell to pay later, but he didn't contradict the D.A.. Samson lowered his lion haunches into a crouch on the floor instead of embarrassing himself by breaking the chair Cruz had vacated. She sat back down and offered up a smile, her blood-red lips far softer than her piercing brown eyes.

"The toxicology on Portia Kolsch came back clean," she said.

It was not the information Samson was expecting. He felt his beak fall open. According to Honey, all the pixies in Fairburn's employ were hooked on dust. It was the reason they'd joined up in the first place. He snapped his beak shut.

"What does that have to do with Honey Centrella?"

"She has agreed to testify against Walter Kolsch in exchange for a severely reduced sentence and witness protection. You see, Honey wasn't one to put all her dust in one basket. She sought out dirt on every one of her associates. Some of that dirt is utterly fascinating."

Samson's head was spinning with the way the D.A. kept switching focus. He wasn't surprised that Honey had hedged her bets, but he resented being taken on this journey via the scenic route. Still, he was in enough hot water with O'Toole. It might be best to play nice with Cruz.

"What did she have on Kolsch?"

"Everything. Portia was cut off by her parents because a pair of board members discovered that good old papa was embezzling funds. They knew the entire company would go down if word got out, so they struck a deal to have the money returned within three months. The only problem is, the Kolsches don't have it anymore. The cash is tied up in properties and cars and all the other things rich assholes buy."

"How much green are we talking?" asked Samson.

"25 mil."

He gave a low whistle. "Three months to come up with that kind of dough would be like plucking whiskers off a manticore, even for high-rollers."

"Exactly. And if they started selling off their assets, that would tip off investors. When her parents cut her off, Portia decided to take matters into her own hands. Some of her rich friends knew a dust supplier, one Glenn Darcie, and she introduced him to her grandfather thinking he could help drum up some cash fast. But Darcie was already working for Fairburn. One thing led to another, and before he knew it, Walter Kolsch was caught up in something bigger than he ever planned." Cruz told the story like a pro, watching Samson's reactions to each revelation.

"A plot to overthrow the Seelie Court," said Sampson. "But why did Fairburn have her dusted?"

"Ms. Centrella isn't clear on that. She guesses that they saw her as a loose end. She was always unpredictable and self-serving. One thing Honey did know, though, was that it wasn't Fairburn who had her killed."

"How does she know that?" asked Samson.

Cruz's eyes seemed to sparkle. She loved this shit. "Because Honey was the one who ordered the hits. She's the one who gave instructions to Dominik Perez and Lance Gruber while they were under the influence of Imperium."

Samson felt the wind leave his body. All this time, they had been investigating the murder of Mandrake Aster, and those responsible were staring them in the face. "Drake was killed by his own friends?"

"Of course he was. Perez can corroborate everything Centrella says, at least the bits he remembers, but it's Portia we care about."

Samson tried not to show how much that particular line pissed him off. He felt his maxilla grind against his mandible, but he continued to play along. "It sounds like you're saying that Kolsch had his own granddaughter murdered."

The D.A. grinned. "Bingo."

"That explains why it looked like a pro job." Another thought crossed his mind. "What about the attack on Hobbes Doyle?"

"That was Fairburn's first attempt to use one of his own drones for a hit, according to Ms. Centrella. He kept pushing her to change the formula for Imperium to make his goons even more pliable, but it never worked out the way he wanted. Ms. Centrella takes pride in the fact that he failed to eliminate a target when her boys never did," said Ms. Cruz.

Samson's feathers stood on end. "She's a monster, and you're just going to let her walk?"

"Kolsch is a big fish, and without her testifying against him, he will buy his way to freedom. As a part of the witness protection program, we can keep tabs on Ms. Centrella. We may even be able to use her talents for good."

He shook his head. Adela Cruz may have gotten what she thought she needed out of Honey, but she was naive to believe she wasn't being played. There would always be men like Fairburn and Kolsch, but it was Honey who made their schemes dangerous. She would disappear, and without stemming the flow of dust, she would set up shop somewhere else. "Imperium is a bigger threat than a corrupt billionaire," he said.

Finally, O'Toole stepped in. "That's your opinion, Detective Wayne. Now, go back to your office. I want to have a little chat with you later."

As Samson was about to oblige, the captain's door flew open again. Detective Hank Adamu burst in. "I apologize for the intrusion," he said, "but I just got word from Bathory. Honey Centrella was found dead in her cell this morning."

52

F our months passed since Chessa's mind had splintered.

A team of Seelie intelligence officers worked with the DFR and other national agencies to monitor the black markets and criminal underworld for any trace of Fairburn or Imperium, and so far, there had been none. Gwen wasn't naive enough to believe that they had eradicated the drug entirely. There were too many hands involved with its production, even if it hadn't yet reached wider distribution. Samson believed that was where Madam Glitz fit into the operation, but if she had a supply, she was far too cunning to tip her hand while the heat was on. She even went so far as to give a statement to the KPD about the meeting she had with Fairburn and Xeos. By all appearances, she was fully cooperating. And by all appearances, Fairburn was dead.

Meanwhile, C&F Investigations was shuttered. Quincy, if he was alive, was on the run, and Norman spent all his days at the Fairy Godparent Academy searching ancient texts for any information on the Unseelie, Faerie, Morgan le Fay, and anything else that might help shed light on either Chessa's situation or the Unseelie plan. He frequently conferred with Cora, who was back in Barbados with Blade but spent half her time learning everything she could about Morgan le Fay and the court of Arthur Pendragon. As for Gwen, she had the Seelie Court to run.

"Your Grace?" Curtis entered the room with a bow. He was the closest

242

thing she had to a friend these days, yet he was careful to observe formalities. It was her fault, she supposed, for the way she kept him at a distance.

"What?" she replied, setting down the most recent book Norman had sent her from the Academy. It was the most complete history of the Unseelie Court that she'd ever seen, but it still didn't tell her anything about the consequences of opening a portal to Faerie.

"This just arrived from Korranthia." He handed her yet another thick, leather-bound book.

"Did he give you the TLDR version?" she asked, dreading the homework Norman seemed to pile on with glee.

"Afraid not, but he bookmarked a section regarding the powers of the Morrigan. He wanted you to read it and talk it over with Laural."

Gwen would rather pull out her own hair. It wasn't that she didn't want to understand the forces trapped within Chessa, Laural, and herself, it was just that the Unseelie threat looming over fae existence made everything else feel like a distraction. She didn't know how to save Chessa, and she had more to think about than one pixie, no matter who that one pixie was. Nobody seemed to understand that.

"Thank you, Curtis," she said.

She opened the book, entitled *Documented Cases of Magical Endowment*. The marked passage read:

__Morgan le Fay__ (/ˈmɔːrɡən lə ˈfeɪ/; Welsh: Morgên y Dylwythen Deg; Cornish: Morgen an Spyrys; all meaning 'Morgan the Fairy'), alternatively known as Morgan[n]a, Morgain[a/e], Morg[a]ne, Morgant[e], Morge[i]n, and Morgue[in]

Daughter of Uther Pendragon and Lady Igraine of Cornwall, born in the year 450.

Entry extracted from the writings of Merlin, wizard of the first order, recovered in the rubble of Camelot.

In a time when Faerie and the mortal realm bled one unto another, so too did the peoples of both. A great fairy by the name of Uther carved out a place of power amongst mortals, blinded as they were to his true nature by a glamour cast both day and night. Yet Uther cared only for his own ambitions and left the ways of the fae behind, all but those of love and coupling. It was his robust appetite that led him to the bed of the Lady Igraine, a powerful faerie in her own right who nonetheless was expected to live committed body and mind to another, Gorlois, Duke of Cornwall. As such, Morgan le Fay was born, a faerie of great gifts, specifically in the ways of love and healing. Gorlois treated the bastard daughter of his wife with scorn, more so when he began to suspect her fae nature. He turned upon all fae in his duchy, passing decrees that saw them subjugated and hunted. Such atrocities were committed against her people, the young faerie became incensed by the actions of the man she called father.

Around this time, a prophecy foretold of a king, half mortal, half fae, who was destined to heal the broken land. The fae of Avalon rallied behind Arthur, son of Uther, and the Lady Igraine instilled the hopes of Avalon into her daughter. Thus, when Arthur was mortally wounded during a hunt, Morgan came to his side. Her healing proved insufficient, and so she called upon the patron goddess of the fae, Danu, for help, yet Danu was deaf to her pleas.

Morgan's rage and anguish for her people echoed through space and time, drawing the attention of a distant goddess, older and more powerful than any known on the shores of Avalon. The Morrigan answered the call and imbued Morgan with power, enhancing what already existed in the young faerie. Divine Iachau and cariad coursed through her veins, but a third power did she inherit as well, dig cyfiawn, and thus she became Morgan le Fay.

"So, Laural was right," mused Gwen the hairs on her neck standing on end. She'd heard murmurings of the Celtic goddess of battle and death, but the Seelie were taught to worship Danu above all, and that's how it had always been. The Morrigan was little more than a footnote in the texts she'd grown up on.

Fifteen minutes later, Gwen and Laural sat together with Norman's face displayed on a laptop screen.

"I'm confused," said Gwen. "Was Morgan le Fay named after the Morrigan?"

"No," replied Norman. "The etymologies of the names are different, and as far as we know, the Morrigan wasn't a presence in Wales or Avalon."

"So, she just popped up out of nowhere?"

Norman didn't offer up an explanation, but Laural shrugged. "There are many great powers and many realms. Gailan didn't come from Faerie, but he found a home in a sick little boy nonetheless and used that child to root himself in a witch who drew power from Faerie."

It was a fair point. Gwen resisted the urge to ask Laural where the demon who had possessed her for half her life originated before she'd expelled it from the child as it wasn't relevant to the current situation. Some hellish realm, she assumed. "True. There are so many pantheons and so many creatures, I struggle to keep them straight."

"That's something I might be able to help you with," said Norman. "It is, after all, your job to rule the fae, and to do that, you should have a working knowledge of all the forces at work within the realm."

Gwen nodded. If they lived through the year, she would see about getting a team together to compile some sort of compendium. Norman would be a good choice to head that effort. The fact that something like that didn't already exist in Avalon was a testament to just how badly the Seelie government had failed the fae.

"I assume you've gathered as much information as you could about the Morrigan?" she asked.

"Yes, Your Grace. She is brutal and vengeful but fair. Perhaps appealing to that aspect is a way to break through to little miss."

"I don't believe our powers were meant to be separated by Morgan or by Chessa," said Laural. "Together, they are balanced, but like this, they are unstable. Every time I call upon my healing powers, I sense a tension building, as if I'm somehow harming that balance."

Norman nodded as if that made perfect sense, but Gwen didn't feel out of balance in any way. Then again, she didn't use Morgan's magic with intention the way Laural did. It was simply a part of her. "If you say so," she said.

Gwen could have sworn she saw Norman shoot Laural a pointed look on the screen of the little laptop, but he didn't respond to her statement. Instead, he carried on. "The ritual I did to unite them only held for a short time. As soon as Gwen awoke, they returned to their separate vessels."

"But for that moment, while we were in that place between life and death and the powers were one, everything felt somehow right," said Laural.

Gwen felt a pang of jealousy. She had no memory of what transpired after the power surge. To her, everything got brighter and brighter until she was blinded, and then she awoke in a hospital bed. "If we find a way to put them back together, do you think that will save Chess?" It was the question the conversation was leading to, and she didn't have the patience to ponder the balance of the universe while everyone pussyfooted around it.

Neither Norman nor Laural responded, but Gwen knew they were all wondering the same thing: how would they even begin to do something like that?

After a long moment of silence, Laural put her hand over Gwen's. "She misses you, you know."

Gwen's stomach turned. After the first few days home, she'd quit going to see Chessa. She was so preoccupied with trying to keep the peace, meeting with heads of different departments, and worrying over what the Unseelie were up to, visiting Chessa became a painful chore she never felt up to. It never led to anything good, anyhow.

"Maybe we could try the ritual again," she said, knowing it was probably an exercise in futility. "Norman, I'll send a hobgoblin to bring you by tomorrow."

53

Chessa finally understood why Gwen hated growing up in the palace of Avalon. She always said it was like a prison, but then, she hadn't been confined to a bedroom, a bathroom, and a balcony. The worst part was that Gwen rarely came to visit herself. Palace staff brought meals, therapists visited daily, and Laural spent a good bit of time doing healing rituals and poking around in her head, but Gwen was off seeing to other matters. More important matters, no doubt.

Chessa wondered if Abi was locked up too. Nobody would give her updates because of the hitlist she'd made back in Bathory. She didn't remember making it, and even if she did escape Avalon, she wasn't sure she truly wanted to kill Abigail Marquis. Where that particular pixie was concerned, her feelings were jumbled. She wouldn't start with her, anyhow.

Damn it, she thought. She shouldn't *want* to kill anyone!

"Norman wanted me to ask you about the sensations you felt when you're having an episode," said Laural. Everyone kept talking about Chessa's episodes as if there wasn't a darkness lurking under the surface every waking moment. Fae were no better than humans at labeling only what they could see. Chessa swore that Laural had been talking for days, going on about the powers of some long-dead fairy. The boredom was intolerable. She wondered if driving a screwdriver through her cousin's throat would make her shut up.

"I've been over this with the therapists," replied Chessa. "It's a wave of righteous anger followed by a compulsion to eliminate all wrongdoing."

"All *perceived* wrongdoing," corrected Laural. "Words mean something."

"You don't think it's wrong to prey upon the weak, to poison the masses, to seek control of others? You don't think it's wrong to imprison those who wish to set the world right while allowing criminals to walk free?"

As she spoke, Chessa felt every word like it was the only one in the universe. Laural should be as angry as she was, and the fact that her cousin merely seemed concerned only enraged her more. A pounding throbbed in her ears, and it took her a moment to realize it was her own pulse.

"Focus on your breathing, Chess. In and out. In and out."

Chessa stood abruptly and walked to the door leading to the balcony. The sun illuminated the grassy tor in a way that felt somehow familiar. Her mind went still, even as Laural began to speak yet again.

"You know Norman's been making some incredible discoveries about the source of this power. He's working to figure out how to manage it from a magical perspective rather than digging around in your emotions. I just want to understand."

"Do you, now?" asked Chessa. "Do you want to understand why I want to see your blood splattered all over these walls? Do you want to understand that the idea of opening your abdomen turns me on?"

Laural flinched. Good. She should be scared.

"Where's Gwen?" asked Chessa.

"Probably putting out more fires than one fairy can handle," said Laural. She was sitting on the edge of the bed, pretending to be comfortable, and a Seelie guard was stationed just inside the door. They were always like this—tense, just waiting for Chessa to turn homicidal. It almost felt like the way people used to be around Gwen.

For a moment, she felt something other than rage. Was it sadness? Then it was gone.

"Has she figured out what the Unseelie are up to?"

"No."

A part of Chessa hoped they were successful. The mortals deserved to pay for everything they'd done to the earth and to her people. Chessa decided to keep those thoughts to herself. She needed to stop antagonizing everyone if she wanted to gain an iota of freedom.

"I could help, you know. If I had my computer, I could work with Norman directly. You wouldn't have to be a go-between. I can see the stress you're under."

Laural sighed. "Believe me, we want you on the case, but you hear yourself right? You're unpredictable. One minute you're the Chessa we all know and love and the next, you sound like a demon. More than anyone, I know how hard this must be for you."

"Why does everything circle back to Gailan for you? I thought I expelled him, but you can't move on, can you? There's no demon here, just me. You're supposed to love me." Chessa felt tears threatening to fall. She hated being like this. She was hurting everyone she cared about, but she was powerless to control it.

"We will figure this out, Chess. I promise. Gwen and I have something we want to try, if you're up for it. Norman will be here in a bit too."

Chessa was always the one who figured things out, and she didn't see a way out of this. There was no way in hell Gwen, Laural, and Norman would figure it out without her. She wouldn't for a moment let herself believe otherwise.

I don't deserve comfort. I killed all those people. I killed Quincy.

The thought pushed everything else out, and Chessa felt a growing hatred for herself spark to life. Morgan's magic came alive. Shit. She didn't really want to harm Laural. Chessa launched at the Seelie guard at the door instead, but he was ready. He ducked and rotated his body so that he could snatch her out of the air and slam her to the ground.

"Don't hurt her," screamed Laural. The note of panic in her voice made the anger recede.

"I'm sorry," Chessa gasped, and the guard helped her up, his face impassive.

She returned to the chair in the corner and sat, staring at the wall. Laural began to hum the song Cora used to sing when she was a young pixie, and eventually, Chessa began to feel more like herself. As if sensing the difference, Laural said, "Chessa, you're the best person I know. Whatever the magic is doing to you is not your fault."

"It is, though. It's just amplifying my darkest impulses."

"We all have dark urges. It just means we're alive. You always see the best in everyone else, and I need you to see it in yourself. Please."

A knock on the door preceded it creaking open. Curtis stepped in. He looked over at Chessa, his eyes filled with sympathy. Perhaps Laural was right and she should show herself a little of the grace she extended to everyone else.

"Her Grace, Queen Gwendolyn would like to speak with you. She would like your permission before entering."

"It's her palace," replied Chessa. "She can go where she pleases."

Curtis gave a nod, stepped out of the room, then reappeared with Gwen. The Seelie Queen, Chessa's former best friend, had dark circles underscoring her gold-rimmed eyes, and her complexion was pale as if she hadn't stepped outside in weeks.

"Chessa, how are you?" asked Gwen. She sounded unsure of herself.

"I'm living in this prison you made for me just down the hall from your own quarters. You can check in on me any time you like." The bubble of rage began to reform in the pit of Chessa's stomach. The part of her that was still logical knew she shouldn't be wounded by Gwen's absence. Laural was right, she had more on her plate than was manageable for one lone fairy. Still, had she listened to Chessa in the first place, returned home to Avalon rather than flying recklessly into danger back in Korranthia, they all would be in a very different situation. For that, she wanted to snap her scrawny neck. The image of Gwen's mangled body flashed across Chessa's memory, sending her further into the hell of her own mind.

"I'm sorry. I want to be here for you, I really do," said Gwen.

Chessa needed to distract herself before she did something horrific. "Has Norman discovered anything about Faerie?" she asked.

Gwen shook her head and remained in the center of the room. "Nothing beyond legends. The books are limited. Once Faerie was sealed off, the Unseelie did everything in their power to destroy all records of it, according to the few history books written well after the initial purge. We do know that without Faerie, our magic dies, even for those practitioners who use celestial magic as a source of power. That's why every document regarding its existence was viewed by the Unseelie as a threat to be exploited."

"They obviously know something we don't if they've discovered a ritual to open the portal."

"Whatever it is, Norman hasn't been able to find a copy of the ritual in any spell book at our disposal here in Avalon or back in Korranthia."

"If there are no records, you should go to someone who was around when the gate was created in the first place," said Chessa. It seemed like an obvious solution to her, but Gwen was never one to see a foot beyond her own experiences. That's why they were in this mess in the first place.

"Except that there are no fae alive from that era." Danu, Chessa hated the note of superiority in Gwen's voice when she was sure of something.

"I didn't say fae." Gwen could be so dense. Chessa hated herself for ever believing anything else of her, and she considered wringing the fairy's neck right here in her childhood bedroom. Instead, she stared at the woman she'd once believed could accomplish anything and waited for her to remember that there were others in the world, ancient powers that predated humanity and fae alike. Finally, it seemed to click.

"You mean Moshup?"

"For starters," Chessa replied. She'd searched for the ancient deity who'd left his imprint on Avalon before returning to Korranthia, but he'd never answered her call. He might respond to the Seelie Queen, however, if she ever cared to reach out.

"Why are you so fucking brilliant?" Gwen asked, grinning like an idiot. She walked across the room and pulled Chessa into a hug.

Chessa stiffened at her touch, swallowing the urge to lash out before relaxing into the embrace. She remembered a time when Gwen was the closest friend she had, and for a split second, she was back there again. Everything felt like it might be okay.

You locked me up in the very place you called hell, she thought. *You abandoned me.*

The intrusive thought pierced her mind like a war cry.

You abandoned me.

Just before the anger took her over, Chessa panicked. No. Not Gwen.

It was too late.

She flitted her wings, flipped around the fairy queen, and caught her in a chokehold. With her arm around Gwen's neck, she squeezed with everything she had, coherent thought giving way to pure rage.

Chessa was vaguely aware of someone screaming, of Gwen's nails ripping into the flesh of her arm, of Gwen's wings twitching frantically and uselessly against her slightly larger body. Curtis hit her like a missile. Gwen, freed of Chessa's death-grip, fell to the ground, gasping and coughing. Chessa's face smacked into the floor, and Curtis pinned her down. With her face pressed against the wooden floorboards, Chessa could see Laural kneeling by Gwen, channeling her healing magic, and a second wave of anger washed over her. Laural should be tending to *her.*

She's the one who freed the witch from the clutches of a demon after Gwen got Corrin, the love of Laural's life, slaughtered by a serial killer.

Corrin. Her beloved cousin never would have died if it weren't for Gwen's obsession with vengeance. Chessa struggled against Curtis in an attempt to get at Gwen, and nearly threw him off, but the other guard jumped into the melee, and they had her subdued in no time. More guards flooded into the room, and Gwen was rushed out with Laural on her heels. Everyone who had ever loved her, gone in an instant.

Blood pooled around her face from her broken nose, but Chessa felt nothing. After the door was secured, Curtis and the other guard stood and waited for her to get up from the floor. She didn't bother.

THE END

ACKNOWLEDGMENTS

This book is dedicated to the memory of Dr. George Hewett Joiner, Jr., who moved onto his next great adventure while I was writing it. He's been thanked in every one of my books because of the profound impact he had on me. While he will be missed terribly, his life continues to make this world a better place.

With each book release, it feels like I thank many of the same people, but that's because I wouldn't be able to do this without them. First, I want to thank my husband Alex, who always prioritizes my writing in every way imaginable. He talks through plot points, loads me up for conventions, and carves out time for my fitful bursts of creativity. This year has been particularly difficult, yet his support has never wavered. Fractured Fae would not exist without him.

Thank you to my two little girls, who put up with the highs and lows associated with a career in this field and who are always eager to celebrate my books with me.

Thank you to Colleen Caron, my mom, for listening to my manic diatribes as I hammer out stories and for always being willing to help untangle my thoughts. Thanks to Paul Caron, my dad, for always showing how proud he is of my accomplishments, and thanks to my brother, Max Caron, for reading my stories and making me feel like a legit fantasy author.

My beta reader team was small but mighty for this book, and I'm so thankful to have both Matt Harshaw and Nicole Bross to offer reader and writer perspectives on my early drafts. I hope the final product makes you proud!

Thank you to John Hartness, my publisher, editor, and friend, for believing in me and always having my back. Thank you to Misty Massey for helping to make my story shine and to Susan Roddey for somehow translating my brain waves into these killer covers! And thanks to Erin

Penn and Kristen Gould for your parts in bringing my stories into the world. I'm incredibly lucky to have such an amazing team for the Fractured Fae Series. And thanks to the Falstaff Misfit family for supporting me at conventions and in life.

Thank you to all the convention runners and track directors who invite me into their spaces and make me feel like what I'm doing matters.

And a huge thank you to people who go out of their way to show their support, either by sharing my books with others, interacting at panels, bidding on Tuckerizations, providing emotional support, or showing up in other ways. People like Dino Hicks, Sara Bond, Ben Humphrey, Tanya and Rick Dorsey, Allison Charlesworth, Jeff Bernard, Jeff Jarvis, Matt Laney, Jason Kormos, Abbie Lane, Vincent Thorne, David Wallsh, Darin Kennedy, Gerald Coleman, James Liang, David Coe, Mel Todd, Cisca Small, Jordan and Tessa Payne, Kim McNamara, Nicole Yackley, Theresa Darin Bush, Thom and Erin Desimone, Ellie Raine, Sarah Madsen, Jessica Nettles, and that one dude who comes to all may panels but never talks to me after.

ABOUT THE AUTHOR

Sarah J. Sover is the author of the Contemporary Fantasy *Fractured Fae* series and the Comedic Fantasy *Double-Crossing the Bridge*, all from Falstaff Books. An active SFWA member, Sarah is a contributor to multiple short story anthologies, to Dan Koboldt's *Putting the Fact in Fantasy*, and to Writer's Digest Magazine. Her degree in Biology and background in animal care informs her world-building. Sarah lives in John's Creek, Ga with her husband Alex, two daughters, rescue pup Gandalf, and possibly immortal snake Santana. Sarah is a serial hobbyist who loves music, stories in all forms, and battling through Hyrule or Hades. You can find her online at www.SarahJSover.com.

FRIENDS OF FALSTAFF

Thank You to All our Falstaff Books Patrons, who get extra digital content each month! To be featured here and see what other great rewards we offer, go to www.patreon.com/falstaffbooks.

PATRONS

Dino Hicks
John Hooks
John Kilgallon
Larissa Lichty
Travis & Casey Schilling
Staci-Leigh Santore
Sheryl R. Hayes
Scott Norris
Samuel Montgomery-Blinn
Junkle
Vickie DeSantos
Quincy J. Allen
Allison Charlesworth

Thank You for Supporting Independent Publishing!

We believe that you should be able
to read your books, your way.
That's why this Falstaff Books
print edition includes a digital copy
at no additional cost!

Just scan the QR code with your device,
follow the directions on Prolific Works,
and enjoy!
You can also join our newsletter when prompted,
and never miss an awesome Falstaff Release!